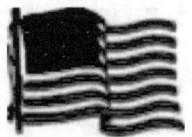

APRIL 15

A NOVEL

ISBN: 978-0-578-68663-9

First they take our money. Then they take our sons.
– American housewife

For are they not like tax collectors? Are they not the dregs of the Earth?
– Jesus of Nazareth

I.

"Somebody's going to pay for this."

The hill overlooking the new I.R.S. compound was covered in straw-colored grass about two feet tall. Here and there, scrub oaks cast long shadows from the late afternoon sun. The air was still and hot.

The sixty-three year old man followed the trail up the hill with some difficulty, although he worked out regularly following a program designed by a University of Michigan strength and endurance coach. He could not fully attribute the hesitancy in his gait to the shrapnel lodged in his left thigh. Was it the nature of the task at hand? He chided himself. This was no time to lose his nerve.

He was wearing a desert camo outfit he had bought, ironically, at one of those punk stores where his daughter used to shop. ROXY, it was called, or something like that. The pale, thin girl who had sold the clothes to him had iridescent blue hair and a tattoo of a snake that crept out of her lacy sleeve onto the back of her hand. She had probably wondered what a guy with graying hair dressed in a suit was doing in her store. The answer: *A patriot's work.*

He reached the crest of the hill and abandoned the trail, low crawling to a position where he could see the sprawling complex from which his target – a randomly chosen stranger – would emerge into the parking lot. It wasn't exactly fair, but it was the fairest solution he could find, and somebody had to pay. From his small day pack he removed and assembled his rifle, a miracle of hypervelocity design at 5.25 pounds, with a flat trajectory that was reliable for a shock-and-drop shot at 500 yards. Locked and loaded, he assumed the familiar prone position and waited. He had determined that the target would be the first individual to exit from the main door after 4:30 p.m.

If this feels wrong, he thought, *I put the next bullet through my head. If it feels right, I'll move forward, and liberty will prevail.*

"Shepherd, I don't think you're listening to me. I said I want this shabby excuse for a United States citizen padlocked, and I want him padlocked today!

Paul Shepherd's boss, Sammy Banks, slammed the palm of his plump but muscular brown hand down on his desk with a loud slap to emphasize his point, but none of the I.R.S. agents in the sea of cubicles outside Bank's glass-walled office paid the slightest attention to the sound, even though the door was open and they could hear him screaming. It was like this every day.

"He has the ability to pay," said Shepherd calmly. "He's signed a 9465. If we shut him down now, we'll never see that money. What the Hell good is twelve thousand dollars' worth of old tire recapping equipment to the United States government?" He ran his hand through his dark brown hair and adjusted his glasses, a nervous habit he had picked up in college. He was thin but in good shape due to the twenty miles he logged religiously every week in the hills behind his home.

Banks reached for the jar of jelly beans he kept on his desk and popped an orange one into his mouth. He had quit smoking just over a year ago, and gained twenty-five pounds in the process. Now, his belly strained against the buttons of his starched white shirt. He chewed thoughtfully for a moment. Then he eyed his agent.

"The good thing is, we make an example of this lazy nigger."

Shepherd thought, *That's it.* Black or not, Sammy had no right to display that kind of disrespect. He said, "I think you'd better get somebody else to do this."

Banks sat back in his chair and folded his arms across his chest. "You ever hear of insubordination, Shepherd?

"Forget it, Sammy," said Shepherd. "I'm contacting the OPM. I'm history."

"Well, that's just fine. You're off the case, effective immediately. You just go back to your office and await further assignment. Until your paperwork goes through, your ass is mine."

Both men stood up. Shepherd turned and headed towards the door when his supervisor called him back. "Don't you get any ideas about any whistle blowing shit, Shepherd. I could tie up your final pay check for years."

Shepherd walked back to his cubicle and began packing up his things. There wasn't much. A picture of Jenny, the Cross pen she had given him for Christmas last year, half a dozen personal books on accounting, an almost-empty bottle of prescription antacid pills – the rest was all government issue. As he straightened up his desk for the last time, he ran though a series of familiar calculations: Four hundred per month from each of his three moonlighting clients. About fifteen hundred to set up his brother-in-law's books. His final check from the government, which would be around three thousand plus or minus. And there was another twenty-five hundred in the bank if they really needed it. But he could get clients. It was easy for ex-IRS agents. Everybody thought you knew things the other accountants out there didn't. To some extent, that was true.

He glanced down at his watch. Four thirty on the dot. Time to make his exit. Tomorrow, he would call in sick. He could submit his official resignation to the Office of Personnel Management via the web. All his cases were in order, with full documentation. Anyone could take them over. He picked up his briefcase and followed the familiar path through the cloth-walled maze of cubicles to the exit. He displayed the contents of his briefcase to the guard and then strode towards the glass door that led to his new life.

"Hold up there!"

It was Banks, out of breath and out of shape but still covering the distance between them with surprising speed. He reached Shepherd and grabbed his arm just above the elbow. "Where the Hell do you think you're going? It ain't five."

"Sammy, let go. You're way out of line." The man had lost it. Didn't he realize this was being captured on video? With a guard observing? He pulled away, but Sammy held his grip, matching him step by step as he headed for the doors. The two of them pushed through simultaneously. Shepherd finally managed to disengage. Breathing heavily from the chase, Sammy pointed a thick finger at him and said in a soft, menacing voice, "You are going to regret this big time."

Two men emerged from the glass doors of the main administration building simultaneously, a young, slender kid with glasses who looked like he was only a couple of years out of college, and an older, much larger black man who seemed to be trying to restrain the kid. The shooter could clearly read their expressions through his scope. The black man's face broadcast rage; the kid's, disgust.

Two targets! His self-imposed rules of engagement hadn't taken this possibility into account, but it didn't matter. In war, the unexpected appeared in front of you every day and, he reminded himself, he was engaged in nothing less than warfare.

It was pretty clear what was going on down there. He couldn't be certain, but certainty was not a part of war. You could only follow your instincts, based on the best intel you had. He took a deep breath. As he expelled it he whispered, "*Sayonara*, asshole." And with that, he pulled the trigger.

Breathing heavily, with sweat trickling down his broad forehead and darkening the armpits of his shirt, Banks looked pathetic. For all his bulk and bluster, he had lost his power to intimidate. In fact, Shepherd felt a sudden wave of sympathy for the boss who had made his life so miserable for the past two and a half years. Banks would be lucky to keep his job after this incident, no matter what the unit performance numbers were.

"Are you listening to me?" Banks yelled, and then suddenly he spun and fell backward. Shepherd stared down at him. Banks' eyes were open, but now lifeless – just like that. A pool of blood was beginning to form underneath his left arm. Shepherd's mind wasn't functioning properly. It put the situation together in slow motion. Not a heart attack... an assassination... I may be the next target... run! By the time he was inside, he realized he had never been a target. Had he been, he would be already be dead. Instead, it was Sammy.

"What happened?" the guard was asking.

"Sammy's dead."

"What?"

"Sammy's dead," he repeated. Then he looked at his watch, because he knew one of the first questions the police would ask was when the shooting took place. His twenty dollar Casio told him it was 4:37, but his mind focused on the date: April 15.

Four Months Earlier

This isn't medicine, thought Matt Stone as he sat awaiting his fate on a mildly uncomfortable banquette with bright orange plastic cushions in the office of Dr. David Feldman, neurologist. *This is a money machine.* The liberals had finally managed to make healthcare affordable, but in the process they had drained all the *care* out of it – and its effect on health was dubious as well.

Stone was old enough to remember a childhood when the doctor actually came to your house when you were sick. He could still see Dr. Wiedenmann in his mind's eye, leaning over the skinny child he had once been, thick, gold-rimmed glasses magnifying the quizzical look in his eyes.

"How are you doing, kid?" he would ask. Always the same question.

The doctors didn't come to visit you anymore. You came to them. And the first question they asked was, "May I see your insurance card, please?"

With his athletic frame, intense blue eyes and only a hint of gray of gray hair at the temples, he looked healthy and out of place in the sterile waiting room. Two mass-produced seascapes in utilitarian metal frames hung on the off-white walls, intended, he imagined, to produce a calming effect on the patients, most of whom were probably terrified. Several rows of glossy magazines were neatly spread out on a low plastic table between the banquets. He had read somewhere that the publishers offered free subscriptions to doctors to boost their circulation figures, and of course, their advertising rates.

To Stone's right was the door where he had entered. To his left, the glassed-in administrative area where two Vietnamese girls in white smocks managed scheduling and billing. For all he knew, his unit had burned down their grandparents' village. *Stupid war!* But he had to stop thinking like that. It was all history now. A lot of the guys in his unit were already dead.

He thought, *I may soon join them.* They didn't set up an appointment to tell you your tests were okay and that you didn't have a problem. There was no billing code for a visit like that. No, there was only one reason why he was here, and he didn't need a doctor tell him. He was a dead duck.

Ambiguous! For twelve hundred dollars, not to mention a time-consuming battery of tests including two CAT scans, he got a diagnosis that was no more help than the first important lesson the war had taught him: You might die pretty soon, or you might not.

It wasn't Feldman's exorbitant fee that got under his skin. Stone had more money than he could ever spend, a private jet at his beck and call, an apartment in Paris for the shopping trips his wife Laura used to take, the whole show. And the doc had done a good job explaining the intricacies of his condition and the reason why it made sense to just wait and see what happened.

Yes, there was *something* near the region of his brain responsible for "cognitive control" that *seemed* abnormal. A tumor in that region could account for all matter of symptoms, from forgetfulness and confusion to hallucinations to plain old headaches. But then again, it was a structure that could have been there all his life. Or something new, but benign. Or even a cancer in remission.

He knew he should feel like celebrating, but in some ways the absence of any solid diagnosis was more unsettling than the death sentence he had half expected – and at moments wished for. He had lost his lust for life when he lost Laura. The demands of running a large and growing company were really nothing more than distractions to help him kill time until they finally lowered his body into an open grave next to the one that had received his wife just eighteen months ago. He didn't really want to play the Game of Life any more.

As he stepped out of the elevator into the gloom of the clinic's underground parking lot, he felt a pang of jealousy for the hope and determination in the eyes of the other poor souls dealing with disease: the harried mom shepherding her two blonde children along the raised walkway where they wouldn't get hit by a car, the frail old man painfully making his way towards the open elevator door with short, uncertain steps aided by a walker, the red-faced woman trying to squeeze her oversized SUV into a parking slot. Whatever their problems, they wanted to live.

Stone had trouble getting the key into the lock of his silver Crossfire. He was shaking. When he finally got the door open and slid in behind the wheel, an inner voice he had learned to obey over the years told him it wasn't safe to drive. He rested in the fine leather seat and waited for calm.

If I don't care about all this, he thought, *why am I shaking like a fucking leaf?*

He certainly didn't want to spend his last days struggling with endless series of medical decisions that ultimately had no meaning, but he wasn't sure he'd be able to say no to the long list of treatment options that would be available to him if it did turn out to be cancer. Most of these so-called cures had horrendous side effects. Did it really make sense to trade brain cancer for "chemo-brain," which sounded just as bad from the descriptions he had read on the Internet.

In the old days, when he got discouraged, Laura was always there to help him, to remind him of all the jobs he had created, all the families who could thank him for their refrigerators full of food and their vacations up north on the lake and their kids going off to college, and how happy he made her every day. That had been enough. Now, the force of those pep talks was fading, and she was gone, gone, gone. *This is not only about you*, he told himself, trying to remember the sense of her words. He still had a thousand people to take care of.

Feeling steadier with this thought, he started the engine of his trusty two-seater and navigated towards the exit. Five minutes later he was in the feeble sunshine that was the best Michigan could offer in early January, easing the Crossfire onto East 94, which would take him back to the factory to review the weekly sales figures as was his habit on Friday afternoons.

He parked his car in the space reserved for him next to the front entrance and pushed through the revolving door into the lobby, greeting Connie, the fifty-three year old receptionist who sat behind a semi-circular reception desk of brushed stainless steel over which the modernistic NUMERICA logo hung from invisible wires. He had had it re-designed at his daughter's insistence when she was a freshman in college under the spell of her first design classes, and he had to admit he liked the impression it made when potential customers walked in the door.

My God, he thought, *What about Kimmie?* If things went south, he needed to figure out a way to keep a roof over her head *permanently*. If he just provided money, she would give it away. Maybe it was time to reach out. The anger he had felt when she skipped her own mother's funeral had finally drained away. Maybe if he could somehow reconnect it would make his days easier.

"Matt, you okay?" said Connie, looking up at him over her rectangular gray reading glasses. The woman had infallible emotional radar. And she probably knew that he had been to see a doctor. She knew everything that went on at Numerica – except for the classified stuff, of course.

"Nothing that a visit to McNally's won't cure," he said, referring to the nearby Irish pub frequented by Numerica's employees of every level. By unspoken rule, work wasn't discussed at McNally's. It was a democratic refuge where everybody could connect on equal terms, in sharp contrast to the rigid hierarchy that prevailed at the company.

He glanced at his watch. "Too early," he said. "Guess I'd better go to my office and do some work. Set a good example for the troops."

"Right," she said with a nod of her head and a sarcastic grin. She beckoned him to come closer. "If you need, you know, some company? Later on? I'm not busy after work. There are other bars besides McNally's."

It was not the first time Connie had made a suggestive offer. And now he was suddenly tempted. She looked as good as the day he had hired her, back when the company was still small. "You know, that could be interpreted as sexual harassment," he said, and wished immediately he could take it back.

Connie locked eyes on him – beautiful green eyes full of feminine energy. At that moment a call came in, breaking the spell. She picked it up and he walked around the desk to the employee entrance, pressed his index finger against the biometric pad, typed in his code and entered the long carpeted corridor that skirted the engineering department. It had grown enormously over the past twenty years, assuming a larger and larger percentage of manufacturing's budget as Numerica's products became increasingly sophisticated. Stone walked passed row upon row of cubicles where men – and not a few women – sat quietly tapping their keyboards as they stared at their monitors in the subtly dimmed light that reduced eyestrain.

He greeted his secretary, Chase, who was years younger than Connie and much more businesslike.

"You have a three o'clock with Bob Swain," she said, looking up briefly from a print-out of the company's monthly newsletter, which was soon to become a podcast under a project she was supervising.

Swain was his personal accountant, and the man's appearance was a tiresome reminder that tax time wasn't that far off. "There's nothing certain except death and taxes," he said with a chuckle, trying to paint a bright veneer over the darkness inside. It didn't work. Just then out of the corner of his eye he saw someone standing by the door dressed entirely in black, but when he turned there was no one there. Only the coat rack.

He rubbed his eyes, briefly shaken. "Anything else on deck?" he asked.

"The sales figures are in."

"Thanks."

He walked around the side of her desk into his private office. When he had started this business, he could literally calculate his sales on the back of an envelope. Soon, the figures began arriving tucked into light green folders supplied by Margie Fox, his first bookkeeper and still an employee. She used to badger his sales force of two to get those numbers, and would brook no tardiness. Now, the figures arrived on an Oracle dashboard which he could view on his large desktop display or his iPhone. Increasingly, he chose the desktop because – he hated this – he could make the type large enough to read and still see the whole page.

He installed himself in the black leather swivel chair behind his desk and tapped some commands into the recessed keyboard. A map of the U.S., color-coded by sales region, appeared on the large screen. The regions were mostly green, with a couple of yellows and no reds – almost too good to be true. But that's what doing business with the government was like. It took a ton of paperwork, but once you were in, you were in. Next, he looked at his top ten deals. All green. Finally, he called up the raw numbers for the quarter. The screen filled with columns of blurred figures he couldn't quite read. He blinked several times and their edges sharpened. But these columns – what did they really mean? Time would destroy everything they represented. He might as well be looking at a field of ashes. Death and taxes. You could postpone them both, but not indefinitely.

Stone brought his attention back to the computer display and shrank back as a hoard of tiny black insects suddenly began to crawl out of the edges of the bezel onto the screen. He couldn't believe what he was seeing. Was there a nest hidden inside the display, some invasive species from China that got in during the manufacturing process, its eggs gradually warmed by the electronics until they hatched all at once? As he stared, trying to think who in the building would have some Raid or Black Flag, the creatures morphed back into numbers, but now his heart was pounding, and a flash of sweat coated his skin.

This had been happening for a while now. A small pile of leaves at the periphery of his vision would become a sleeping animal, or he would see a pair of shoes sticking out from a snow bank instead of two black stones. They weren't hallucinations, he told himself. *Sometimes my eyes play tricks on me.* Those were the words he used to reassure himself. And Feldman had concurred. Given the test results, it was no big deal. But this time it was a little scary. What if it had happened while he was driving? He told himself what he used to tell his men. *Fear is good. Fear makes you focus.* Maybe so, but today, focus was out of reach. He could barely maintain a steady demeanor in front of his employees.

At that moment, his phone chimed. It was Chase, calling to announce that his accountant had arrived.

"Send him in," said Stone. He wasn't looking forward to this encounter. Dealing with taxes always put him in a foul mood. And today – what if a hoard of cockroaches came pouring out of his accountant's briefcase? The craziness of that thought shook him. He took a deep breath to compose himself as best he could. The door swung open.

Bob Swain was in his early fifties, but already a bit stooped from years of bending over ledgers, and more recently, computer keyboards. His hair was mostly gray and thinning, and he wore silver spectacles that looked like they came from another century. He offered Stone a less than firm handshake and a smile that quickly faded.

"You okay, Matt?" he asked. "You look a little pale."

Fuck! thought Stone. He couldn't afford displays of weakness or uncertainty. Not at work. *The tests were ambiguous*, he told himself. *You're okay, at least for now.*

"I think I'm coming down with something," he said.

He sat down behind his desk and gestured to a seat in front of it for Swain. They had known each other since high school, but had never been friends. Swain's father had done the books for the job shop Stone's father had set up in the 'fifties, and today Stone found this continuity comforting. Even if the path was becoming meaningless, he wasn't on it alone. He just needed to focus on the next step... and a succession plan. Numerica needed the leadership of a man with fire in his belly, not someone who had started reading his old dead wife's college philosophy books in the lonely evenings, consuming far too much scotch.

"How's Kimmie? asked Swain.

Was it too late to bring a successor in from the outside? Somebody at the senior vice president level from a company like...

"Matt?" said Swain, his mild face now wrinkled in genuine concern.

"Oh, sorry. I'm juggling a lot of balls right now. Life's all about solving problems, right?"

"How's Kimmie?"

Kimmie was not one of the balls Stone was juggling, but he wasn't surprised that she would come up in the context of problems. She had been wild in high school and everybody knew it.

"She's still out in sunny California," said Stone. "We chat every couple of weeks." This was a lie, of course. "She's involved in art therapy." Another lie, but a plausible one. "How about your boys?"

"Bobby Jr. is taking his family to Italy this fall. Some sort of liaison job for Chrysler. Garth is still at State.

"The Big Ten's new powerhouse," said Stone, raising an eyebrow. "Maybe he should have tried out as a walk-on."

"We all knew he couldn't play football at that level, Matt, and to tell you the truth, I'm glad. The game's gotten too damned dangerous."

Stone nodded, saying nothing. There were levels of danger that civilians simply couldn't comprehend.

"Shall we get started?" said Swain, lifting his bulging black briefcase onto his lap. "This won't hurt a bit."

Stone sighed. The IRS got you coming and going. They even taxed social security these days. Billions of dollars into the rat hole called the U.S. Government. What could you do? He picked up his pen and signed over sixty thousand dollars of his own money for last year's final quarter. When Swain left, Stone could find nothing to do but sit and stare at the black door through which his accountant had departed. Finally, he stood up, put on his jacket, straightened his tie and walk out the door himself. Then he paused, returned to his desk and shut down the computer. You never know who might wander in and take a peek. Sales figures weren't classified, but he himself had decreed that no screen in the building should ever be left unattended.

He headed out but halted at the door once more and returned to his desk. This time he peeled off a yellow Post It from the pad he kept handy and scribbled a quick note. Then he finally left, giving Chase the best smile he could muster on his way out. When he reached the reception desk he handed the note to Connie.

Meet me at the Roadhouse after work.

The Roadhouse had evolved from a restaurant serving travelers on the old Highway 42 heading to Cincinnati, to a popular pick-up bar for twenty-somethings during the 'nineties, and most recently, to a quiet refuge with fine scotches. Stone was on his second when Connie arrived. She ordered a dark beer. When the waitress delivered it, she raised the frosted stein in a toast. "To creating new memories."

Stone gave her a long look, then repeated the words.

"So," she said after a pause long enough to be awkward, "What made you change your mind?"

"I haven't exactly changed my mind."

"You mean, you're not going to sexually harass me?

Stone laughed. It felt good to be here with Connie. But he couldn't let things get out of hand.

"Not tonight. Too much booze."

"Too much booze? You've had – what?– two, three at most."

"I'm not finished. Neither are you."

Stone started talking about the early days of Numerica, when it was still ValveCo. This was safe territory. Then they talked about their kids, her life as a single mom, his estrangement from Kimmie, which he hadn't kept a secret from her, although he hadn't shared the details either. Gradually, the alcohol took effect, and his sense of time began to change, until what had been a relentless downward escalator from which there was no escape resolved into a series of moments that stood still and felt like they would last forever. They ordered steaks, and a bottle of French red. "This is not a smart thing to do," he said half a dozen times at least. He didn't know whether she believed him. He wasn't sure he believed himself.

When they had polished off a heavy chocolate desert, she took his hands in hers and gave him a *This is serious* look.

"Mathew Stone," she said, "I do not have a crush on you. I just like you, and I care about you. And I will give you whatever you need." She paused. "Starting with a ride home. You can't drive tonight."

She was right. He was drunk. He handed her his keys, and they made their way out the door into the cold air and harsh light of the parking lot. She would drive him home in his car, and then take a cab back to the restaurant.

It was a short drive, and before he knew it they were on his front porch. The taxi was already waiting at the entrance to his driveway, more than a quarter of a mile away.

"The cabbie can't see us," she said, putting her arms on his neck.

"I know."

She pressed her lips against his, and he let himself respond. Then he pulled away. "Thanks for everything." It sounded so inadequate. "I don't know what else to say."

She stepped back, shaking her head. "I knew you were the kind of guy who wouldn't put out on the first date."

Stone awoke to the harsh ringing of an alarm clock that dated back to his army days. He had been in the rack almost five hours, but it felt like he hadn't slept at all. The buzz from last night's wine had evolved into a dull headache. A couple of ibuprofens would fix that. The vague unsteadiness in his legs would fade by itself. He knew this from experience – far too much experience, he thought, since Laura had passed.

Peeing a deep yellow stream into the toilet bowl, he thought about the consequences of what doctors now politely referred to as alcohol abuse. It was hard on your liver. He thought, *I need to cut back*. But why? His drinking wasn't affecting his performance, and in fact the tests showed that his liver function was perfectly normal. He needed whatever consolation he could get. That's what Connie would say.

By habit, Stone stepped into the shower and from there moved through his morning routine, shaving, pulling on his clothes, knotting his tie, popping the vitamins, setting the alarm system before he left, all the while wishing he could undo the events of the previous night.

He had almost broken one of the cardinal rules of business: *Don't get your meat where you earn you bread*, as his dad had expressed it. He had almost invited Connie in for a nightcap. Worse, he had been on the verge of telling her he really didn't want to live anymore.

He knew he ought to talk to somebody. It wasn't good keeping things bottled up. So the grief counselor had said, and unlike most of her bullshit, it was pretty good advice. He made a mental note to call Herb and Ginny when he got to the office and invite himself over for dinner so he could tell them what they would see as unambiguous good news about his exam. If the weather held, he'd pick up some steaks on the way over. They could grill them on the deck and have a couple of martinis in the process. He was almost getting used to the idea that Laura would never be with him for Friday night drinks with those two, or trips up north to the lakes, or anything. But he was by no means fully healed. It still didn't seem fair that she had to suffer, or die without being able to know for sure if Kimmie had found a comfortable place in the world. That she of all people should be singled out for an early death seemed too random, and too much like the deaths he had seen over in Vietnam, which didn't have any purpose at all.

The commute traffic was light, a grim reminder that in spite of the stock market's encouraging performance, the economy as a whole was still in the toilet and the auto industry a shadow of its former self. Fewer cars on the road meant fewer people going to work. It was a simple as that. For all the positive press releases issuing from GM and Ford, Detroit would never again attain the world dominance it once enjoyed. Thank God he had diversified Numerica's customer base. He drove an American car, but he was secretly proud that not a single part in it was manufactured by his own company. The days of being an insignificant link in a Big Three supply chain were long gone. Now it was all about precision: valves for big pharma that the Chinese just couldn't be trusted to make, artificial knee and hip joints... and the robots – highly classified and highly lucrative little machines.

Sometimes the new directions Numerica was taking made him nervous. So much of the value add was in software, an area of expertise where he was, to put it bluntly, clueless. That made his chief of software development less expendable than Stone would like, but as Laura used to say, you had to go with the flow. And the man seemed loyal. He was sure as hell well-paid.

The guards waved Stone through the gates, one of them offering a friendly mock salute which Stone returned. He parked in his usual slot, grabbed his briefcase and braced himself for the inevitable encounter with Connie.

She was behind the imposing reception desk as always, not one blonde hair out of place, her speaker tube curving delicately towards the lips he had kissed only a few hours ago.

"Morning, Matt," she said in her usual cheerful voice. "Somebody dropped this off for you. I didn't recognize him." She handed him a small, folded note. Puzzled, he paused to open it.

I know, I know. Never again. I understand. But you have to admit it was pretty hot. – C.

He looked up and their eyes met. He gave her a quick nod and a reluctant smile, then stuffed the note into his pocket. On the way to his office he stopped by the admin bay and personally fed the note into a shredder. Fooling around with Connie was a Bad Idea. But the evening had brought his loneliness into focus. Maybe it was time to start dating... although the very idea of a date seemed more than a little strange.

Now on auto pilot, Stone greeted Chase, poured himself a large cup of coffee to make up for the espresso he had skipped on his way in, walked through the outer office to his desk, checked the dashboard on the large flat-screen monitor for red bars that would indicate a problem on the factory floor and, finding none, reached for the phone to call Ginny about dinner. An IM from Selena Moreaux, his new chief information officer, interrupted him. He was still getting used to her informal style, which included scheduling meetings no more than fifteen minutes in advance if she felt like it. He had deliberately gone young with her hire because, like it or not, young was better in IT. He had hand-picked her number two, Carl "Jinx" Jenkins, who had worked his way up to management from the shop floor. Jinx was smart and tough-minded, and she had wisely made him her point man when she wanted to sell new technology to department managers who were easily old enough to be her father. The two of them were an unlikely team, but an effective one.

She strode into his office, dressed crisply in a dark suit and silk blouse, accented by a colorful scarf in red, white and blue. She wore one almost every day, even in the summer. All business, she sat down on the couch to the left of his desk and began talking without preamble.

"I think all the senior executives and the team leaders on the floor need iPhones like you. Here's why."

Stone studied her as she made her case, speaking rapidly with a slight French accent. Glowing Mediterranean skin, dark hair, large gold earrings, a little too much make-up, noticeable perfume. He wasn't really listening. He trusted her, and when he learned it would only be fifteen thousand for the first year, he said yes without even asking any questions.

The day proceeded like every other, but the meetings had an unfamiliar quality, as though he were part of a play where everyone's lines were predetermined and where, no matter what revelations or betrayals might take place, nothing mattered in the end. It was only a play.

Before he knew it, five o'clock had arrived. He auto-dialed Herb and Ginny's home phone as he pulled out of the parking lot, but got the recorded message. That was actually a good thing. Neither one had gotten home yet, and he would be there to surprise them with a treat. Herb's business, much more closely tied to Detroit than Stone's, had fallen on difficult times in the past couple of years, and steak was no longer a regular item on their menu.

Stone took the Fisk exit and made a stop at Ralph's, the town's one gourmet market, where Laura had shopped for years. She had taught him so much – how to live, really, beyond the rough and tumble of making money and building a company. He would certainly never have landed in Ralph's on his own. He had been a meat and potatoes guy in high school and his first two years in college. Laura had changed all that, although he feared he was slipping back to his old habits now that she was gone. Stone chose three rib-eyes and a nice bottle of red and then, just to be safe, a bottle Tanqueray. Today, Ralph himself was behind one of the check stands, another sign of the tough economic times.

Stone wasn't prepared for the display of flashing blue and red lights that met his eyes when he rounded the corner to his old friends' comfortable tree-lined street. Slowing to a crawl and fighting a rising tide of anxiety, he forced himself to assess the scene with a soldier's eyes: three police cars parked haphazardly in front of Herb and Ginny's modest white clapboard house, like vehicles that had arrived in a hurry. Yellow crime scene tape stretched across the open garage door and the gate to the picket fence that fronted the sidewalk. A uniformed cop down on one knee examining the tail pipe of Herb's seven-year-old Dodge RAM. A second cop stationed in front of the gate, hands behind his back in a posture of parade rest.

Not good.

Stone parked and trotted over to the cop who was guarding the gate. Young and gangly, he eyed Stone uncertainly.

"This is a crime scene, sir."

"I can see that," Stone snapped. "What happened?"

"There's an investigation in progress."

Stone began to lose his patience with this *kid*. "Who's in charge?"

"That would be Detective Reiser."

"Where is he?"

"Inside."

Stone fought to contain his exasperation at this dribble of information. Beyond Numerica, Herb and Ginny were his life. He understood that the kid was only doing his job. You don't blurt out the details of an investigation to any damn stranger who comes by. But Stone had a screaming need to know.

"Look at me, son," he said. He hated to play this card, but had no choice. The young cop gave him a quizzical look. Then his face blanched as recognition dawned. Matt Stone. White Lake High football legend. War hero. President and CEO of Numerica, the town's primary source of employment, and its tax revenue for that matter.

"I'm not asking you to break any rules," said Stone. "But I've known the Grimes family for forty years. Whatever's gone down, Reiser's going to want to talk to me."

The kid hesitated, then reached for the microphone at his belt. At that moment, the front door opened and a man emerged, tucking a small spiral-backed notebook into the pocket of his ill-fitting tan suit as he descended the three wooden steps from the small front porch to the walkway. He looked up and nodded at Stone, who brushed past the young cop, swung open the low gate and ducked under the tape. There was a trick to the gate. The hinges were broken and you had to lift it up or it wouldn't clear the concrete of the walkway. He extended his hand as Reiser approached.

"Matt Stone"

"I know who you are," said Reiser, offering a half-hearted handshake. The man looked tired and, Stone thought, a bit sad. What the Hell was going on here?

"Friend of the family?" asked Reiser.

"Since high school," said Stone.

He and Herb Grimes had been teammates on the first White Lake football squad to win more than half its games in ten years. Stone was the volatile quarterback, Grimes the reliable left tackle who always had his back when he needed protection. They had taken different paths after that happy year. For Stone, football had lost its luster. Beyond that, although he had the leadership skills and the brains to play at the college level, he lacked the physical tools you needed to throw a perfect spiral sixty yards. He *did* want to go to college, and to pay for it, he committed to an ROTC scholarship at the University of Michigan. As it turned out, the classes in military theory and the summer training only supported the romanticized view of war he held back then, before he knew any better. War, he had thought, put football to shame.

Herb managed to swing a deferment from military service and went to work at his father's eighteen-man job shop right after graduation. He took over at age twenty-eight when his father died of an early heart attack.

Stone had a similar option when he returned from Vietnam after his compulsory service. His father also owned a small, third-tier manufacturing shop specializing in valves for automotive air conditioners, but Stone saw working there as a thinly-disguised form of indentured servitude to General Motors, the shop's only real customer. Beyond that, he couldn't imagine taking orders from his father after what he had been through as an officer in Vietnam. Stone loved his father, but the man was meticulous to a fault, and often impossible to please. Stone managed to get a job at Xerox and ended up a young sales star. He was competitive by nature, and eventually acquired enough cash to buy his father's business outright.

Liberated from a demanding travel schedule, newly married and faced with the reality of having to meet a payroll every two weeks, he turned to his old friend for companionship and, at least at the beginning, advice. Although they had been separated by circumstances for several years, when they were together it was just like the old days, except with jobs and wives instead of homework and girlfriends. When the gap in the scale of their businesses grew, their friendship didn't suffer. Herb kept him grounded, in touch with his roots, and Laura saw in Ginny the older sister she had always wished for. But now....

"What's going on here?" asked Stone.

Responding, Reiser's eyes had the look of a man who had seen far too many crime scenes. "I think you should talk to Mrs. Grimes." he said. "She's inside."

Stone descended the steps into the Grimes living room. Ginny was sitting on the couch, staring into space. Beyond her, through sliding glass doors, was the patio and the Weber grill around which they had gathered so many times, drinks in hand, cares drifting away like so much cigarette smoke. Stone felt a bolt of concern as Ginny stood up. Her appearance was ghastly. It seemed that not only the color, but the life itself had drained from her face. She was dressed in jeans and a loose sweatshirt, as though she were planning to go over to the shop and put in a shift, which she often did now that the kids were out of the house. She approached him with uncertain steps, and when they embraced she felt unnaturally hot.

"What happened?" he said, but he already knew.

"He's gone, Matt," she said softly. "It's over."

"What?"

"He's dead. D-E-A-D."

Stone pulled back. The room seemed to spin.

"How?"

Now anger brought some life to Ginny's eyes. "He killed himself, Matt. The I.R.S. padlocked the shop and he came home and taped the doors to the garage and got into the truck and started it up and breathed the carbon monoxide until he passed out and then... he died. I was at the grocery store. When I came home I called 911, but just because, you know, that's what you do. I knew he was gone. Shit."

Stone stiffened. "Wait a minute. The I.R.S. padlocked the shop?"

"They're seizing all the assets. You want some gin? I've had a couple. I think I want some more."

Ginny walked stiffly into the kitchen. Normally she has a graceful way of moving that made the few extra pounds she had been carrying the last few years seem attractive and not at all worth shedding through the difficult diets she undertook every January. Laura used to say that Ginny had a Gauguin body. Right now she just looked heavy and worn out. On the Formica counter Stone could see a bottle of cheap gin and an empty tumbler. She retrieved a second large glass from the cupboard and poured more than an inch of gin into each. Stone walked over and put a restraining hand on hers before she could drink.

"Maybe you should hold back a little," he said.

"I've been holding back my whole life," said Ginny.

Stone let this cryptic comment pass. He released her arm and she took a restrained sip from her glass.

"Have you contacted the kids?" Herb and Ginny had a son who was on his second tour of duty in Afghanistan and a married daughter who was a nurse. She lived somewhere in the South – Georgia, if memory served him right, which was not always the case these days. Anyway, it would be a day or two before either one arrived.

"You can't stay here alone tonight," he said.

"I know," she replied woodenly. "Bad idea." She took another sip of gin. "I'll call my sister She'll come over. Or I'll go there. I mean, I'll have her come and get me. Don't worry, I'm okay. Do you know what they'll do with the body?"

Stone looked into her eyes, their crystal blue now clouded with confusion and too much gin on an empty stomach.

"I don't suppose you're hungry." he said. His mind went briefly to the steaks in his car. Shouldn't they be in the refrigerator? The thought alarmed him. His best friend had just died and he was thinking about steaks.

She shook her head in answer to his question. There was a long silence.

"I guess I'll lose the house," she said at last.

Stone put his hands on her shoulders. "You're not going to lose anything. Forget about that."

"Matt—"

"We'll fix this." It was a stupid thing to say. There was no fix for death. Hot anger filled his body. The I.R.S. had murdered Herb as sure as if they'd taken him out behind his shop and shot him. This was not the country he had risked his life for in some bullshit war. Three men under his personal command had died, and thousands upon thousands more – for what? So a bunch of government leeches could rob a hard-working man of his livelihood?

The cascading disaster of his friend's suicide began to play out in his mind. Herb wasn't the only victim here. What about the business? The lost jobs and the foreclosures that would inevitably follow? The U.S. Government had taken a wrecking ball to a lot of lives today.

Ginny could feel his anger. "Matt, calm down. I'll be okay."

He took his hands off her shoulders and walked back into the living room, as though turning his back on her could somehow make the flashing lights and the yellow tape and everything else fade out of existence, like a nightmare that gradually dissolved as you showered, shaved, drank your double cappuccino and engaged in the new day.

He returned to the kitchen.

"Ginny, who did this?"

"I don't understand."

"Do you have the name of the agent Herb was dealing with?

"I don't know. What does it matter? Herb's dead. We went through this with Laura. He can't come back. It's all over."

"No it's not. This time, somebody's going to pay."

II.

Strike at What Is Weak

Driving home on a two-lane back road with only his headlights to illuminate the flat, rural landscape, Stone felt a sudden urge to vomit.

What the fuck? He hadn't felt sensations like this since he was a child.

He pulled over and hit the safety flashers before he swung out of the car and wretched, steadying himself with his hand on the cold metal of the open door. The blinking lights made him feel sicker. He leaned in, hit the flasher button again and then stood up and took some deep breaths. The cold winter air felt clean and fresh. Gradually, his nausea faded. There would soon come a time, Stone had recently realized, when he would no longer be able to depend on the once rugged engine that was his body.

He looked up at the stars, replaying thoughts that had flashed through his mind years ago during a lull after his first fire fight. Was there a God? Stone couldn't believe there was. What divine being would create such a fucked up world? In this world, you had to go it alone. He got back into the car and headed down the long, straight road that would eventually take him home. With each mile, the realization grew in him that avenging Herb's death was more than a random fantasy born of anger. He could do it. He had the resources. He could find the weapons. And he had nothing to lose.

The fence posts to the side of the road flashed past with a hypnotic cadence, reminding him of the weeks in his life. Time speeded up the older you got, the closer to the end. The end. Was he really planning to go out like some left wing wacko, busting into an IRS office and shooting the place up until a SWAT team arrived to take him out? What kind of a statement was that? Where was the dignity? And what good would it do?

Better to punish the asshole who went after Herb. That would serve justice. And it would also very quickly lead to prison. He'd be an obvious suspect. He'd already as much as revealed his intentions to Ginny. *This time, somebody's going to pay.* Beside that, no matter how careful he was, he'd leave clues. FBI forensics would find him out sooner or later, and most likely sooner. There was no death penalty in Michigan, so he wouldn't even have the honor of dying for his country. That was how he would want it framed. Not just personal revenge. A statement. But it could well be a statement made by a sick and frail old man. Prison medical care wasn't exactly up to the standards of the Mayo Clinic. He didn't want to die that way. Even for a noble cause. He just wasn't that strong.

Which left him... on a country road with a couple of steaks nobody would ever eat and a bottle of gin that would vanish all too quickly.

Back in his office on Friday morning and surrounded by the same furniture he had known for more than a decade, the previous day's events seemed far removed. Connie had given him her usual wry morning smile as he walked past the reception desk, Chase had handed him a print-out of the day's schedule on his way into his office as she always did, the coffee pot on the credenza opposite his desk was full, and the expensive Herman Miller chair his back now demanded awaited him.

It seemed so normal! But what did he expect? A cloaked figure carrying a scythe walking by the window, flaunting the meaninglessness of life with his silence?

He called Ginny and learned from her sister, Hope, that she was still in bed. Hope was a somewhat obnoxious born-again Christian. According to Ginny, her sister had lived a "dissolute" life, but Stone had no details. He only knew Hope had given up smoking, drinking and, of all things, dancing, and had long considered Stone and his wife a negative influence in Ginny's life.

"You shouldn't have let her drink so much, Herb," she said over the phone. "She's got enough headaches without a hangover."

Stone bit his tongue. "Please have her call me when she gets up," he said, wondering if this woman would actually pass on the message. "I'm helping her out with the I.R.S. situation," he added.

"What I.R.S. situation?"

"She can explain it," he said. "I have to go. I'm really sorry this happened. I'm going to try to help."

"God works in mysterious ways."

"That he does," said Stone in a soft voice, cradling the phone.

His next call was to Jack Hastings, his corporate council. He needed to get that padlock off Herb's shop so he could get to Herb's books, assuming Federal agents hadn't confiscated everything. Hastings picked up on the first ring.

"It's Matt. I need a good tax lawyer. Got any names?"

Hastings cleared his throat, one of his numerous delaying tactics. "Can you talk about the nature of the problem, Matt?"

"I'm looking into some Nigerian investments and I need to understand the tax implications."

"What? Matt, listen—"

"I'm joking, Jack. But I do need a name. I'm trying to help a friend who got into some trouble with the I.R.S. He ran a job shop. We're not talking high finance here."

"Do you want a lawyer or a high-level CPA?"

"A lawyer. I need privilege."

Hastings, himself a lawyer, hesitated a beat before responding, no doubt wondering what kind of trouble would involve attorney-client privilege. "I'll drop by your office in a few minutes."

"Email is okay."

"No it's not. You know that. It's like sending a post card."

"You just want to find out what Chase is wearing today."

Serious to a fault, Hastings ignored this. "I'll see you in a few minutes."

Next, Stone dialed the president of the White Lake Community Bank and arranged to have five thousand dollars in cash delivered by messenger. That would be enough to tide Ginny over for a few weeks.

That done, he turned his attention to the day's schedule. It was mostly internal stuff – a nine thirty meeting to settle a turf war between his VPs of engineering and manufacturing, a quarterly briefing from HR, an afternoon rehearsal demo from the robotics group, an update on the new government quality control requirements that were going into effect in June, a presentation from the PR agency. He pinged Chase and told her to reschedule his afternoon. Then he took a deep breath and rehearsed his 'We're all on the same team' speech for his first meeting.

With the morning behind him and five thousand dollars in his pocket, Chase drove out to Herb and Ginny's house, and once again was struck with the veil of normalcy draped over the externals of his life. *Death is also normal*, he reminded himself as he swung open the creaky wooden gate that led to the walkway. But not Herb's death. Suicide was the most unnatural of acts.

Ginny greeted him at the front door in a pink terrycloth robe that had seen better days. She looked a little puffy, but at least there was some life in her eyes. She hugged him and then held onto his hand as she led him down into the living room. He could hear the clatter of dishes being washed in the kitchen. Hope was at work, and from what Ginny had said about her sister in recent years, she wouldn't quit without scrubbing the floors. *Cleanliness is next to godliness*, he thought. Ginny had always been a little messy, while her sister, once even worse, had become a fanatic since her conversion.

They sat down side by side and Stone handed Ginny the cash, shushing her with a finger to his lips when she tried to protest.

"You need to buy groceries," he said.

"Don't get me wrong. I'm very grateful," she said, putting her arm on his shoulder. The gesture exposed almost all of one breast. Stone looked away.

"I guess you can see we've been skimping on everything. Of course, Herb would never ask for help. I guess I wouldn't either." She looked down at the gray carpet, then glared at Stone.

"The bastard! Why did he do this? We could have just retired and lived on the farm. I mean, sure, renting it was our main source of income, but we could have worked something out."

Stone had spent a weekend on that farm a few years back when Ginny's mother died and she had inherited the property. It was dilapidated, but livable, and only a couple miles from Lake Michigan and some good fishing. And it was theirs, free and clear—unless the IRS had levied it as well, he reminded himself. He would have to track that down. What a mess. He was beginning to wonder just how deep a hole Herb had dug for himself. Why had he deserted this woman who had stuck with him through thick and thin?

"I want a cigarette," Ginny declared. "And a gin fizz and a couple of cyanides," she added with a bitter laugh.

"Are you having suicidal thoughts?"

"Now you sound like a therapist."

"Have you?"

"You know I wouldn't do that."

Stone had no trouble believing her. For Ginny, being cheerful was a duty. She would prevail, even over this.

At that moment Hope entered the living room with a dishtowel in her hands. Like her sister, Hope was chubby, but she moved without grace, and with none of Ginny's muted sexiness.

"Do you want some lunch, Matt? I'm making tuna fish sandwiches." There was a note of criticism in her voice, as though there ought to be more in the pantry than a couple cans of tuna.

"Thanks, but I've eaten," Stone lied.

He waited until she left the room.

"Listen, Ginny, I went ahead and hired a lawyer to help straighten this out."

She shook her head and sighed. "You're just a take charge kinda guy, aren't you."

"I want to know what happened. But if you don't want me to – "

"Christ, Matt," she said loudly. "I need all the help I can get."

"I'll thank you not to take the Lord's name in vain," called Hope from the kitchen.

"Sorry," Ginny called back. Stone got the feeling they had had back-and-forths like this for decades.

"I'll know what it takes to get the padlock off by tomorrow," he said. "We'll take things from there."

"Is there any chance we could re-start the business?" she asked. "People keep calling up and I don't know what to tell them. I mean, they express their condolences, but what they really want to know about is their job."

"I don't know, Ginny. We'll have to see."

"Tell me the truth."

"It's not likely. The Three don't want to deal with a shop that's in financial trouble. And, frankly, they don't like to deal with small shops period. Those days are pretty much gone."

"What ever happened to loyalty?" she asked, glancing upward as though her sister's God might have an answer. Loyalty was a commodity in short supply. Stone knew this from his own experience, and it was that deficit that led him to take his own company out of the Detroit Three's fold in the first place. If he hadn't, he might well have ended up in poor Herb's shoes.

"It really wasn't Herb's fault, was it?" said Ginny. "It was the whole system."

Herb thought, *of course it was his fault*. He said, "The system sucks,'" borrowing language he had learned from his daughter in her teenage years.

They both stared out into space. Ginny began to softly cry. "Shit," she said. "I want him back."

It was an appropriate day for a burial, cold, with a leaden sky. At least it wasn't snowing. There was a large flower arrangement at the head of the open grave, a reminder that the wild flowers and the long, hot days of summer would return just like that had last year, and the year before that. But Herb Grimes wouldn't be back. Ginny stood next to Stone, holding his hand as Herb's coffin descended into the earth with awful finality, her face covered by a black veil.

Almost a hundred people were gathered around the grave, the men grim and uncomfortable in suits they almost never wore, the women plump and tearful. Many of the men were connected to the Blackhawk Regiment, a pathetic amateur militia that Herb often referred to as "the last resort." That was the only point of contention between the two men. Stone simply saw no reason to put on camo fatigues and spend his very limited leisure time eating lukewarm MREs and running around a forest playing glorified games of capture the flag.

Most of the men who made that choice had never dropped into a hot LZ or taken hostile fire in any form. If they had, Stone had always thought, they would never want to do anything that reminded them of the experience. In a couple moments of weakness he had contributed to the cause, funding in one case a heavily armored APC and in another the concrete work for a private rifle range where Herb had practiced regularly, but Stone always felt that militias were fueled by paranoid thinking that had no basis in reality.

Now, he wasn't so sure. Herb always brought up the Waco siege as an example of what the government could do whenever it wanted. Eighty-two people were killed there, and surely most of them were innocent of any crime. And as proof of the difference militias could make, he would cite a highly publicized incident in Nevada, where heavily armed militiamen had successfully faced down the Bureau of Land Management in a weird grazing rights dispute.

Who could know what would have happened had Herb shared his predicament with his weekend brothers in arms? Stone surveyed the group, trying to pick out the Blackhawks, and imagining them dressed for battle, weapons locked and loaded, entrenched in defensive positions around Herb's shop. Just at that moment Ginny squeezed his hand, and he felt a surge of rage he could hardly contain.

After the first ceremonial shovel of dirt had been thrown onto the coffin, the mourners got into their cars, no doubt grateful for the warmth their heaters provided, and made their way to the Grimes house, where Ginny's sister had set out a buffet and, reluctantly, Stone imagined, a generous stock of beer, wine and liquor. Stone's first act was to pour himself two fingers of scotch from an unopened bottle of Glen Livet, a single malt Ginny knew he favored. He wondered if she had conveyed this information to her sister. That was Ginny, always thinking of the people around her, even when she was in dire straights.

Right now, she was politely chatting with a young couple. Probably ex-employees, Stone thought, or perhaps a young Blackhawk with his wife. Ginny appeared not to have shed even one tear. That would come later. Right now, in spite of the circumstances, she was playing the gracious hostess.

A stocky man in his mid-forties approached the makeshift bar holding a glass of half-melted ice cubes. Stone vaguely recognized him from his occasional visits to the range with Herb. The man nodded somberly at Stone and poured himself a refill of bourbon.

"It ain't right," he said, shaking his head.

For a moment, Stone thought the man was criticizing his and Ginny's hand holding during the graveside ceremony. The man was a Blackhawk, and saw himself almost as a brother to her. He might well view Stone as an interloper.

"There's an IRS agent out there who deserves to have his name inscribed on a bullet. A three fifty-six hollow point, preferably," said the man.

Stone didn't dare agree out loud. The last thing he needed was a tweet on the Internet that had him, the president of Numerica, advocating violence against the U.S. government. And everybody tweeted these days. Not just kids and athletes. Blackhawks too.

"I know how you feel," said Stone. "I've known Herb since high school."

Recognition dawned on the man's face. "You're...."

"Matt Stone," he said, extending his hand.

"Numerica, right?" said the man.

Stone nodded. "And you are?"

"Steve O'Brian. I remember you. You ought to come out to the range more often. There's some guys who would like to meet you."

A stocky man with blue eyes and early hints of gray hair now approached them. He was about Stone's age, with the same muscular build. He was clearly not a shop rat like many of the Blackhawks. He offered his hand and shook Stone's with a firm grip. "Mark Stetson," he said. "Pleased to meet you."

"Mark's giving us some fresh leadership," said O'Brian, as Stetson poured himself a drink. Stone studied this new source of leadership. He certainly projected a sense of command.

O'Brien lowered his voice. "Somebody's got to put an end to this shit, know what I mean? They think they can do any fuckin' thing they feel like."

They. The U.S. government. What ever happened to government of the people, for the people and *by* the people? Stone, in spite of everything, still called himself a patriot, if not in the sense that the Blackhawks used the term. He held a soft spot in his heart for the government under whose flag the generals and bureaucrats managing the war in Vietnam had betrayed him – had betrayed a whole generation for that matter. The nobility of purpose and wisdom of the founding fathers were nowhere to be found in that war, nor the new ones in the Middle East, for that matter. Still, he clung to the hope that the ideals that launched his nation could somehow be rekindled from today's ashes of cynicism and stupidity.

It was naive, and he knew it. The government was like a buddy of yours who had gotten hooked on heroin. You knew he would lie to you and even steal your money to score his H. He wasn't himself anymore, but you didn't want to believe it. Power was the government's heroin. And they would do 'any fuckin' thing' to keep it.

O'Brian was right – and everybody in the room would surely agree with him, along with millions of Americans who weren't in the room. The government was out of control. But what was to be done? Stone scanned the gathering, once again trying to pick out the Blackhawks. The "regiment" was about thirty men strong according to Herb, and they were both well trained and well disciplined. On the other hand, many were near Stone's age, and not the fighters they once might have been. When all was said and done, in the mathematics of conflict they were a rounding error.

On the other hand, as a guerrilla force, with carefully selected targets and the element of surprise, they could do a lot of damage.

Stetson rejoined them, raising his glass, which was now full.

"To freedom," he said.

"And the right to bear arms to protect it," said O'Brien, raising his. Stone got the impression that this was a ritual toast, a call and response repeated again and again.

He raised his own glass and joined them. "To freedom," he said, wondering where in God's name this was all going to lead.

Stone sat in the dim light of Herb's cramped office, staring through the open door at the idle lathes and drill presses soon to be sold off to the highest bidder. It was almost ten o'clock, his routine bedtime, but the QuickBooks documents spread out on the battered desk held his attention, like a novel too compelling to abandon in favor of sleep. Two sets of books. This fact told a tale in itself. And a sad tale at that.

The first set, the more optimistic of the two, was obviously intended for potential lenders. Herb had recorded more than a dozen preliminary bids to the tier two companies that were his customers as actual deals—deals that had not only been closed, but shipped and invoiced as well. In doing so, he had created $235,000 in fictitious receivables. There were plenty of sleazy finance companies that would accept receivables as collateral for a short term loan – the practice was called factoring – and some of them were no doubt sloppy enough to be fooled by Herb's fakery. Stone suspected if he combed the office he would find a folder of forged purchase orders to back up the cooked books. He couldn't bring himself to snoop like that. He had seen enough.

There was only one word for what Herb had done: fraud. But he obviously hadn't gotten caught. It was the second set of books – the real ones so far as Stone could tell – that had brought the I.R.S. to the door. They showed an operating loss averaging about twelve thousand dollars per month for the current year, and Herb had dealt with those losses by not paying his bills. He had most likely sweet talked his suppliers and convinced them to wait for money that, in reality, wasn't even in the pipeline yet. Everybody in Michigan was stretching out their payables, starting at the top. You were lucky if you could get net ninety days from GM or Chrysler, and Ford was at net forty-five. So Herb had a credible story. But there were some bills he couldn't escape paying. And he had covered these by borrowing from the payroll tax account. That was the fatal mistake. How could Herb have been so stupid? Surly he knew that could send him to jail.

There was more. Stone had learned from the tax lawyer that Herb hadn't filed personal tax returns for three years, and that meant an automatic tax bill of ten thousand per year until Herb came up with the real numbers. That might not have been the easiest task in the work, Stone reflected, but when it was done, Herb – or rather, his estate such as it was – would owe a lot less. For now, Stone had covered everything the Feds wanted with a personal check. "It's the only way to buy a government hacksaw," the lawyer had quipped, referring to the padlock that had come off this morning.

Stone arranged the documents he had printed out into two neat stacks and stood up from the ancient swivel chair where he had been sitting, stretching to get the kinks out of his back. He had known Herb for decades, and Herb was no risk taker. If anything, he was overly cautious. Why had he risked jail?

Rounding the desk his hip brushed against Herb's old wire-frame IN box and sent its contents spilling onto the concrete floor. As he retrieved the collection of unpaid bills and advertising flyers, his eye fell on a stapled sheaf of papers with the Autoline logo at the top of the first page. It looked like a contract, and from one of GM's top suppliers at that. Stone reached into his shirt pocket for the reading glasses he had put away and studied the document. It was a contract for three hundred and fifty thousand dollars.

A contract that would save the business.

He flipped through the legalese at the front end of the contract until he reached the addendum that spelled out the details of payment and delivery, each number initialed. He could do the heart-breaking math in his head. Had the I.R.S.

not padlocked Herb's shop, he would have been out of the woods in sixty days.

He could have made it. He could have – should have – hired somebody to help him buy time. Stone had learned from the tax lawyer that there were several work-outs available. But Herb would see that as giving in, doing what *they* told him to do, playing by *their* rules. He could hear his friend's voice in his mind, talking about a run-in he had had a few years back with the Occupational Safety and Health Administration, better known as OSHA.

"All I have to do is kiss their ass and they'll let me go," he had said. Then, after a pause, "I'd rather die." Stone knew that Herb would bring the same attitude to his tax situation.

That was the problem right there. If you didn't like what your mayor or your congressman was doing, you could vote them out of office. But the I.R.S. was out of control. Literally. Those agents could do any goddamn thing they felt like, and their victims had no recourse

Stone's nerves began to hum with quiet rage. The bureaucratic bastards just couldn't wait to get their pound of flesh. He stared down at the contract, worth hundreds of thousands only two days ago, now reduced to nothing more than scrap paper for the recycle bin. It infuriated him that there was nothing he could do. Yes, Ginny was right. Herb was gone, and he was never coming back. And the business was dead as well. But there were a lot of Herbs out there who were in the same boat and weren't dead yet, not to mention the millions of other poor souls who had been fucked over by the I.R.S. for the privilege of being United States citizens. Someone had to pay for this. And Stone had a name.

Agent Daniel Chan, age forty-seven, was a native of Michigan, having grown up in Pontiac not fifteen miles from White Lake. He was married, with one son who was majoring in economics at U of M. He had joined the I.R.S. in 1993, and had risen to the rank of senior agent, a position he would likely hold until retirement. He was a registered Democrat. He drove a 2007 Honda Accord. His address was 2716 Magnolia Avenue, Priliox, MI 94337.

It would be very easy to take him out, and the thought had drawn Stone into countless fantasies. He wouldn't do it sniper style. He'd kidnap the man. Chan worked out of the IRS office in Detroit, which was near the river not far from the Renaissance Center. Stone would intercept him in the parking lot and have him drive up I 98 at gunpoint to the old Stone family cabin in the Upper Peninsula. He imagined the smiling face on Chan's LinkedIn page incandescent with fear as he cocked the pistol he would use.

An eye for an eye and a tooth for a tooth.

It didn't stop there. Stone imagined a small organization like Ireland's IRA, but composed of sober patriots, not teenagers out for random trouble after too many pints at the pub. The military arm of a revived Tea Party, men of action who could turn principles into realities. A few well-chosen assassinations would make case workers like Chan think twice about the hardball tactics they now used with impunity. The key to success would be to keep things loosely organized. No online forums. No bank accounts. Just a common purpose, a little practical training on targeting the right people and, although he hated the word, a manifesto. A set of concrete demands. A vision. But what, precisely, was that vision to be? Taxation, like government itself, was a necessity without which society would descend into chaos. Laws and the means to enforce them could not be done away with. But how to prevent their abuse? That was the question. His instinct was to fight fire with fire, with surgical strikes against the worst, most blatant offenders, but the thought of recruiting a cadre of men who could be controlled and trusted to carry out that mission would be tough. And he couldn't make the impact he needed to make as a lone shooter. He didn't have enough time.

Stone shook his head and brought himself back to the present moment in Herb's dim shop. These were crazy thoughts, and he knew it. He needed to think things through, not indulge in Rambo fantasies, and he couldn't do that right now. What he really wanted to do was share what he had learned with Ginny. Herb had engineered an amazing deal for a small company like his, and she ought to know about it. There had been a lot of praise at the funeral for Herb's kindness and dedication, but the subtext was that he had died a failure. The contract from Autoline shed a new light on everything. If Herb hadn't been ambushed at the last minute, he would be a hero right now. Stone glanced at his watch. Ten fifteen. She would still be up. He would swing by.

Five minutes later he was opening the squeaky gate and bracing himself for an onslaught from Rex, Herb and Ginny's German shepherd. The dog always followed the same pattern. He would snarl, charge, and then at some point recognize Stone's familiar scent and put his head down to be scratched. He must be inside, Stone thought as he mounted the steps and knocked on the front door.

A moment later Ginny's face appeared in the door's small glass viewing window. She flashed him a bright smile, the first he'd seen from her in days, and opened the door.

"A late night visitor!" she said enthusiastically, offering him a hug and then leading him down into the living room. She was dressed in a summer robe with a pattern that featured large pink flowers. Ginny had lost quite a bit of weight in the past couple of weeks, and was close to regaining the Marilyn Monroe figure she had enjoyed in high school. Stone tried, unsuccessfully, to ignore the prominent nipples poking out against the sheer fabric.

There was a half-empty glass of white wine on the coffee table in front of the sofa, and next to it, an open copy of the novel she had been reading, *Fifty Shades of Gray*.

"Herb didn't like me reading stuff like that," she said, glancing at the novel. "But now, I figure, why not? You have to live one day at a time. Would you like a little wine? Maybe a brandy? There's so much booze left over from the funeral! I'll never drink it all by myself."

Stone opted for a brandy, and Ginny disappeared into the kitchen to fetch it.

"Where's Rex?" he asked, calling after her.

She reappeared with a snifter in her hand and a questioning look on her face.

"Rex died two years ago, Matt. He had hip dysplasia, don't you remember? You were there when we put him down."

A cold wave of fear passed through Stone's body. Of course he remembered. They had made a little ceremony of it, complete with a last meal of premium beef for the old dog, who by that time could hardly get into a comfortable posture to eat. But a moment ago, it was as if none of that had happened.

"I do remember, but... Is this what they call a senior moment? Good God! I'm not that old, am I?"

"Don't worry about it, Matt," said Ginny, resting her hand on his shoulder as she handed him the heavy snifter of brandy. "You're tired and you've got a lot on your mind."

"I've had a lot on my mind for years. I've got a thousand employees right now and every two weeks I have to pay them. I always managed to remember that."

"Do you realize that's the first time you've said anything about Numerica in this house in years?"

"I guess I've always thought of your place as somewhere to relax."

"Matt, Herb accepted your success and he wasn't jealous. He liked having a smaller business. Of course, it wasn't easy when things started going down hill with the big outsourcing trend and all."

Stone took a swallow of brandy and gave himself a moment to enjoy the warmth it brought.

"Herb was on the edge of a big turnaround, Ginny. If Agent Chan hadn't been such a...." Stone searched for an inoffensive word.

"Prick?" Ginny offered.

Stone raised his eyebrows. "That'll do." Ginny had never talked that way before. When the shock passed, he felt his anger once again rising, mingling with the heat of the brandy.

"That son-of-a-bitch," he said. "I'd like to cut his hands off."

"I know you would," she said, briefly touching his hand. "But we have to be Christian about this. We have to move on."

"That contract was an amazing piece of salesmanship. I don't know how he did it. It was worth more than a quarter of a million dollars." Stone's voice tightened and rose in pitch as he spoke. "It would have fixed everything. He was days away!"

"Please don't yell, Matt. There's no going back. That's what we have to remember."

"You should be proud."

"I am. Herb got up in the morning and did his best every day. He supported eighteen families for years, and many of them have kids in college now. He just got worn out. Who wouldn't? Sometimes I get mad, but most of the time I don't blame him." She reached into the pocket of her robe for a tissue to dab her eyes, then rested her hands on her lap.

"How are you doing, Matt? Have they given you a treatment plan yet?

"There is no treatment plan. It's called watchful waiting. I told you that."

"I know, but shouldn't you at least get a second opinion?"

"Why?."

"Well, I for one want you around for awhile."

"I'm going to be around for awhile." Instinctively, he knew what he said was true. He had a reason to live now. He would not go until he saw the IRS in flames.

Stone stood up and Ginny stood as well. he stood as well. "Matt, don't go yet. You can't fly on one wing. Have a nightcap with me."

"I have to drive. The last thing I need is a DUI."

"You didn't have that much."

"I know, but I didn't eat any dinner. I came right over from the plant."

Ginny put her hands on his arms and looked up into his eyes. "You're not taking care of yourself. You're not eating properly. And you're probably drinking too much. I know, I'm the pot calling the kettle black."

"Who said anything about pot? I haven't had any weed in years."

"This is nothing to joke about, Matt," she said crossly. Then, deliberately lightening her tone as though to make her own inappropriate joke. "You're all I've got right now." She put her hand to her mouth. That was too close to the painful truth.

"Oh, I shouldn't have said that. I'm sorry. I've got plenty of resources. And I can get a job. I *am* going to sell the house. You know, ghosts and all that. I know I can find a place with a little garden." At that, she burst into tears. She clutched his arms harder and pressed her face against his shoulder. He slid his arms around her in the most welcoming hug he could manage, more than a little uncomfortable because, in this moment of her grief, he could feel more than a touch of sexual desire mixed with his compassion. He had to push that down, and fast. Sex just complicated everything.

He waited until her sobbing subsided and gently released her.

"I'm sorry," she said. "It just happens sometimes."

"Ginny, I know. I've been there. I'm *still* there."

"But it goes away, right?"

"I guess." He reflected on this *it* they now shared, the *it* that hid in the most ordinary situations and objects, ready to attack at any moment with overwhelming force.

"Things change. Anyway, they have for me. Ginny. I'm no psychiatrist. I only know what I know from my own experience. Life goes on. Diminished. But maybe not diminished forever. We just have to live one day at a time." He paused. "Sometimes one hour." He felt like he was repeating stupid clichés out of some pop psychology book. But it was surprising how often those clichés were on the mark.

He took a step back. This time she didn't restrain him. At the door he gave her a chaste kiss on the lips, barely touching her.

"Be careful," she called after him as he got into his Crossfire.

This night he would. Spurred by revenge, he wanted to see tomorrow. He was on a mission.

Kat Selig wiped her strong, thin fingers against her black apron and glanced up at the café's old-fashioned railroad station clock. Nine more minutes and her shift would be over, with plenty of late afternoon sunshine left for her second run of the day.

It had been a pretty good shift. Everybody had showed up, and that made things go so much smoother. She was getting used to being behind the counter and serving the pals she used to sit with in the mornings before going off to her old job.

Before she got fired. And just for trying to do a good job. But that was capitalism for you. They'll screw you any way they can.

Losing that job had thrown her off for awhile. But this new set-up was going to work, so long as she could keep getting at least thirty-five hours a week. She idly wondered if she was going to have to fuck the manager to get the schedule she needed. It wouldn't be that bad.

That was a stupid thought. This was a good honest job, like they used to say. And Jerry, the manager, was a good guy who kept his promises. Everybody on the staff said so. As a customer, she had known him for three or four years. He was married, coached Pop Warner football, and never flirted with anybody. She turned away from the counter, and in doing so painfully banged her wrist against the old fashioned cash register. The world found a way to punish you when you let yourself have thoughts like that. She deserved it. Where had that thought come from?

Rubbing her wrist, she turned around to see one of her favorite customers walk through the door. He was at least in his mid-fifties, she guessed, stocky and muscular, and well-dressed in an expensive suit and dark tie. He had an air of authority that made you want to please him, and just a touch of – what was that expression? – *world weariness.* That was it. World weariness. The other day she had actually told him he looked like he needed a massage. As soon as the words were out of her mouth she had wanted to take them back. She had actually blushed. But he had just smiled.

"Everybody needs a massage by this time in the day," he had said, and she could tell he hadn't taken her words in the wrong way. She almost wished he had. He seemed like such a strong, steady man. She was pretty sure he was married, although maybe not. She hadn't actually seen him wearing a ring. She thought that maybe she had seen a tan line and a little indentation where a ring used to be. But what difference did it make if you didn't get too involved?

"Dark roast with a shot of espresso to go?"

"You've got a good memory," he replied.

Somehow, it didn't feel like a compliment. It felt a little like he was trying to manipulate her, but not in some evil way. That was just the way he acted. There was something almost automatic about it.

"You're hard to forget," she said. *Oops!* she thought. *Why did I say that? What's wrong with me?*

"I guess that rules me out for that spy job with the CIA. The bad guys would pick me out in a crowd every time."

"I guess," she said, flustered. His eyes were blue, the same shade as hers, but while hers were soft and aqueous, his seemed to shine, like probing spotlights. She called his order over to the barista and then turned her attention to the cash register, more to escape his gaze than ring up the order.

"It's $3.56 with tax."

His face darkened.

"Did I make a mistake?" she asked.

"Was I scowling? Sorry. Taxes are kind of a sore subject with me."

She nodded and then stepped away to pour his coffee. She passed it to the barista to receive the shot of espresso, slid on a paper sleeve and set it on the counter.

"Got a lot of thinking to do?" she asked. She was being too chatty but she couldn't help herself.

"Actually, I'm going for a run. The caffeine helps, and it's legal."

She offered a smile as he took the cup, and he smiled back Then he was headed for the door.

"I'm a runner too," she whispered, but of course he couldn't hear her. Brushing a strand of fine brown hair away from her face she watched him exit the café, allowing herself a brief fantasy of the two of them on the trail that circled the lake, running easily, exchanging an occasional smile. There were moments when life could be so simple.

At 6:30 p.m. sharp that evening Kat walked into Lily's Fine Seafood wearing a cotton pullover and torn jeans that evoked a harsh look of disapproval from the middle-aged hostess. Kat thought, *I could have dressed up a little.* Her sis would probably be mad, but there just hadn't been time. Her run had taken an hour and a half, and she had to stretch and shower afterwards.

The hostess led her through the main dining room past a dozen round tables draped in white linen and adorned with sparkling place settings, most of which weren't occupied. Times were tough, even here in the Eastlake district. Her sister Jen awaited her in "their" booth, where they met once a week. She stood up and gave Kat a welcoming hug. Five years older than Kat, she was thirty pounds heavier, and it seemed like the weight she had put on had grounded her emotionally in a way that would be forever out of reach for Kat. Jen was motherly and sympathetic. It seemed she had been born that way, and with two young kids and a husband who faithfully brought home the bacon, she was living the life she was meant to live. People who met her and Jen together at weddings or holiday parties could never believe they were sisters, placid Jen and haunted Kat.

The menus arrived, tucked into thick leather covers. Jen ordered Crab Louis and a glass of Chardonnay. The crabs were flown in from Chesapeake Bay daily, the menu proclaimed. Ordering goopy salads was Jen's way of pretending she didn't over eat. Kat ordered a hamburger and a beer, even though she knew it would embarrass her sister. Imagine, ordering a hamburger in a place like this! But she was craving beef – protein to replenish her muscles after the run. She hadn't eaten anything all day long except a banana nut muffin. At the café they let you have as much coffee as you wanted, but only one pastry per shift.

Jen was trying to be light, talking about her little problems as the secretary of the P.T.A. and the family plans for a summer vacation at Myrtle Beach, but a cloud of tension hung over the table. Finally, while sharing a fancy chocolate sundae, Jen approached the topic Kat had been braced for.

"So..." she began, "How's work?"

"Jenny," said Kat, "I really like it. I'm part of a team. We make people happy. It's good work."

"Mom and Dad are freaked out."

"I'm sure they are. Did they tell you they're *disappointed?*"

"They spent a lot of money sending you to college. And you're working at a Starbuck's! What happened to that job in Ann Arbor? You said they really valued your computer skills."

"It's not a Starbuck's. It's a family owned café and they've been in business thirty seven years."

"You know what I'm saying."

Jenny reached out to take Kat's hand in hers. Kat tensed, but didn't pull away. There was always something comforting in her sister's touch, even at those times when she just didn't *get it*.

"We just want you to be okay."

"I *am* okay." Kat could see her sister wasn't convinced. She kept glancing at the big bruise on her wrist where she had hit herself on the cash register. Self-consciously, she withdrew her hands, as though that would somehow make the bruise fade away.

"I know you hate it when I ask, but... are you taking your meds?"

There it was! Jen just didn't understand what those drugs did to your brain. You felt like you were a zombie. Okay, that was an exaggeration. But... you weren't *you* anymore. And you certainly couldn't write good code.

"I'm okay. The running and the caffeine are all I need. I'm being careful. I'm going to make it" She could feel her mind spinning as she spoke. She knew intellectually that it wasn't going to be that simple, but what was life without challenges? She could only believe that things would work out.

"Are you really going to stick with this job? I mean, where will it lead?"

"That's not the point."

Jen sighed. "Okay. But listen. We're sisters, right?"

"Of course we are."

"Well then, as your sister, I'm going to tell you that I've socked away about seven thousand dollars that Frank doesn't know about. So if you need money, it's there. I won't ask any questions."

Kat felt unwanted tears in her eyes. She didn't deserve this. And she didn't need it. She could make it on her own. But maybe she couldn't. It was so hard to ask for help, and here it was, offered without any strings.

Kat brushed away the tears with the back of her hand, wincing slightly at the pain in her wrist. "I don't know what to say."

Her sister rested her chin on her palm and closed her eyes as though pondering. Then, without any sarcasm, she said, "How about, 'Thank you?' I think that would work."

Kat stared into her sister's eyes. They were so calm. So peaceful. "Thank you," she said.

Stone awoke to dark clouds. A storm was on its way, which meant an early morning run or none at all. His muscles balked at the idea, but it was better than getting soaked at the end of the day and risking a lightening strike. He got out of bed, peed, and then checked the iPhone on the little table for the schedule Chase always transferred onto his iPhone before she left for the day. He was clear until eleven.

Stone pulled on shorts, a faded blue U of M T-shirt and a pair of ECCO BIOMs he needed to replace soon. Laura used to take care of things like that, but now it was up to him to manage, and he was getting a little sloppy. Stone's eyes suddenly filled with tears. She really *had* taken care of him, with love, and he had not acknowledged it nearly enough, although he had tried. All that love, gone forever, with nothing left behind but cruel reminders. Ginny had taken charge of clearing Laura's things out of the house, so at least he was spared having to stare at the cookbooks she had so lovingly collected over the years, or open a drawer to find a sweater he had given her for some Christmas long past. But the house itself was reminder enough: the furniture, the landscaping, all of it. Her footprints were everywhere.

He needed to move to a new place. But with the continued medical uncertainty he was facing, was it worth it? Was this damned run worth it? Was *anything* worth it? Yes. Retribution was worth it. In his heart of hearts, he knew that was how he wanted to go out.

Stone left the bedroom, slamming the door behind him, and trotted down the stairs, now furious and wanting nothing more than to drive over to Detroit and strangle agent Chan with his own bare hands this very day. He took a deep breath and walked out of his house. An ominous scent of rain was in the air. Today, instead of the monotonous track at the high school, he would run the lake, and choose beauty over efficiency for once. Laura would approve. Besides, being near the water would calm him down. What ever he was going to do, he needed to think it out carefully. The revenge part would feel good, but that wasn't enough. He was aiming at permanent change and nothing less.

The small parking area near the north end of the lake was usually deserted at this time of day, but this morning someone had parked a silver Ford Escort next to the trail that cut through the trees and wound through the dense vegetation down to the water. The car had seen better days. Stone parked next to it and headed down the trail, idly wondering how people could neglect their vehicles like that. Within twenty steps the parking area was no longer visible and he could only hear the sounds of nature.

The lake's secluded location had long made it a popular make-out spot for teenagers on warm summer nights. As a guy, all you needed was a blanket and a little luck. Stone had spent his share of time down here when he was in high school, and had even brought Laura once, long after they were married. He had thought it would be romantic, but she had been too spooked by the thought of bugs to relax.

The trail led to a well-maintained dirt and gravel path wide enough for two runners. As Stone rounded the last bend in the trail, he stopped dead in his tracks and gasped. Laura was kneeling down in the middle of the path to tie her shoe not half a dozen yards in front of him.

It could not be Laura! Laura was dead. But there she was, wearing dark shorts and an oversized T-shirt, her hair tied up in a kerchief that looked like it came straight from the 'seventies – just what Laura would pick if she were a runner. Stone's pulse started to race and he felt a cold sweat breaking out on his forehead. Was science wrong? Was she somehow reaching out to him from "the beyond?" Every since he had first known her, she had taken guilty pleasure in reading those sensational tabloids the supermarkets used to display next to the check-out stands. "Sure, most of it is made up," she would say. "But how do you know that some of it isn't real?" As was often the case with her, he could come up with no ready answer.

Now, as he continued to stare, Laura stood up and smiled at him, and it wasn't Laura anymore. It was the girl from the coffee shop. Stone struggled to put the images his eyes were presenting to him into some sort of perspective.

"Hello! What a surprise," she said, walking towards him, swinging her hips lightly. "Men usually don't start stalking me until at least the third date. Hey, what's wrong? You look like you've just seen a ghost."

"Sometimes my eyes play tricks on me," said Stone, gathering his wits. He was the CEO of a $600 million company! He couldn't appear dazed and confused in public like this.

"I mistook you for my wife," he explained. "She passed away more than a year ago, so it was a bit of a shock."

A cloud settled over her features. "I'm sorry," she said. Then, after a pause, "Do I look like her?"

"No, not at all." Laura had been blonde, with a buxom figure and a flowing grace to her movements. This young woman bordered on skinny, and her movements were quick, almost birdlike. She approached him and extended her hand. It was bony, and warm to the touch. "Kat O'Brien," she said.

"Matt Stone," he responded, waiting for her reaction. None came. An out-of-towner then. He felt himself relax.

"You run here often?" she asked. "I don't think I've seen you here before."

"I usually run at Laker High."

She raised her eyebrows. "You have a key?"

"I do." He didn't add that Numerica had funded forty percent of the new athletic facility.

"I run that track now and then," she said. "It's a hassle picking the lock, but the track feels so good under your feet once you're running. Don't tell anybody I'm sneaking in, okay? They might get a lock that's harder to pick."

"Your secret is safe with me, Kat."

She eyed him with a crooked grin. "I'm not so sure about that, Matt. But now that I told you, I guess I'll just have to take the risk. Wanna go for a run?"

She started off at a slow jog without waiting for his answer. He quickly caught up with her and they ran side by side for half a mile in a silence broken only by an occasional trout leaping out of the water.

"What happened to your leg," she ask after a few minutes.

"Old wound," he said. They had been running at a fast clip, and that words came out in short, controlled bursts.

"We've all got 'em. Some just aren't physical."

They exchanged a look. Then she suddenly speeded up her pace. "Catch me if you can, Colonel, or at least enjoy the view," she called over her shoulder.

"Captain," he shouted back, increasing his own pace.

The point where they had begun their run around the lake had come into view. He willed his legs to move faster, ignoring the ache building in his thigh. He estimated he had just enough energy left in him to close the gap – *if* she held steady. She did. He couldn't help noticing the way her shorts clung provocatively to her ass. Was that "the view" she was talking about? Somehow she had managed to turn a simple run into an erotic game, and he had become a willing player.

But no. He was reading too much into her taunt. "Enjoy the view" just meant take it easy. Soak in the quiet beauty of the lake and its surround. Nothing more. Or was he wrong? He'd been away from situations like this so long he didn't know how to read them. Well, the situation with Connie wasn't hard to read, but he had to stay away from her. Still, her kiss had opened up a door that had been locked for eighteen months, and he didn't imagine that it was going to shut itself. Stone cleared his mind and dug in, gaining ground. This was what he knew how to do best. Compete.

They crossed the trail marker – the finish line in his mind – in a dead heat. He rested his hands on his knees, panting and glad it was over.

Kat flashed him a smile, her face flushed. "I'm impressed, Matt," she said.

"I need a shower," he replied. it was a lame response. How could this woman half his age so easily put him off balance?

"Me too. Great running with you. We should do it again."

Matt felt his face flush. Did she notice? It was hard to tell. He heard himself say, "I'd like that."

Selena Moreaux entered Stone's office, dressed formally as usual in slacks and a blazer, and plopped down on the couch as though she were an old time friend or a member of the family he had known since infancy – anyone but a subordinate reporting to her boss. The new CIO's lack of deference both pleased and annoyed him. It clearly rubbed some of his senior managers the wrong way, which was not good. Even though she was their peer on the org chart, she was also twenty-five years their junior, with no experience in manufacturing, and on top of that, she was a woman. Who was she to walk into their offices without an appointment, and ignoring their secretaries to boot? Her Silicon Valley style wasn't designed to win friends in Michigan, and in business, no matter how smart you were, there were times when you needed friends.

On the other hand, her bluster often worked as a weapon. She caught people off guard, unprepared to counter her more radical positions. And she had an amazing first year track record. "Gotta admit it," one senior VP had said, "Her gadgets work, and she does hire smart people."

She looked up attentively at Stone, who was seated behind his desk, a stylus poised over her iPhone. "You called, Oh Master?" she said sarcastically, and in a tone that was far too familiar. Why did the brilliant techies always have to be such problem children? "Is it about the General Dynamics story?" she asked. The Virginia-based weapons system contractor had been hacked. It had been the number one story on the Google news feed she had set up for him and, more importantly, the morning's lead story for both the Wall Street Journal and the New York Times. He was sure to get a few calls from nervous customers within the next couple of hours, wanting reassurances that their projects were safe. He needed to know what to say. He also had some questions that had nothing to do with Numerica's security posture, and today's scare would give him the opportunity to ask them without raising any suspicions in his CIO's mind.

"I assume we're in full compliance with the DoD's regulations," said Stone.

"That goes without saying," she said, stiffening at what for her was an implied affront. "We are 'on top of it,' as you say. We have very strict access control and logging on all our systems, we examine every packet of incoming traffic for malicious code, and the email traffic we generate is automatically encrypted when appropriate, even for mobile devices. Your secrets are safe."

"They're not *my* secrets, Selena. They're my government's secrets."

"Do you think I'm not doing my job? It sounds like it."

Stone thought, *Are all French women like this?* He said, "Of course I think you're doing your job. Will you please relax? I'm just going to need to calm some people down today and I want to get the facts straight."

"I'm sorry," she said, "I had a bad night. I'll try to be a little more professional." As she spoke, however, she gave him a look that said, *With me, you take what you get.*

Stone found himself trying to imagine what a bad night might mean for this woman. A bad night in bed? He knew nothing about her personal life. She was leaning forward now. Her blouse had a bow at its collar that struck him as overly prim. He found himself wondering what would happen if he untied it, and tried to brush the thought away. He couldn't seem to get sex off his mind.

He paused a moment, as though trying to frame a question he had already planned to ask. "What you're saying is, nothing bad can get in and nothing valuable can get out."

"That's the goal of any security system, and we've achieved it."

"So nobody can read my email except the intended recipients."

"All of your messages are encrypted."

"That doesn't answer my question."

"Are you corresponding with a secret Chinese girlfriend?" she asked with a smirk.

Stone suppressed an angry response. *Stick to the point*, he told himself, forcing a bright expression. "You know, that's exactly it. I mean, that's the perfect hypothetical. What if I sent a design to an offshore destination? As an attachment."

"It wouldn't get there. It would be blocked and – let me think – a guy named Scott Gibson would come to you for face-to-face confirmation that you intended to send it. I'm not sure you know him. He's the chief security officer for the engineering division. If you told him it was okay, he'd release it. But he'd also know who sent it. There would be a digital trail leading back to you."

"Everything can be traced, then?" That was the real question. What lines of communication would be secure enough for his new mission?

"Traceability equals accountability. It's a cliché of security."

"What if an engineer bought one of those throw-away phones and used it to – I don't know – send some key specifications to a competitor?"

"We would know. Well, unless he was using TOR."

"Tor?"

"It stands for The Onion Ring. It's a network of anonymous servers. It's free, so there are no financial records. And it's completely decentralized, so there's no person for an agency to go after or send a - What do you call it?" She pulled her iPhone out of her purse and began tapping at what Stone assumed was a French-English dictionary. "Just a minute..." she said, not looking up. "A subpoena. That's it. If you use TOR correctly, your email can't be traced. You can download it and look at it yourself. It's at TorProject-dot-org. Any engineer would know about it."

"So, with this TOR, communications can't be traced?"

Stone had read in *The Economist* about the existence of the Dark Web and its now defunct Silk Road, which was a sort of eBay for drugs, contraband and, of particular interest to him, weapons. If what Selena was telling him was true, he could browse the Dark Web with impunity. And for the mission that was taking shape in his mind, he would need to do that. He would need the right weapon. It wouldn't be hard to find out where to look.

"Does that answer you question," said Selena.

"I'm sorry," said Stone. "I guess I drifted off.

"I said that you're correct. With TOR, communications can't be traced."

"So I could download this TOR and flirt with my Chinese girlfriend and no one would know?"

"Actually, TOR is blocked on our network. But you could download it at home."

Stone laughed. "I think I've got better things to do with my time."

He stood up to signal the end of the meeting. Then he walked around his desk and extended his hand. In Europe, he knew, you shook hands after a meeting as a matter of courtesy. "I appreciate your interrupting your schedule for me. It's the way I operate. Well, you've seen that. It was less disruptive when the company was small, and now...." He hesitated for a beat. "I guess I'm too old to change."

"You're not so old," she said, shaking his hand. With that, she turned and left. Stone glanced at his calendar and then his watch. He had ten minutes until his next meeting. Would it never end?

The next day, Stone awoke with a sore back. It was nothing new, and would go away with a hot shower, but he found it hard to accept the slow failing that was your fate over time, no matter what you did. "We just need to live every day to the fullest," Ginny had said, and of course she was right. It made sense. But all the slogans in the world couldn't compensate for the loss.

In any case, today was going to be full for sure. He had two generals coming in for a demo in the afternoon, with dinner and more bourbon than a man his age should drink to follow. Five years ago he would have been pumped for a demo of this magnitude: a jointed "crawler" that could give stealth teams like the one that had taken out bin Laden eyes and ears at a distance of one kilometer, with no need for line-of-site communication. SADIE, they were calling it in the engineering department: Stealth Ambulatory Device with Internet Extensibility. The project was on time, within budget, and exceeded all the specs. If the demo went well, and it would, Numerica would be the recipient of a multi-million dollar contract – the second one this quarter – but as he dragged himself out of bed he realized that he couldn't care less.

That was terrifying. His mind told him the feeling of meaninglessness would pass. Once he got to work there would be people to deal with, problems to solve, and it all would seem important again. At least, that's what had happened so far. Work was like a drug. It made you forget the real truth of things.

In the shower he decided to try another morning run. He needed to generate some endorphins! It crossed his mind to run the lake, but that trail would be too muddy after the recent rains. Also, he didn't want to encounter that cookie from the café. Not today. He would run, grab a coffee at the new Starbuck's, and then change at work. Chase always kept extra business clothes ready in the office for days like this.

The air felt damp and cold against his legs as walked from the black asphalt parking lot to the track, which was surrounded by an eight foot chain link fence. As he approached, he noted that the gate was ajar, its padlock hanging open. A few yards beyond the gate, next to the track, was the girl from the café. Kat. She was once again tying her shoes, in exactly the same posture as he had first seen her at the lake. His heart leapt. Somehow, subconsciously he supposed, he had known she would be waiting for him at the track. That was how he put it to himself: *waiting for him.* Where did that thought come from? There was no way she could have known he'd show up here. Still, her presence didn't feel like a coincidence.

She looked up with raised eyebrows. "I thought you said you didn't like to run in the morning."

"This is my only shot," he said. "I hope you don't mind sharing the track."

She stood up and put her hands on her hips. "Can we avoid bullshit in this relationship, Sir?" She cocked her head to one side. "I looked you up yesterday. You own this track."

"It belongs to the city."

"Well, you built it, Mr. Mathew Stone, CEO of Numerica and largest contributor to the Republican Party in Oakland County. I'm a socialist, by the way."

"Duly noted," he said. "Why don't you just call me Matt?"

"Yes, sir," she said with a mock salute. Then she turned and broke into a slow jog. Stone was soon at her side.

It felt good to be running with a partner. Kat's stride was smooth and light, and it seemed like that lightness flowed into him as they ran, smoothing out the kinks in his own stride. By unspoken agreement, they had set an easy pace that made it possible to talk.

"So, what's it like to run a big company?" she asked.

"We're not exactly that big."

"Nine hundred and seventy-eight employees isn't exactly that small."

Stone pulled up abruptly. "Hey," he called after her, "Come here."

She trotted back to him, a bemused smile on her face.

"How do you know how many employees we have?"

"Chill! I just guessed."

Stone had no idea how many employees were active at the moment, but nine hundred seventy-eight was definitely in the ballpark.

"You just guessed?"

"Well, maybe I peeked."

"What's that supposed to mean?" said Stone, his voice rising involuntarily.

"I'm smarter than I look, Matt. There are plenty of online sources for a number like that. All you need is a laptop and a little creativity. I'm very creative," she added, with a seductive edge in her voice.

Stone stared at her. She wasn't wearing a bra. He felt a sudden pulse of inappropriate desire and had to struggle to hold the thread of the exchange. Could this *girl* put Numerica at risk?

"Please tell me you didn't hack our systems."

"I didn't hack your systems," she said, as though she were an actress repeating a line he had just written for her.

"I'm serious. Where did you get that number?"

"I got it from the U.S. government, if you must know. Now do you want to run or not?"

"Kat, you have to understand—"

"If we're going to talk, let's go get a coffee at the new Starbucks. Nobody important will see us together over there," she added, as though that might be a concern of his. She reached into her pocket and pulled out a collection of keys tied together with heavy twine. "My car's on the other side of the track behind the gym. I'll meet you at the Starbuck's, okay"

Stone nodded in agreement. He couldn't let this slide. If she could track down semi-private data about Numerica like the exact number of employees with what seemed like no effort at all, what else could she uncover if she tried a little harder? More accurately, what more *could* be uncovered—not necessarily by her, but by a competitor or, worse, a foreign government? He had to know. But that wasn't the whole story. This skinny girl was sexy.

Stone locked the gate behind him as he left the track and got into his car wishing he had never had that drink with Connie. With one kiss she had opened a floodgate of random sexual desire he couldn't manage to shut. There was a part of him that *wanted* this Kat, and the sooner the better. At the same time, he felt he was being drawn into a game he shouldn't play. There was something just a little weird about their "chance" encounters. What if she was some sort of operative? It wasn't such a ridiculous thought. Shit like that happened all the time with defense contractors, and the only reason you didn't hear about it was because they did whatever it took to hush things up. What better way to hook a widower with no woman in his life than with a quirky young girl? And what better bait for that hook than the hint of a data breach?

By the time he sat down across from her at a metal table under the familiar green awning, his cloak and dagger fantasies seemed more than a little far-fetched. But he couldn't drop them all together.

"I have to ask, Kat. Are you a hacker? You make it sound like you know what you're doing."

"Hmmm, a hacker? I've never heard that line before," she said with a grin that displayed a dimple. "And I've heard a lot, believe me."

As this sank in, Stone thought, *This is a date!* He hadn't been in a situation like this in years.

"I'm not easy, though." She took a sip of the triple espresso she had ordered, studying him.

"Look, Kat, we hardly know each other, but I'm going to tell you this anyway, Numerica has a lot of online traps. If you were to try to hack us you could get into real trouble. We're a defense contractor."

Her expression softened. "You really mean it! This could take some getting used to, Matt. Men usually want to get me *into* trouble, which I do very well myself, by the way."

"Are you listening to me?"

"Yes, Sir. Numerica has a lot of online traps. I could get into real trouble. But I won't. I will only use my skills for the benefit of humanity."

"So you do have a background in computers?" he said, ignoring her sarcasm.

"I've been taking a break for awhile. That world isn't healthy, particularly for somebody like me. Working at the café is good for me. It's simple. It's almost like a family."

Stone nodded. He felt suddenly awkward, not a familiar state for him. What was he doing here?

"Look," she continued, "Maybe I think you're an interesting guy, I'll admit that. But I'm not the slightest bit interested in artificial hip joints or military robots or whatever it is you build. I have to tell you though, unless everybody in your company is on TOR, your email is very hackable. That's just a fact of life. You need to be careful. And not just you. Everybody in your 'not that big' company."

Stone thought, *TOR*. Selena had mentioned TOR. The Onion Ring. *Maybe this girl is smarter than she looks*. And potentially a hell of a lot more dangerous. He needed to put an end to this conversation at once. He needed to get over to the factory so he could run through his script for the demo a couple more times. This Kat was nothing but trouble, any way you looked at it.

"What's up?" she said, breaking into his thoughts. "Your body language entirely changed."

"I have an important meeting today. I need to review some documents so I'll be ready when they grill me."

A look of disappointment crossed her face. "You must have a lot of pressure," she said. "I mean, every day."

"Comes with the territory."

"Running's good for that. Hey, you've got a willing partner now."

"Thanks," he said, standing up although his cappuccino was virtually untouched. "Sorry, it's later than I thought. I really have to take off."

Kat pulled a laptop out of a backpack she had stashed under their table. "I'll just stay here and hack a few major U.S. corporations. I've got four hours before my shift starts." She reached out and gave his hand a quick squeeze. "I'm kidding, Matt. Good luck with your meeting."

For just a moment her eyes held him before he was able to turn away and head for the exit. For a brief moment he was back in the Laker High cafeteria, walking away from Cammie Baker, trying to pretend she didn't have him wrapped around her little finger, star quarterback or not. Enough! He had to be sober. He was on a mission.

The day passed without surprises, a CEO's dream. The two generals had dressed in civvies, and seemed more interested in getting to a bar as fast as possible than they were in the demo, which was a home run as far as he was concerned.

Shortly after five o'clock they were driven to Lily's Fine Seafood in a secure limo Chase had arranged, complete with a wet bar. Stone was careful to pace himself. He had made a tentative plan to drop by Ginny's at the end of the evening, and he didn't want to show up drunk, particularly after he had been lecturing her to go easy on alcohol. As a result when the chauffeur dropped him off at the brightly lit Numerica parking lot, he felt only a slight buzz, which vanished instantly when he saw the folded sheet of paper tucked under his windshield wiper.

It was a single page print-out of an email message from Selena to someone named Angelique, and although Stone's French didn't extend much beyond menus, he could clearly see it was a love note. It had been sent only a few hours ago, from a Numerica address. At the bottom of the page there was a note in back-slanted handwriting so small Stone had to squint to read it.

> Please don't be mad at me. Wanted you to know you're more vulnerable than you think. I won't do this again.
>
> – Kat

The note sent an icy chill through Stone's whole body. Selena had specifically assured him that the email system was safe. And now this! He got into his car and tapped out a message to her on his iPhone.

> We have to talk. It's about Angelique. 8:00, my office.

His hand hovered over the SEND button. Anyone could read this, he thought as he tapped the button. Or listen in to the conversation if he dialed the cell phone number Kat had emailed him in in the middle of the day in case he wanted to, "you know, hang out sometime." At the moment when he got Kat's email, he had simply stored it in his own phone, with the guilty thought that he had no business doing so. Now it occurred to him that he had never given her his e-mail address. Had she simply guessed? That would be a stretch.   Most   employees   had firstname.lastname@numerica.com,   but   his   was captain@numerica.com, a remnant from earlier, lighter days.

Stone put the iPhone in his pocket, slid into his car and started the engine. Then he pulled it out again and actually used it as a phone to call Ginny and tell her he couldn't make it. He had to think.

Sitting in the old leather chair in his study, Stone sipped his second double Glenfiddich and stared into space. He needed to focus, and he couldn't. The security breach Kat had engineered was more than a distraction. It was a slap in the face demonstration that Numerica's security was far from adequate. That stung, especially in light of the assurances Selena had given him this morning – perhaps at the very moment Kat's hack was taking place. Beyond that, it was a reminder that he himself could be tracked very, very easily. E-mail was a joke, and if you searched the web, Google knew everywhere you went. So did the U.S. government for that matter. It was public knowledge that the NSA had a record of every telephone call every U.S. citizen made. They could no doubt record those calls as well, probably on an automated basis using voice-recognition software to pick up key words and phrases.

The physical world, he reflected, was no better. Chrysler could track his every move if they wanted to with the embedded GPS device that gave him directions and traffic information. There were cameras at half the street corners in most big cities. If you travelled, Visa or MasterCard or

American Express had a record of every breakfast, lunch and dinner you ate, every hotel room where you slept, even where you parked your car. For the first time in his life, these facts of modern life mattered, because the mission he was contemplating couldn't be carried out by one man alone. It would take a team, and they would have to communicate. How the fuck did bin Laden pull off September 11? And wasn't what he, Stone, had in mind pretty much along those lines?

No. This had to be a mission with zero casualties. Destruction, yes. Death, no. His tentative target, the new I.R.S. data hub in Colorado, was ideal in that respect. It was what they called a "lights out" data center, fully automated, with no human technicians on-site who needed to turn on the lights so they could find their way among the maze of server racks and storage bays. Stone didn't believe any facility of that complexity could operate without occasional human intervention, but anybody on the premises could be warned off or rounded up prior to the strike—yet another detail to attend to! He had to get his act together. The clock was ticking.

Right now, he felt tired and worn out. Besides battling the most powerful government in the world, he had a company to run, and that was a demanding mission in itself: turf wars, contract negotiations, paranoid customers, new regulations – it was endless.

Then, there was the issue of Kat. *This woman is trouble*, he repeated to himself for the fiftieth time that day. *Obviously neurotic.* He pulled his cell phone out of his pocket and stared at the contact information she had given him for a long moment before putting it away. He didn't need Kat in his life. He needed people he could trust, people who could help him think things through, and then put a plan into action. His premise was simple: Taking out the physical infrastructure that supported the I.R.S. in its current form would clear the decks for a new system, and create a crisis atmosphere in Washington that would make action possible. Was that a viable plan, or yet another Rambo fantasy?

Stone downed the remains of his drink and stared at the ice cubes, which for a moment looked like a collection of little transparent skulls. He quickly set down the glass and went upstairs to the room that had been Laura's office, the one room he had decided to handle himself after she was gone. In fact, he had set foot in this private space of hers only once, a few weeks after her death, to check up on a couple of unpaid credit card bills. Now, it drew him back into the past with a rush. The desk with its stacks of papers and books and catalogs, the roller cart crammed with art supplies, the half-finished canvases leaning against the wall, the old Picasso prints from their college years which she had refused to exchange for the real Picasso sketch he had offered her as a fortieth birthday present, the tennis shoes in the corner, the total messiness that he had come to love over the years in spite of his penchant for neatness and order military training had instilled in him.

He had lived alone his senior year in college, she with two roommates. As their romance evolved over the fall quarter from dating to something more serious, she had come to spend more and more time at his apartment, and she couldn't seem to leave without leaving something behind: a book, a sweater, a bag of laundry to be washed within the next few days, a portfolio containing old sketches.... It added up, and led to one of their rare arguments. Quite heatedly he had said, "Look, if we're going to live together, you have to start putting things away where they belong," and she had responded, "Is that a proposal?" Then, with a grin that showed she knew just how much power she held over him, she started humming "Here Comes the Bride." Six months later, they were married.

How could a life go by so fast? Being in her office, he felt like she had just gone off for a short trip to New York. She would return in a couple of days, cook a fancy dinner, come to bed in the expensive lingerie for which he had such a weakness.... but no. That was not to be. Never. He wondered how she would feel about this last mission. He would never know, but one thing was sure: she would warn him to be careful.

That was why he was in her office. He started searching the drawers of her desk and quickly found what he was looking for: a box of stationery with a book of stamps. He sat down at her desk and rolled a sheet of the smooth, off-white paper into the classic Olivetti portable electric typewriter she had loved so much.

Dear Bobby,

I'd like to meet next Tuesday, 13:00 at our favorite watering hole in D.C. This is top secret. Do not contact me. Fall back is breakfast Wednesday, 07:00 at the Starbuck's two doors down. Burn this.

Stoney

Stone addressed the letter to his friend's Bethesda home, hoping he hadn't moved since the last time they'd had any contact, at Laura's funeral. Stone licked the envelope, which had no return address. Even in the age of the Internet, there were ways to send a message that couldn't be traced. He didn't know how his old friend would react when he revealed his plans. What he did know is that the man would never rat him out.

As Stone entered the dim interior of Rigoli's Tavern he had the anxious thought that he had chosen a poor location for a secret meeting. Just beyond comfortable walking distance from K Street and fitted out with curtained booths along the walls, it was an obvious spot for a rendezvous that a congressman and a lobbyist wanted to keep off the record. If he were a reporter looking for dirt, he'd have his lunch at Rigoli's polished, brass-railed bar every day. But these were paranoid thoughts. He was a small fish in a big pond here – a non-existent fish, to be more accurate, and Bobby fell into the same category. Or did he? That hadn't really talked about *work* in a long time.

Stone was ushered into one of the small booths where a waiter in a formal red jacket quickly appeared to take his order, a Stella Artois on tap. A few minutes later, Bobby walked through the door, on time to the minute. He was thin and lithe, and moved with a grace and confidence that left no doubt that he was completely comfortable in his coal black skin. The two men embraced and sat down facing one another. The waiter arrived again almost instantly. Bobby ordered a San Pellegrino and then they were alone, together for the first time since Laura's funeral. Strangely, it seemed as if no time had passed. The connections you made when you were young never changed.

"How are you doing, my brother," said Bobby, speaking with the light ghetto accent from the 'sixties that he reserved for close friends. In meetings and at cocktail parties he sounded more like a Harvard professor.

What a question! thought Stone. "These are heavy times," he said.

"You think I don't know that? Hey, you're looking good."

"You too. How's Beth?"

Beth was Bobby's girlfriend of more than twenty years. They had never married. "My work is too dangerous," Bobby had said on numerous occasions, but Stone had always wondered if there were some deeper reason. He was certain that Beth wanted a ring. Would that be so difficult? He had pressed his friend on this point more than once, but all Bobby would say is, "I hear you."

"Beth is good. She sold three paintings at the gallery this summer. Paid for a week in the Cayman Islands."

"That's great."

The two fell silent. They hadn't come here to chat about vacations.

"Time to get serious?" said Bobby.

"Let's wait for lunch."

Both had ordered light fare: Stone a bowl of minestrone, Bobby a three-bean salad. They had come a long way from the martinis and creamy fettuccini alfredo of the old days. When they had finished eating and the waiter had brought their espressos, Bobby opened the thin, black leather briefcase he always carried and produced a stainless steel cube about an inch square. He put it on the table.

"Jammer," he explained. "Can't be too careful these days."

Stone nodded. The thought that there were hidden mikes under the table or digital cameras hidden in the corners of the booth was absurd, yet it felt good to know that their technology would be foiled if they were there. *This is what it feels like to be a terrorist*, he thought.

Bobby was watching him intently. In the restaurant's subdued light, his eyes seemed almost to glow. For the first time, Stone truly felt the weight of what he was about to attempt.

"You want to help me blow something up?" said Stone, trying to lighten the mood.

"It's what I do," Bobby replied.

This wasn't precisely true. It was what he *had* done. Now, his company supplied security services for corporate compounds located in countries where it was no longer safe to be an American. Bobby had become a salesman, an administrator, and a trouble shooter when things went wrong. He logged a lot of first class miles, and his hands were neatly manicured. But he still knew how to blow things up. And, more important, he knew how to obtain the ordinance you needed to make that happen.

"Did you ever meet Herb Grimes?" Stone began.

"I think I met him at the funeral. Long time friend of yours, right?"

"Since high school. And now he's dead. Drove his truck into the garage, closed the door and left the motor running."

"I'm sorry to hear that, Stoney," said Bobby, and Stone could tell from the look in his old friend's eyes that he truly *was* sorry. This was a new faculty for Bobby, developed and nurtured over the years, Stone suspected, by Beth. Back in Vietnam, Bobby had never shown emotion.

"What happened?" he asked.

Stone related the whole story, ending with the bitter twist that Herb had scored the contract he needed to put his house in order, and would have succeeded had Agent Chan not chosen to play hardball.

"This country's out of control, Bobby," said Stone. "It's not the good old U. S. of A. we risked our asses for. Something has to be done, starting with the IRS."

Bobby regarded at him with alarm. "You're not thinking about taking the law into your own hands with this Agent Chan, are you?"

"No," said Stone, staring down at the table for a moment. "Although nothing would give me more pleasure. But I have a broader vision. We only have so much time left on this Earth, Bobby. Somebody has to do what has to be done."

"Tell me more about this 'broader vision' of yours, Stoney. I'm not sure I'm pleased with where this is going."

Stone hesitated. He hadn't anticipated Bobby's skepticism. But a skeptical ear was just what he needed to sharpen his thinking.

"I guess I should get to the point."

"I guess you should."

"I want to take down the IRS."

Bobby sat silent, staring at Stone as though he were a stranger. Finally, he spoke.

"That's crazy. That's fucking crazy." He paused, gathering his thoughts. "Stoney, if that could be done, which is questionable at best, it would destabilize the whole country. You may not like this government's policies, but there has to be a government."

"Of the people, by the people and for the people, as I recall."

"That's never been the reality. You know that. What is up with you?"

"What's up with me is, the IRS murdered my friend. And he's not the only one they hurt. Or *will* hurt. Americans shouldn't have to live in fear of their own government. That's wrong, and you know it."

Bobby nodded almost imperceptibly, indicating attentiveness, but my no means approval. His movements had always been economical, and that hadn't changed over the years. Had his resolve? That might be a meaningless question. He was hardly buying into Stone's pitch.

The waiter appeared. Without asking Bobby, Stone ordered two single malts. His friend didn't object.

Bobby took an appreciative sip of his scotch and then rested his arms on the table. "Just what do you propose to do to *correct* this situation?"

Stone felt a flash of anxiety in his chest. Was Bobby still the friend he once was? Or was he collecting information to use in ways Stone would come to regret? He realized he dare not let himself think that way with Bobby. For better or for worse, there were some people in your life you had to trust, and accept the consequences if you were wrong.

"I'm not sure, and I'm not being cagey when I say that. The more I think about it, the more I think revenge isn't enough."

"What else is there?"

"Structural change."

"I couldn't agree more. There must be some threat that would get them to make those damned tax forms simpler. They're a bitch."

Stone's face reddened at this smarmy comment. "I'm not talking about tax forms, Bobby. I'm talking about making those fuckers think twice before they destroy somebody's means of livelihood. I'm talking about fear of retribution."

Bobby held up his hand as though warding off an attack. "Stoney, be serious. This is not – "

"I *am* serious." Stone paused to gather his thoughts. Bobby was looking at him as though he were a maniac. He had to find a way to get through to his old friend.

"Look," he continued, "Let me take a step back. I think the IRS has far too much power in our so-called democracy. Are you with me there?"

"No one could disagree with that. Except the guys that work there."

"Okay. Then, just hypothetically, what if there were a way to curb that power, with changes that could be written into law?"

"That's pretty damn hypothetical. The process of writing laws...." His voice trailed off. He looked down and shook his head.

"But what if the process had a little help?

Bobby raised an eyebrow.

"Hypothetically," Stone quickly added.

"What kind of help are we talking about?"

Stone shook his head. "I don't know. I genuinely don't know yet. I want you to help me think things through."

"Look, if you want me to help you plan the next Oklahoma City massacre, I can't do that."

"No casualties."

"No bang-bang period. If we're talking about something more subtle... I still don't know."

"Roll with me on this for awhile. I need your clarity."

"I will roll with you, as you put it, because I am feeling an irrational impulse to protect your ass. Do you understand what I'm saying? At this point I'm in for one reason and one reason only, and that's to make sure you fail."

"Fair enough."

Sitting alone in one of the dim back booths at The Roadhouse sipping his usual expensive scotch, Stone glanced for the fifth time at the stainless steel Breitling Laura had given him to celebrate Numerica's first million dollar contract with the government. Kat was about twenty minutes late now, and he was beginning to wonder if she's show up at all. He considered texting her, but he hated texting. It stripped away the tone of voice and pauses that were such an important part of a voice exchange, and it was hopeless when you needed to go back and forth about anything even slightly complex, like deciding where and when to meet. But it was also the only way he could communicate with her. If he called, she wouldn't pick up. If he texted, she'd respond in a couple of minutes, and often in a few seconds. Just like his daughter used to do.

Stone had been texting Kat quite a bit lately. They had arranged this meeting at The Roadhouse with text messages, which was why he wasn't sure he was in the right place at the right time. But he *was* sure she had suggested The Roadhouse. She seemed to take it for granted that he didn't want to be seen in public with her. In fact, he didn't really care who saw them together. Yes, they would get some strange looks if they went to Lily's. But so what?

"Hey! Isn't a gentleman supposed to stand up when his lady arrives at the table?"

Stone jumped in his seat, a startle response he hadn't experienced in years. Then he stood, somewhat awkwardly, as Kat slid into the booth opposite him. She was wearing a dark blue, 'forties-style dress, elaborate earrings, and even a bit of lipstick. He had been braced for torn jeans and a sweatshirt.

"Nice outfit," said Stone.

"Thanks. I wanted to show you I know how to dress like a grown-up."

A waiter arrived, sparing Stone the need to respond. Kat studied the menu and ordered a French Chablis "for starters." He wondered if she knew anything about wine, or had simply picked the most expensive one on the list. When the wine arrived she swirled it in her glass, just like Laura used to do. The first sip brought a huge smile to her lips.

"This is so good! Do you want to try it?" she asked. Then his half-empty glass caught her eye. "Oh, you're on scotch tonight. Hard day at the office?"

"Nothing a colonel can't handle."

"I thought you said you were only a captain."

"I promoted myself."

"I guess if you run the company you can do anything, huh?"

Stone thought, *If it were only that easy.*

She put her hand on his for a moment, a move that sent a surprising thrill up his arm.

"You look tired," she said. "Can we just relax tonight? You know there are studies that show your productivity goes down if you don't get enough rest."

"I know, but my time is limited."

Kat's face fell. "You've got another meeting after this?"

Stone laughed. "No, I meant in general. You're right. Maybe I need to relax a little more. Let's make a deal. Give me ten minutes and then business is off the table."

"We'll see."

Now came the moment of truth. Stone had been doing some homework on computer security, and he didn't like what he was learning. Yes, the private "cloud" that Selena had put in place was literally saving Numerica hundreds of dollars an hour, and it tripled the company's computing power. But it also introduced an element of risk that bordered on unacceptable. True, the risk could theoretically be contained, if every engineer in charge of every server were perfectly vigilant, and never forgot to check the right boxes on the right screens to block unauthorized access to the sensitive data continuously flowing through the system. But that sort of vigilance was a fantasy. What Numerica needed was a pair of intelligent *eyes* operating inside the IT department – someone who could fit into the existing structure, but who had the mind and instincts of a black hat.

Was that person sitting across the table? There was something about her that was off center, but they were all that way in the IT department – at least the ones under forty. If you didn't let your programmers wear T-shirts and sandals to work and show up at odd hours you couldn't get anybody who was really good. Those were the facts of life these days. She could definitely fit into that culture. But there was more to it than that. Kat had real psychological problems. She had told him as much, and her weird departure from her last job bore that out. Was that a problem?

Beyond all these considerations, would she accept an offer?

He took a deep breath and plunged in. "Kat," he said, "Would you consider a job at Numerica?"

Her face fell, and then he detected a flash of anger in her eyes.

"A job at Numerica?" she repeated.

"Yes."

"Is that why I'm here? You want me to work for you?"

"I'm not such a bad boss,"

She stared at her wine glass for a moment, then into his eyes.

"I thought you wanted to be friends."

Stone felt a wave of panic. She was right. At the end of the day, he just wanted to be here with her and spend time together. It was that simple. But instead of accepting that obvious reality, he had tried to make her into a puzzle piece in a problem set. He was losing clarity. How was he to steer the ship that was Numerica, much less disarm the most powerful agency in the U.S government, with no reliable compass?

"Are you okay?" said Kat.

"It's been a long time since I've had a friend."

"Do you think I'm too young? I'm not as young as I look. I mean, if that's what's bothering you."

He shook his head. "I know. Hey, look at that dress." He paused for a laugh, but she remained stone faced. "I've just got a lot on my mind. It has nothing to do with you."

"Do you want to tell me about it? I'm a great listener. You can just skip over the classified stuff."

At that moment, Laura walked into the room. She was wearing a tan suit and carrying a briefcase. For some reason, Stone had the impression she had just returned from a business trip. That was strange, because she had never taken a business trip in her life except to accompany him. She waved from across the room and headed towards the booth where he and Kat were seated... and walked right past to hug a woman who had emerged from the booth behind them.

Stone couldn't conceal his reaction to this hallucination.

Once again, Kat put her hand on his. "Please tell me what's going on."

"Something very bad happened," said Stone. "And I don't know what to do. I'm afraid it's affecting my judgment." He looked down at the glass of scotch in his hand, the second on an empty stomach. The alcohol was affecting his judgment as well. He couldn't drink like he used to.

"It will feel good to talk about it."

"I've been alone for eighteen months now," he began.

Kat felt a surge of guilt as she piloted her car along the dark road that led back to town. Mathew had put down two scotches and most of the bottle of wine he had ordered with the dinner. He was definitely over the legal limit when he gave her a good night hug in the parking lot. A hug, but no kiss. She should have offered him her lips. She should have driven him home! *Too many shoulds*, she told herself. And yet, there was no question in her mind that she should have said no to his job offer, even though it was just for six months. After that she could go back to the café. He would arrange it. That was the deal. Her whole purpose was to double check the security systems and find any more flaws like the email problem she had uncovered. She would pretend to work as a secretary under some guy who knew the secret of why she was really there. A "low pressure guy," Mathew had called him. She would have plenty of time for her runs. In fact, she and Mathew would run together. Once a week. That's how she would report to him.

At least she'd get to see him. Maybe they could be friends after all. Friends with benefits. He wasn't married or anything. Why not? She felt safe around him. She could tell he was hot for her, even if he wouldn't admit it to himself.

As she passed the weathered sign announcing the White Lake city limits, the glowing digital clock on the instrument panel told her it wasn't even midnight. On impulse, she pulled off the road and killed the headlights. Then, in the darkness, she pulled off the dress she had worn to dinner and wriggled into a pair of jeans and an old black T-shirt she had ditched in the back seat. She was a little old for the club she had in mind, but it had great music. Besides, by now everybody would be too stoned to think about her age, and if anybody gave her funny stares, they could go fuck themselves! She needed to dance. That was the right way to balance your endorphins. Maybe Trevor would be there. He was a little creepy, but he could actually dance. You could get into a flow with him, it was almost like sex but without the complications.

Kat drove through the old downtown with its 'fifties-style stores into the warehouse district. The street lights here were few and far between, but she knew her way and easily navigated the shadowed maze of corrugated iron buildings until she found the one with a crowd in front and the dull thump of techno drums leaking out of its half-open door. The smell of weed was thick in the air as she passed through the crowd of twenty-somethings, their intent faces seeming to float in the ghostly light of their iPhones.

It's okay for me to be here if I want to be here, she told herself. *This is what I need.* A biker type she vaguely recognized stopped her at the door.

"You clean?" he asked.

"I'm too old for drugs," she said.

He gave her a strange look and waved her in.

Why did I say that? she thought. But it didn't matter. You could say anything here, do anything here, except bring drugs inside. That was what she liked about it. No rules. The cavernous warehouse amplified the music: high-pitched drum hits, a penetrating bass you could feel in your whole body, unintelligible screamy lyrics. It was like your mind on a bad day, only amped up. Near the ceiling, she imagined, there was a quiet space that was untouched by the activity below, the space they said you could reach in meditation, although it had never worked for her.

Kat slid past gyrating bodies into the center of the floor, letting the music tell her how to move. Almost immediately she had a partner. He was obviously stoned, and he wasn't really dancing. It was more like flailing. She managed to escape into the embrace of a woman about her age who offered her a sweet smile and a sexy sparkle in her eye. They danced close for awhile, and Kat let herself enjoy the soft press of her new partner's breasts against her body. When the woman offered a kiss, Kat disengaged.

"Sorry, I'm taken," she said in a voice that seemed too loud – but how else could she communicate over the music? It was so loud it seemed to condense the air, making it thick, like warm syrup.

I'm taken! How could she think that? She had gone on a couple runs with Mathew, and one dinner date which wasn't really a date at all. He wasn't interested in her. He was interested in what she knew, or what he thought she knew, actually. She wasn't going to uncover anything important. A new thought crossed her mind. Had he talked her into working for *Numerica* to put her off limits and take away the temptation of a wild young girl who could get him into trouble? As an employee, she would be unequivocally off limits. At least to him. He was that kind of guy.

Kat felt a hand on her ass and spun around to see Trevor. He was a head taller than she was, lanky, with dark, shoulder-length hair and pale skin that took on an unnatural sheen in the club's harsh spotlights. She slapped his hand and he smiled, revealing an incongruous dimple. He began swaying his hips, inviting her deeper into the mass of bodies. It was even warmer in the center of the crowd, and there wasn't really room to dance, only to rub against one another. She could feel herself slowly sliding into a trance where all the complexities of living in the world could dissolve.

Thoughts weren't actually real. They were just thoughts. Her sensations right now were the true reality. But thoughts had power. They were like ghosts. They couldn't physically harm you, but they could scare you. So you had to ignore bad thoughts That could be hard to do.

She brought herself back to the dance floor and realized that Trevor was getting hard. Not what she wanted.

"I have to go," she practically yelled, and then spun away. Would he be mad? In a way, she had led him on. She shouldn't have done that. But her days of casual sex were over. Long over! He could find somebody else. She was taken. There was that thought again. Maybe it wasn't such a bad thought.

Kat pushed through the mass of dancers and found the door. Time to sleep and build up energy for her mid-morning shift. She wondered if they would be sorry to see her go, but she'd never really know. That was how things worked here on Earth. You never really knew what other people were thinking.

The two men approaching Stone's table with Bobby could have walked right out of a bad action movie. Vaguely middle Eastern, they both wore expensive but ill-fitting tan suits with white, open collar silk shirts and shiny Rolex watches exposed at the wrist. The taller of the two, Monzer al-Shami was the name he gave, had a prominent scar on his left cheek. He seemed tense and distracted. His companion, balding and chubby, wore gold-rimmed glasses and reminded Stone of the accountants he sometimes asked to sit in on meetings if the discussion got down to actual numbers. He introduced himself simply as Hoss." Stone stood up to shake hands. They spoke with an accented English that matched their appearance. Stone felt like he had walked into a car dealership where the salesman was sizing up his clothes to assess which models he could afford. Bobby gave him a wry smile: *Be careful what you wish for.*

Their meeting place was Morton's, a dim D.C. establishment with tables spaced far enough apart for private conversations. It was perfect for secret lovers... or arms dealers. Stone briefly reflected on how much time he had spent in only slightly more reputable D.C. bars like this over the years, and how many gallons of scotch he must have drunk. He added to the total with a Glenfiddich. Bobby's two "associates" ordered vodkas, while Bobby himself got a San Pellegrino. Stone wondered if his friend had a health problem he wasn't discussing that limited his alcohol consumption. Out of long habit, Bobby wouldn't volunteer information like that. It could be perceived as a weakness.

Stone let his friend steer the conversation, and as it wandered back and forth from vacation properties on the Black Sea to smart phones to fluctuations in the platinum market with no seeming direction, Stone began to fear he was in over his head. It seemed at moments that his three companions were speaking in some sort of code. There were surely rules in this game. There were rules in every game. But he was at a loss to figure them out.

They were well into the second round of drinks when Bobby finally touched on the issue they were here to discuss, and he did so indirectly. "With all the chaos in the Middle East and the former Soviet Union," he said, "many American leaders are worried that weapons of mass destruction will fall into the wrong hands."

"What sort of weapons are of concern?" asked al-Shami. Stone noticed he had a slight tic in his left eye.

"Nuclear warheads are at the top of the list, of course," said Bobby.

"In that case, I think the worry is misplaced," the man replied. His companion nodded. "A nuclear warhead would fetch a good price," he said, "but none are on the market. Whoever has such a device wants to keep it." He laughed with disturbing coldness. "If they were for sale, the Taliban would own one."

"Do you think there *are* any realistic worries then?" asked Bobby.

"There are shoulder launched RPGs that can take out a 757." The man shrugged. It was as though they were talking about golf clubs. "For a bridge or similar target, Russian Tochkas are available. They have the advantage of mobility."

"Mobility?" said Stone.

"A mobile launch platform. They were designed for combat."

"And the range?" asked Bobby.

"Fifty, maybe one hundred miles. It depends. The newer ones have a longer range, but then...." he rubbed his thumb and fingers together with a humorless smile to indicate the price went up along with the range.

"How much money are we actually talking about?" asked Stone, thinking *Why not ask? Isn't that why we're here?* At the same time, he wondered if the alcohol was loosening his tongue.

"The Tochka? Well, the market fluctuates. And it also depends on where you buy it and whether it has to be disassembled for shipment. There are a lot of variables."

"I understand," said Stone. "But what's the ballpark? I mean, roughly speaking."

"Around two, perhaps."

"Two thousand dollars? That can't be right."

The man with the scar laughed humorlessly. "Two *hundred* thousand."

"That makes more sense," said Stone.

"But there are deals from time to time," said the man whom Stone had pegged as the accountant.

"What about reliability?"

"You can get a CEP of around seventy-five meters.:"

Stone thought, *circular error probability*. It was a standard measure of accuracy for missiles, an acronym not everyone would know. Was this man testing him?

"If the fuel tanks aren't rusted out," said Stone.

"The Tochka has a solid fuel propellant."

"You know what I'm talking about. Some of these birds are thirty years old."

"And some age more gracefully than others," came the reply.

Bobby interrupted, raising his glass. "May we all age gracefully. That's my goal. And here's to a world where all the unrest and hatred that make these weapons necessary is long gone."

The accountant, as Stone had come to think of him, clapped Bobby's shoulder. "Without unrest and hatred, my friend, you would be out of business."

Stone was caught off guard by this casual comment. Were there dimensions to Bobby's business of which he was unaware? And, for that matter, didn't what the accountant had said apply equally to Numerica? The classified business now accounted for more than half his revenue.

Al-Shami joined in. "Yes," he said. "Until that day when the lion lies down with the lamb, men who are truly committed to achieving their goals must arm themselves and their followers, or accept insignificance."

"Logistics must be a problem for these truly committed men," said Stone, with the hope of getting the conversation back on a more practical footing.

Al-Shami shook his head. "Not as much as you would think. Of course, some destinations are more difficult than others. But there is no obstacle that cannot be overcome by men who are truly committed."

Stone thought, *again that phrase. Men who are truly committed.* Was it a subtle hint? As yet, he himself didn't fall into that category if a truly committed man was meant a customer ready to buy. But surely these two arms dealers didn't expect him to show up at their first meeting with a shopping list and a briefcase full of cash. He had told Bobby to make it clear that this was an exploratory first step.

Stone reached for the bill, which had been sitting on the table for some time.

"I appreciate your insights. You obviously know what you're talking about."

"It was our pleasure. Perhaps we'll meet again," said al-Shami. "I'm sure you understand there are times when digital meetings are preferable. With today's technology, time and space are no longer barriers to private communication. And in business, with BitCoin, there's no more need for cash."

Stone nodded as though he knew what the man was talking about. He had heard the term, but he had no real knowledge of what a bit coin was.

Outside the restaurant they went their separate ways. Stone was scheduled to regroup with Bobby at five. Having more than two hours to kill, he decided to join the tourists on Constitution Avenue and walk down to The Wall.

So many had fallen over there in Vietnam! And with every passing year, taking a stand against the ideology of Communism in a little country that was nothing more than a collection of rice paddies and thatched huts seemed stupider and stupider. For all the deaths, nothing was different, and Communism had collapsed under the weight of its own bureaucracies with no help needed from Uncle Sam.

Stone was convinced that American ideals *were* worth defending. He himself was proof of the opportunities that existed nowhere else in the world. He was also convinced that internal forces were the greatest threat to the ideals he believed in. It wasn't just the IRS that had overstepped its bounds. The intelligence community was out of control as well, and about to become his enemy, he reminded himself. It wasn't that these institutions shouldn't exist, but they had lost their way, subverting the very ideals they were created to support.

He deliberately didn't seek out the names of the men he had known. He just stayed with the pace of the somber crowd, drawing strength.

"Those two are quite a pair," said Stone, seated across from Bobby at an outdoor café not far from the mall. In deference to his friend's new aversion to alcohol, he was sipping a sweet iced tea.

"You don't find many Boy Scouts in the arms business, Stoney, which is one of the many reasons for abandoning this project of yours."

"I was at The Wall this afternoon."

"And?"

"I just feel I have to do something. To honor their sacrifice. To fix things. Maybe even set an example."

"By blowing up Government buildings? Sounds like a great example for the youth of America. Especially boys and girls of color."

Stone briefly closed his eyes and was greeted by a visual of Corporal Howie Monk, who was walking about ten feet ahead of him on a rural highway just at the moment his head exploded. Stone had thought those flashes were a thing of the past, but lately they had returned full force.

"Are you okay?" said Bobby.

"Just a flashback. I thought they'd gone away."

"I get them too. I don't think they'll go away until we're dead."

The two fell silent. It was a perfect late afternoon in the capitol, warm but not hot, with a slight breeze, and no hint of the humidity that was the norm. The terrace was filled with ordinary citizens who had come, Stone surmised, to be inspired by the sights.

"Bobby, I've hit a wall. I can't seem to come up with anything clean."

"Clean?"

"It's like chemo. There are lots of drugs that will kill cancer cells, but most of them kill normal cells as well, and they can end up doing more harm than good."

"You care to elaborate on that?"

"Take that new facility they just completed outside of Denver. The one with the central database that's supposed to save us so much money. I think I could blow it up. The whole fucking thing. But I'd have to go nuclear."

"Jesus Christ!"

"Calm down. It's not going to happen. If I did that, my legacy would be a mountain of radioactive rubble that would be uninhabitable for ten thousand years. Who wants that? It makes the IRS look like the good guys. Targeted assassinations have the same problem. The collateral damage is unacceptable. Widows, orphaned children... I can't be responsible for that kind of shit. It makes me no better than they are."

"Targeted assassinations? You actually considered that?"

"This IRS shit cannot go unchallenged."

"Wait a minute. This is no joke. I want you to tell me you're not planning to kill anybody. Because if you are – "

"I'm not planning to kill anybody. Don't worry. But I have to tell you, I don't know what's right anymore."

Bobby's eyes drilled into him.

"Do you mind if I get a scotch?" said Stone.

"Of course I don't mind. I'd join you if it weren't for this damned joint infection. I'm on metronidazole, and it's got interactions with alcohol."

"Our bodies are falling apart."

"I'd drink to that if I could."

At that moment Stone felt a spasm of pain in his lower back, as though to confirm Bobby's comment. He ignored it, and it went away.

"Why don't you make a film?" said Bobby.

"You're not serious."

"You can afford it. With today's technology, you can do a documentary on a shoestring. You could probably get Michael Moore to direct it if you put your mind to it."

"Are you kidding? He hates guys like me. I'm a capitalist pig."

"Your enemy's enemy is your friend."

"A movie is not going to stop the IRS."

"Face it, Stoney, nothing is going to stop the IRS."

The message from Ginny had come in around three thirty, while he was in the middle of a conference call with two suppliers who were balking about sharing production data over the Internet. It was a situation where Stone held all the cards. If push came to shove, he could threaten to terminate their contracts, but he wanted them to see the benefits of the deal and get on board voluntarily. After all, they were loyal vendors who had been there for him when he needed favors. He didn't want to push them around if he could avoid it.

When he finally managed to bring them around, he immediately listened to Ginny's message, fearing trouble. But instead, it was a dinner invitation, a "celebration," as she put it. When he called back, her voice was bubbly, a tone he hadn't heard in weeks.

"I hope you don't have another date," she said.

"Another date? Give me a break." In fact, he had been toying with the idea of a run by the lake. There was a good chance Kat would be there, even though it wasn't their day to meet. He wanted to... what? Get past the resentment she obviously felt towards him for railroading her into a job she didn't really want? Share a bottle of good wine? Somewhere in there. But he didn't even know with certainty she would be there. Besides, if he wanted to spend time with her, he should just call her up and say so. Actually, he would have to text her.

"Earth to Matt," said Ginny. "Are you deciding whether or not to blow off your secret girl friend for a night? I know my cooking is risky, but I'll make up for it somehow." Did he hear a tipsy edge in her voice? And how did she come up with that secret girlfriend idea? Women had ways of knowing things he would never understand.

"That would be terrific," he said. "What time should I show up?"

"Just come on over after work."

"Around six, then?

"I'll be ready for you."

She kept her word. When he arrived, she was waiting for him just inside the open door holding up two chilled martinis, one in each hand. "Here's to the future," she said, brushing her glass against the one she had given him as he entered.

She led him down into the living room where they sat side by side on the sofa, sipping their drinks and nibbling on nuts from a small wooden bowl flanked by two tall candles she had arranged on the old coffee table. He felt a little strange sitting on that couch in his business suit with Ginny next to him in jeans and a pullover. She looked good, he noted, as though by losing those pounds she had also shed some years.

In what seemed like only a few minutes their glasses were empty, and so was their store of light conversation. There was a long silence.

"Aren't you going to ask me what we're celebrating?" she said at last.

"Shoot."

"There was a life insurance policy. I found it in a drawer under his winter underwear. Don't ask me why he hid it there. But I get to keep my home, Matt. Maybe even fix it up a little. I'll still have to work, but I won't have to live up in our U.P. cabin like a hermit.

"That's wonderful," he said with genuine enthusiasm. "I know staying here was important to you." He turned and gave her a hug and she clung to him, slightly trembling. When she pulled away her eyes were moist with tears.

"The important thing is that he thought of me, the rat! I get so mad at him, Matt, and then I think about how hard he worked – for years! – and I just start crying my eyes out. I go back and forth like that all day long. I wish I could just get used to all this and get ready to be a grandmother. Anyway, tonight it's just you and me, right? No spouses allowed."

Ginny smiled as she stood up and collected the empty glasses. "Let's open the wine and have something to eat. Are you hungry? I made spaghetti with meat balls. I'm not the cook Laura was, but at least nothing's burned." She kept talking as she walked into the kitchen. "Oh, and there's a big salad. Have you ever had that Paul Newman salad dressing? It's really good. I got it at Ralph's. I know Laura used to shop there all the time."

"Hey, no spouses, right?"

Ginny sighed. "I can't get anything right, can I? Please sit down at the table. Food's coming up."

Matt approached the dining room table, which was located adjacent to the living room, set off by a half-height wall. The glass doors that looked out onto the back patio were only a couple of feet away from him. He glanced out at Rex, the old family dog, curled up under the barbecue, and then realized with a start that he was looking at a black garbage sack. Rex was dead. He knew that.

Ginny came out of the kitchen carrying a large platter of spaghetti. "Your setting is there," she said, nodding her head at the table. There was an envelope on Matt's plate with his name written on it in Ginny's lightly slanted school teacher script.

"What's this?"

"Open it."

The envelope contained a thank you card, with a check for eight thousand dollars tucked inside.

"I'm paying you back."

"You don't have to do that."

"It's important to me. Otherwise...."

"Otherwise what?"

"Eat, Matt. I worked my butt off cooking this for you."

Ginny spooned a little parmesan cheese onto his spaghetti as he tucked the check into his jacket pocket.

Suddenly, it felt like they were an old couple who had lived together for years, who would turn on the TV later on and then get into the same bed. He felt a wave of melancholy. So many things were lost forever, his childhood, his time with Laura, the early days with Numerica, so full of hope...

"Don't let your food get cold," said Ginny, cutting off his reverie. She was sitting across from him, fork in hand. She really looked good, any middle-aged guy's dream date, actually. Was this a date? It seemed like every situation he got into with a woman lately was ambiguous. He needed to give that some thought, but not now.

Stone was hungry, having skipped lunch. He accepted a second helping, and with that Ginny opened a second bottle of wine. The dinner ended with a slice of apple pie fresh out of the oven and a cup of old-fashioned American coffee, which they took back to the couch. Now, for all the hours they had spent together over the years, the moment became awkward.

"I have some nice brandy," said Ginny.

Stone refused. He was drinking too much, and accepting any more was as much as asking to be pulled over by a cop.

"Aw, come on," said Ginny. "You're no fun."

"I'm already over the limit, and I have to drive home."

"No you don't, Matt."

Something in her tone made Stone turn and stare. Was she suggesting he sleep on the couch? Or...

"It sounds great, Ginny, but I have to get up early tomorrow. It's a school day for me."

"You're just worried about what the neighbors will think if they see your car parked here all night. You could park it in the garage, I guess." Her lip trembled as she spoke. "Sorry, one of those minutes."

"I know them well," said Stone, standing up.

Ginny stood up and they hugged tightly. "I miss him too, you know," said Stone. He had been so focused on anger that he really hadn't let the reality of Herb's death sink in. There were some things he could only talk about with Herb, and now Herb was gone.

Driving back, he felt a strong sense of Laura's presence. They had driven this road home so many nights together. All too often his mind would be on work, while she would attempt to cajole him.

"You need to get laid, Matt." It was Laura's voice. Somehow, she was there. It seemed so natural. And why couldn't she come back from where she was for just a few minutes in the middle of the night on an empty road?

"Know anybody who might be willing?" he responded, certain from experience that his wife would volunteer in lurid detail. Then he swiveled his head to give her a suggestive smile, only to find emptiness filling her side of the car. Of course, she wasn't there. But that hadn't been a memory. He had *heard* her voice.

"Laura?" he said. "Honey?"

There was no answer. Stone started to shake. He slowed the car and gripped the wheel tightly, fearing his eyes would be next to deceive him. He wasn't far from home. He knew he would make it. But where had that voice come from?

On Friday night at seven thirty in the evening the dimly-lit Numerica offices were creepy, fully of empty cubicles where any wacko could easily hide. But wasn't that exactly what *she* was doing? Hiding? No, Kat was *waiting*. For her boss. In spite of all the secrecy, this was really just a business meeting – and he wasn't going to like what she had to tell him. Too bad. The truth was the truth. She had done exactly what he had asked her to do, and these were the results. It wasn't her fault.

She still wasn't sure whether or not to tell him how she had gotten into a classified database in a little under two weeks with none of the resources that any state-sponsored organization would have. She didn't want to get anybody into trouble.

It had been so simple. She had started in the company cafeteria, just hanging out and observing the loners, then making a little conversation and finally managing a coffee date with Rick Carpenter, a junior systems administrator whose duties included overseeing the Oracle Identity and Authentication Managers that controlled access to all of Numerica's engineering department systems.

He wanted to talk about his job. In fact, that was all he wanted to talk about, and particularly the endless stupid problems he had to solve because his managers didn't understand modern code. At one point she had managed to interject a complaint about Numerica's password system.

"It's a pain in the ass," he had agreed.

"I use signs of the Zodiac," she had offered.

"Planets from Star Trek," he had responded, and just like that, she had what she needed to get in. Well, not quite.

She had spent several days reading online documentation to see how the Oracle systems worked. Then she had needed to write a little script that would attempt to log on to the system once every five minutes with a different password taken from an exhaustive collection of Star Trek planet names she had found online. A ping every five minutes wouldn't attract any attention. She also had to sit through one more coffee date, to make sure he didn't figure out their first date was all about fishing for his passwords.

It had taken her three days to get into the system. And now she was about to demonstrate what she, or any determined Russian hacker, could do. Actually, what any junior high schooler could do, and really without that much determination.

At exactly seven thirty she heard the door click open, and then Matt's voice.

"It's me," he called. "Ready for the demo?"

"As ready as I'll ever be, I guess."

Stone entered the cubicle, sat down on the other chair and scooted over next to her, close enough so that she could smell the faded scent of his cologne. Actually, it could be deodorant. When it came to stuff like that, what did she know about executives? Half the guys she had dated didn't even wear deodorant. *I am not dating this man*, she reminded herself. But there was something going on.

"Let's see what you've got."

She rested her hands on the keyboard and called up an application that could access one of Numerica's classified databases. When the challenge screen appeared, she typed in Rick Carpenter's user name and password of the month. Instantly, a list of graphics files appeared.

"How did you figure out the password?" asked Stone.

Kat answered without taking her eyes off the screen. "They're not that hard to guess. There are lots of lists of the most common passwords on the web. You just try one after another until you get a hit. It usually works."

Stone was staring at the screen now, as though he recognized the file names.

"Is there a particular file you'd like to see?" asked Kat.

Stone instantly rattled off a file name. She clicked on it, and a schematic drawing of what looked like a mechanical insect appeared.

"Fuck," said Stone, whispering under his breath.

"What is it?"

"Shut it down. This is highly classified."

Kat closed the window and then shut down the computer itself. "It's really bad, huh?"

"Yes," said Stone.

Kat had never seen him upset like this. "Is there anything I can do?" It was a stupid question, but she didn't know what else to say.

"How did you get the password?"

Kat swiveled in her chair. She suppressed an urge to put her hand on his knee as she answered him.

"I know your impulse is to punish somebody. But that won't help. You need to change the system."

Stone gave her a stricken look. Her words had clearly touched a nerve, something that went far beyond the computer system vulnerability they were discussing, which could easily be corrected.

"What is it?" she asked. "What did I say wrong?"

"Nothing. Sorry. I'm just under a lot of pressure."

"Matt, listen. There's something called two-factor authentication. It makes it so a password isn't enough. Your coders are only human. Not everybody has...." She hesitated. "Not everybody has your strength and discipline."

Stone nodded, and she could tell she had gotten through to him. "Two factor authentication," he repeated.

"I don't know what the details of the regulations are, but on a practical basis it should work."

"I don't know either. That's what I pay Selena for."

"Please, Matt. Just let her fix it."

Stone was shaking his head. "This is unbelievable."

"Just tell her you got an anonymous warning. Don't involve me, okay? It will make my life miserable." She swiveled in her chair and put her hands on his arms. "You got me into this."

"Two factor authentication," he repeated half to himself.

"Right. It will work. And you can have it in place in a few days. In the meantime, she'll make everybody change their passwords once a day or something like that, and you'll be okay. This isn't rocket science."

Kat was amazed at the confidence in her voice, but she knew he needed reassurance at that moment, and to her surprise, it was there for her to offer. How did that happen? It was him. He was good for her. He made her realize she really could manage things. And now, what he needed was to take her to the Roadhouse for a couple of those expensive scotches he liked so much. She couldn't bring herself to suggest it. That would be stepping over a line he didn't want her to cross. Or did he?

Stone stood up and pulled his iPhone out of his pocket. He tapped out a quick note and a moment later she heard the sound of an email message taking flight.

"I'll meet with Selena in the morning," he said. "Thanks for staying late to show me this."

"I'm just doing my job."

"You did good."

They walked out together.

"Have a good night," she called as he got into his sports car.

"With the help of some good scotch, I will. This may be a Roadhouse night," he called back with a laugh.

"Want some company?" she whispered once he had closed the door and she was sure he couldn't hear her.

Kat's feet pounded the secluded path around the lake in rhythm to the words that repeated themselves over and over again in her head,

I-DO-NOT-BE-LONG-IN-HIS-LIFE.

I-DO-NOT-BE-LONG-IN-HIS-LIFE.

Dressed in nothing but a thin T-shirt and running shorts, she felt cold and stiff in the damp, early morning air. It served her right. She should have had enough sense to at least put on a hoody when the temperature was only 45 degrees. Beyond that, she should have had enough sense to say no about getting involved in this whole bullshit project of Matt's, whatever it was.

He couldn't fool her. There was nothing wrong with security at Numerica now. Two factor authentication and the new auto-encryption system had taken care of that. Now, if an engineer got careless and sent some eyes-only specifications to a sub-contractor via email without hitting the encrypt button, that email would still look like gibberish to anyone who might intercept it. And if someone managed to sweet-talk one of the technicians out of a system password, the intruder would still be blocked because the passwords were now tied to physical tokens that could double as key chains. And if a laptop got lost or stolen, it could be remotely wiped clean in seconds.

In spite of all these changes, which were all that French woman's idea, by the way, with no help from Kat, Matt kept quizzing her about security during their runs. Were there hackers out there who could target a specific email account? How did that work? If you logged on at a Starbucks, did that make you harder to trace? Could someone tell if your were using TOR when they got an email from you? Often, she didn't have definitive answers to these questions. But when she suggested he ask Selena, who was his CIO after all, he made lame excuses about not wasting her time or getting her side-tracked. But it was obvious he didn't want to involve her. He was clearly planning something. Something that was probably illegal. And Kat was his research assistant. That was her real job. He had even gotten her a computer that had direct, un-monitored access to the outside world, so there would be no traces of the excursions he sent her on.

Her big task last week was setting up a fifty thousand dollar account with BitCoin, the leading internet currency which, like all of them based on block chain technology, couldn't be traced. It was common knowledge that BitCoin's main purpose was to facilitate drug deals. But the idea that he was involved in drug trafficking just didn't make sense. What was going on? She had to admit, there was something very sexy about a man who could just order up that much money and then make it disappear into thin air without anybody asking any questions, or at least not anybody inside the company. Apparently, there were classified bank accounts that only he controlled.

"Don't worry," he had said. Nobody will miss it." How could you not miss fifty thousand dollars? And how did he intend to spend it? Was it really his money to spend? Or was she – what was the word – an *accessory* to some crime?

The stuff about the Federal government was even scarier. He was concerned that the Feds were trying to collect data about Numerica that would put him at a disadvantage in contract negotiations. Even though she had assured him they couldn't get into Numerica's systems, he had asked her if she could find out "what agencies have what," which entailed a rather complex sorting process. He was particularly worried about the IRS. It was like an obsession. In a way, you couldn't really blame him after what happened to his friend, but some of his questions were weird, like wanting to know where different kinds of IRS data was physically stored. What did it matter? What was he going to do, blow up the data center where information about Numerica was stored? That was crazy. She should just quit and go back to her quiet life at the café. She was skating on the edge of something that felt too risky. And she didn't need those big pay checks.

All she really wanted to do was hang out with Matt. She didn't want their secret coffee meetings and their runs to end. A part of her just couldn't believe he was doing something illegal. And what if he was? What was so hot about the laws of the U.S. government? There were higher laws. The truth was, she *wanted* to help him. And she wanted to make him happy. There were things all men wanted, no matter how involved they were in their work or their cause or whatever. She was good at that stuff.

Stone felt the cold heat of anger building in him as his headlights illuminated Ginny's driveway. He would never again see it without remembering yellow police tape. *That agent should die*, said a voice inside his head. But it was just a thought. Not like hearing Laura right next to him. He parked his Crossfire, yanking far too hard on the emergency break. As he approached the front porch he took several deep breaths, trying to calm himself.

Ginny opened the door wearing a bright smile and a spring dress that was new to Stone's eyes. She was, he guessed, at least two sizes thinner since Herb's death.

"Let's start with a martini," she said. "I've cut back on my drinking way too much."

"Sounds great," he replied, although in fact he wondered if alcohol was a good idea. He entered the house to receive a long, comfortable hug. They had established a pattern of dinners every Wednesday.

"Have you started working out again?" she asked. "You feel different."

"I've been running a lot."

"How about running to the kitchen and playing bartender? Our dinner's in the oven. It'll be ready in about half an hour."

A wave of sadness hit Stone as he entered the kitchen and went about pouring the gin and vermouth into the cocktail shaker. In the past, this was where he and Herb would have time for a brief private exchange away from the women. Now, there was no one left on Earth he could talk to like that.

When he had finished preparing the drinks he joined Ginny on the couch.

Stone raised his glass. "To the old days?"

"No," she said instantly, "To the new, happy days that lie ahead."

They sipped in silence, unable to avoid thinking about the old days.

"I saw two for sale signs in front of old employees' houses last week. I feel awful."

"There's nothing you can do about that. There's nothing anybody can do about it. The damage has already been done, Ginny."

"I know. I keep telling myself that *I'm* out of a job too. But I've learned QuickBooks now. I think I can get a job as a junior bookkeeper right away, and then when I learn more and take some courses I can have a little business. There are job openings at H&R Block right now and they train you, but I just can't bring myself to take a job helping people pay their taxes. Am I being dumb?"

"No."

"You're not exactly talkative tonight."

"Sorry."

"The whole purpose of a martini before dinner is to loosen your tongue." She punched him lightly on the shoulder. "Hey. It's me. Ginny. You can talk to me about anything."

Stone raised his eyebrows, then laughed.

"Matt, I'm serious. I know what's on your mind. You've got to drop this whole revenge thing. There's nothing we can do. You just said it yourself. Even if you ran for Congress like you talked about a few years ago, you'd just be one out of how many? Five hundred and some odd members? It's like me trying to save the people who are losing their houses."

She stood up, not waiting for a reply. "It's time for some red meat and red wine."

Ginny led him to the dining room table, sat him down, and then disappeared into the kitchen. She returned with a beautifully crusted pot roast on a platter, ringed by small potatoes, each with its own sprinkle of parsley. Stone felt his heart catch for an instant. It was a recipe she had gotten from Laura, meat and potatoes taken to a new level. Ginny went back into the kitchen and returned with a bowl of green beans.

"I know we're not supposed to try and re-live the past, but I also know you love pot roast like this. I hope it's okay.

You know, sometimes I just want to give you things I know are missing from your life."

There was an unopened bottle of red wine on the table, and now she handed him a cork screw. "We may need this if I goofed up on the roast."

Stone laughed and uncorked the bottle with practiced hands. He filled both glasses generously. This time they clinked without a word. Then she handed him the carving knife.

As they ate, Ginny talked about her progress towards the goal of independence. True to form, she was following the plan that she had devised step by step, with a little progress every day. She seemed slightly nervous, pouring herself a second glass of wine before he was half through his first.

Desert was peach ice cream, a favorite of his, and she knew it. He suddenly realized to his chagrin that she had been making little mental notes of what he liked and didn't like for years. He had never observed those details about her. And when her life suddenly blew up, the only way he knew to console her was to give her money. Looking back, it seemed so clumsy.

"Matt, are you with us?"

"Sorry, I was lost for a minute."

"Are you in love?"

Stone sat up straight in his chair. "What in the world would make you say that? Surely you jest."

"Are you?"

Matt hesitated a beat. She was serious!

"You are! I knew it. Well, it was inevitable."

"I'm not in love, Ginny. This is silly."

She leaned towards him. "I've had fantasies about sleeping with you for years, Matt. Did you ever think about sleeping with me?"

"Ginny, I think we need to monitor our alcohol intake a little."

"Oh, come on. You never mentally undressed me?"

"I didn't need to. I saw you once. In the shower at the cabin on the lake. You were taking a shower. The door was unlocked so I just walked in. You didn't notice me, and as a gentleman, I left immediately."

She sighed. "I can see my hints aren't working. What you saw is available, Matt. My body is a little older than it was back then, but it's still pretty darned good. Do I have to be more blunt?"

Stone stared at her. She had soft brown eyes. Alluring eyes. Had he been younger, he couldn't have resisted her.

He shook his head. "I just can't," he said.

"Why not? Herb's dead, for Christ's sake." Her voice rose in pitch. "And so is Laura."

Stone couldn't look at her. It was too painful. He didn't want to get entangled. That was the truth of it. Sleeping with Ginny would be no one night stand. She would want, and deserve, more attention than he had to give. He needed to be focused. He didn't even have a plan of attack yet, much less a team to execute it.

"It just wouldn't feel right," he said. It sounded lame and selfish.

"Well then, will you just come around the table and hold me for a little while?"

Stone did as she asked, holding her soft body against her. She smelled luscious.

"Matt," she whispered in his ear, "If this lady treats you badly, tell her I will scratch her eyes out." She pulled away and started laughing. "Okay, you win. Just know that I am your true friend, and I am so grateful for what you've done for me."

"Your are a beautiful woman, inside and out."

She cocked her head to one side. "You sure you don't want to do it with me? Just this once? I miss it!"

"You know that once wouldn't be enough."

"I know. In my heart I know it's a bad idea, but my body doesn't agree."

Then ended up taking a neighborhood stroll in the cool night air. Each house had its own story, and Ginny knew them all. Why was he putting up a wall between himself and this compassionate woman who found meaning and purpose everywhere? And what was this thing about being in love?

Back in his empty home, Stone brewed himself a pot of coffee, knowing that drinking it would make sleep difficult, and not caring. Spending the evening with Ginny had been a painful reminder that almost two weeks had passed since his meeting with Monzer al-Shami, and he had done nothing. Perhaps al-Shami's veiled suggestion that he wasn't a "truly committed man" had a grain of truth in it.

No, that wasn't the problem. He was as committed as a man could be. But he could as yet find no path to the goal. The two hundred thousand dollar price tag for a missile powerful enough take out the Denver datacenter wasn't a trivial obstacle. He would have to sell his house, and then figure out a way to launder the profits. He could use BitCoin for laundering purposes, but that "currency," if BitCoin was even worthy of the name, was unstable, and he could end up losing his ass with nothing in the way of destructive force to show for it.

Beyond that, say he won a few hundred thousand dollars at Las Vegas and could buy any weapon he wanted. Then what would he do? Send the Denver datacenter a communication saying he would blow the place up if they didn't meet his demands? The IRS received crackpot threats like that every day. To make his threat credible he would have to prove he really had a weapon, that it was within range, that he knew how to use it and had the will to do so – all of this without revealing his identity or whereabouts. He had no idea how that could be accomplished.

Stone sat down at the dark, highly polished dining room table where he and Laura had enjoyed so many dinner parties over the years and took out his laptop. There was one thing he *could* do He fired up the laptop and googled "Tor." At the top of the list of entries was

Tor Project: Anonymity Online

Anonymity. Just what both Selena and Kat had promised. Anonymity was essential for moving forward, no matter where this mission might ultimately lead him.

Among the on screen options below the main heading for Tor was one titled Download. He clicked on it, and after a couple of tries was able to see the Tor browser icon on his desktop. It was a stylized onion. TOR, he recalled, was an acronym for The Onion Ring, but to his eyes it looked more like a bomb. He double-clicked on it.

The initial screen was full of warnings. He began to read through the list of additional precautions required to achieve true anonymity, and began to wonder if he was in over his head. At least he was not on the corporate network, so no one in the company would realize that their CEO was fooling around with a web browser most often associated with illicit arms and drug deals. But beyond that, he wasn't sure who knew what about his actions this night.

He had to be sure. He went back to the precautions list and began to execute its directives one by one. When he came across terminology he didn't understand, he googled the terms until he got an explanation that enabled him to move forward.

Shortly before one a.m. he reached a place where he felt relatively confident that he was truly safe from prying eyes. He was by no means going to reach out to al-Shami and put in an order – he wasn't that confident – but he did launch Google Maps and take a long look at the satellite views of the datacenter. Then, unable to resist temptation, he switched to Street View for a ground-level inspection of the chain link perimeter fence. There were a few places where some animal had dug under the fence. There was no way a man could get through, but a stealth robot by the name of SADIE would have no trouble. What if he didn't need to buy the delivery system, but only the bomb?

One problem solved – at least potentially. There were a string of others, but you could only take one step at a time.

Ninety percent of golf is played from the shoulders up. Putter in hand, Stone visualized his ball rolling into the cup, holding Arnold Palmer's admonition firmly in mind. He and three upper level Numerica executives were on the eighteenth hole of the exclusive Indianwood Golf Course about forty miles north of Detroit. He was putting for par on this hole, which would tie him with Jim Cotter, his bespectacled VP of Engineering. Cotter approached golf like he approached everything, with meticulous attention to detail. He was thin, and lacked the muscle to hit deep drives, but his strategy was flawless. He played within himself, as sports commentators were so fond of saying, never attempting shots that were beyond his skill, but getting every ounce out of what he had.

The other two men in the foursome, both directors, only played golf because they had to, or at least that was Stone's impression. You could tell they weren't passionate, although they put on a good show.

Stone imagined what Kat would think if she could see him now. It was the cliché image of capitalist executive privilege, and she would tease him without mercy. Cotter cleared his throat, bringing Stone back to the present moment: the brilliant late morning sunshine, the velvet-textured putting green, the ball as white as the moon. He stroked it, and knew at once that he had not hit it with enough force to take it to the cup. Game over, as his daughter's friends used to say. It came to a stop a few inches short, he casually tapped it in, and that was that.

When Stone proposed lunch at The Nineteenth Green as the four of them changed in the locker room, the two directors begged off. That was strange. You don't turn down an invitation for lunch with the big boss! As he and Cotter entered the clubhouse, lovingly restored to its early twentieth century glory, Stone began to wonder if this was a set-up. Was Cotter carrying a message?

They both ordered burgers and beers. Stone spoke as soon as the waiter had left their table. "Do you have something to tell me?"

Cotter wasn't taken aback by Stone's bluntness. He was used to it.

"Yes. You haven't been yourself lately."

Shit! thought Stone. *What does he know?* Of course, he couldn't know anything. "Can you be a little more specific?"

"You don't miss putts like that."

"Hey, even Willie Mays dropped some easy fly balls at the end of his career."

Cotter leveled his eyes at him. "Are you at the end of your career?"

Stone was amazed. A highly competent engineer with a good head for business, Cotter was one of the two most obvious candidates to take over for Stone when the time came. But to suggest that time was near was in bad taste to say the least.

"Are you getting itchy to run the company?" asked Stone, attempting to put a lighter spin on the conversation.

Cotter laughed. "I think we got off on the wrong foot here, Matt. I *am* a little concerned. You seem distracted. You've always been honest with me, and I'm just being honest with you."

Stone nodded.

"I know how hard losing Laura was for you, and we all have a lot of respect for the way you carried on. But lately, well, I just feel it's my duty to ask you if everything is okay. You're the kind of guy who would tough out any situation, but sometimes that's not the smartest thing to do."

"Jim, I have to ask you. Are you the spokesman for a committee here?"

"Nope, just a loyal team player."

It was easy to believe him, and a relief to hear his answer. He wasn't ready to deal with a cabal right now. The strain of living what he had come to see as a double life – CEO by day, anti IRS guerilla by night – was already sapping his energy to the point where his direct reports were taking notice. How was he to respond to this trusted lieutenant? How much of the truth would put him at risk down the road? And how much dissimulation would lead Cotter to conclude he was lying – or worse, faltering? Stone had never dreamed he would have to make decisions like this.

He sighed. "The truth is, I'm beginning to wonder if the country we're making weapons to defend is still worth defending."

"I don't understand."

Stone recounted the story of his friend's suicide, and the circumstances that led to it.

"He was a close friend?"

"Since high school."

"Those bastards." Cotter shook his head. "I'm sorry, Matt."

"We might as well be living in Russia, and I want to do something. Right now, being successful making hip joints and stealth robots doesn't seem as important as it did a while back. That's what's been on my mind. I hope you'll keep it to yourself."

Had he said too much? The best lies were laced with a good measure of truth. But, *I want to do something*. He had gone too far. He imagined Cotter sitting in his living room with a couple of FBI agents, relating this conversation. Was that a paranoid thought?

"The truth is," Stone continued, improvising as he went along, "I've been re-thinking the idea of running for office."

"You would challenge Conners?" asked Cotter, always the practical man. Frank Conners was the sitting congressman from their district. Both men knew him. He was in his late sixties, in good health and well-liked. He would be difficult to unseat.

"I would try to talk him into retiring. That would be the first step. It's probably a crazy idea. But if I decide to pursue it, I won't keep you in the dark. Right now, I think the chances are about ten percent."

"I like that number. I'd like zero even better."

Stone eyed him and nodded. Cotter would not leave the table wondering what *I want to do something* had meant. His thoughts would be focused on this unanticipated shot at CEO.

When the two parted in the parking lot, Stone was left with a sense of emptiness. He wasn't going to run for Congress. He probably wasn't going to blow up the new IRS facility in Denver. He had no concrete plan to make *anyone* pay for the outrage of Herb's death. And he was play-acting as CEO of Numerica. In fact, there was nothing in his life that made him want to get out of bed in the morning. With nothing better to do, he got into his car and headed back to White Lake to buy some groceries and pick up his laundry.

Why live?

Stone awoke with this question echoing in his mind and it would not depart. His plans to right the wrong of Herb's untimely death had been shattered by the realities of what it would take to do so, and the energy to regroup had abandoned him. The thrill of success in business was gone and had been gone, he now realized, since Laura had died. Ginny could manage on her own now and – this hurt the most – his own daughter really didn't want him in her life anymore except via email or text on birthdays and holidays. His body and mind were slowly giving way, and although he knew he would never take his own life, he would welcome a disease that would take it for him.

A part of him knew that this collection of black thoughts was a chimera with no power beyond what he granted it, but that knowledge was no help. Nonetheless, he threw the covers back, pivoted out of the bed and headed for the bathroom, the shower, the shaving mug and the rest of it. Something would eventually come along to make the day bearable.

He would begin with a river run. He had read within the last week of a new study confirming that the brain responded to exercise much like a muscle, and that regular aerobic work-outs did more for seniors' brains than crossword puzzles or that new craze Ginny had taken up. Sudoku. *Seniors*. Did he fall into that category? If not now, soon enough.

The sight of Kat's beat-up gray car jolted him. She was the real reason he was here. He was kidding himself if he thought otherwise. But now what? Have an affair with a girl maybe not as old as his daughter and put millions of dollars in contracts at risk? One of the best CEOs at Hewlett-Packard had been kicked out for nothing more than expensing a couple of fancy dinners with some busty PR consultant. Stone, with no authority to do so, had enabled an IT consultant to hack into a classified database. Granted, that hack had taken place under controlled circumstances, and for a reason, but he was still playing fast and loose with the rules. He could easily be forced out of his leadership position at Numerica if word got out, and possibly end up in prison.

He followed the path down to the lake and there she was, standing on the trail with her arms crossed against her chest. This time she really was waiting for him. He could feel it. As he approached, she opened her arms and the next moment they were caught up in an embrace that felt as natural as it was unplanned and unexpected.

"Just turn off your mind," she said, pressing her hips against his and then opening her mouth to receive his tongue.

"Come on," she said, breaking away after a long moment and taking his hand in hers. "I brought a blanket just in case you showed up. I knew this was going to happen eventually."

She had spread out a plaid wool blanket in a spot that Stone had first discovered way back in high school, and he felt like he was in a time warp, like the ones in the science fiction novels he used to read. He was once again seventeen, and the force of his desire was so strong it overruled all thought and caution.

They lay down on the blanket and kissed endlessly. "We can't quite go all the way this morning," she said, rubbing his stiffness, which had reached the point of aching, "but I'm going to make you feel really, really good."

She scooted down until her head was at his hips and loosened the knotted cord of his running shorts, pulling them down so he was exposed.

"Oh wow," she said softly. Then she took him in her mouth. The sensation was amazing. His whole body was buzzing as she coaxed him closer and closer to the edge.

"Just let go," she said, staring into his eyes and pumping him. "Just let go. Just let go." She repeated the words over and over until he finally gave into them.

Afterward, she cuddled up to him, pressing her face against his cheek. "Did that feel good?" she asked. "I hope I didn't go too fast."

"Don't be silly."

"I've been dreaming about that for a long time."

Stone said nothing. He knew if he closed his eyes he would fall instantly asleep. He felt so peaceful. At this moment, everything in the world was as it should be.

"Hey," said Kat, "I want you to know that I'm a girl who can keep a secret."

Her words jolted him back into the world where everything was most certainly not as it should be, the world where he had responsibilities he couldn't seem to fulfill lately.

"You need time like this," said Kat. "You can't push yourself day in and day out. Not at your age, colonel," she added with a smile.

She was right. He had been living in a very narrow world. There was more to life than obligation – but his obligations were nonetheless very real.

"We have to get you a security clearance," he said.

"Wow, what a romantic," she shot back, pushing herself away from him. "I just gave you the world's greatest blow job and you tell me I need a security clearance."

"I'm sorry, I didn't pick the best time to bring that up. But if we're going to –"

"Fuck a lot?"

"You really have a way with words, Kat."

"So I've been told."

"We need to clean things up."

"I thought I swallowed it all."

Stone gently turned her head so he could look into her eyes and get her to be serious, but she looked so beautiful to him just then that he had trouble gathering his thoughts.

"There are some digital links," he managed.

"Can't we talk about this later?"

For a brief moment, Stone thought he saw a hint of pain in her eyes.

"Of course. You're right. It's... just how I am sometimes."
Stone inwardly cringed. How many times had he and Laura
had this conversation?

Stone sat nursing a double espresso in the rear corner of the
Starbucks where he and Kat had chatted after their second
run together. This was no night for alcohol. He had to get
off his ass and figure something out! For reasons he couldn't
understand, his encounter with Kat had stoked a new sense
of urgency. She invaded his thoughts at every turn, and he
couldn't say she wasn't welcome. But not now.

On the table next to his half-empty cup was a worn
copy of Sun-Tzu's *The Art of War*, and a tablet of yellow
lined paper upon which he had copied some of the ancient
Chinese general's epigrams.

> *Great results can be achieved with small forces.*

> *Begin by seizing something your opponent holds
> dear. Then, he will be amenable to your will.*

> *The way of war is to avoid what is strong, and strike
> at what is weak.*

His problem was that the IRS had no weaknesses. It was
a legion comprising tens of thousands of agents, with the
power to intimidate not only ordinary citizens, but senators
and congressmen as well. Furthermore, the whims of those
agents had the force of law. Stone knew from bitter

experience that the way to attack a monolithic enemy like that was to pick targets of opportunity and inflict a death by a thousand cuts, exactly what the Viet Cong had done to America's massive forces in 'Nam. But Stone had neither the resources nor the time to conduct a campaign like that, even if he could imagine what form it might assume. And when all was said and done, taking out the Denver datacenter would not right the wrongs that had led to the death of his closest friend.

Begin by seizing something your opponent holds dear. What was he supposed to do, kidnap the IRS Commissioner's daughter? This train of thought was leading him nowhere. He emptied his cup in one gulp, gathered his things and headed for the door, frustrated and angry. The weapons of war were death and destruction. Take these out of the equation, and what was left?

As he drove through the dark streets, his mind turned the problem over and over. There was no army, no organization and, for that matter, no *man* without weaknesses. Where to attack? And with what weapons?

When Stone approached his driveway, floodlights came on and the garage door lifted. He had put these security precautions in place for Laura's protection. Now, they were meaningless. He let himself into the house through an internal door in the garage and walked through the kitchen into the living room where the bar was, turning on lights as he passed. Three day's worth of letters and a couple of catalogs lay in a pile beneath the mail slot next to the front door, yet another symptom of his distracted state these days. One of the letters was from the IRS. Standing by the door, he opened it by sliding his finger under the flap. Inside was a bill for exactly the amount of the check he had already written more than a month ago.

Another IRS fuck-up. What a surprise! The software they had was so antiquated they were lucky they could collect taxes at all. He had read somewhere that crashes and inaccurate data were a regular part of life at an IRS offices, and that security was notoriously weak.

Weak.

Stone let the mistakenly issued tax bill fall from his hands and flutter to the floor. *There* was the weakness, and an open door to what his opponent held dear: data.

III.

A Fatal Vulnerability

Kevin Fallon had been a bug hunter for almost five years. He had slid into it, just like he had slid into everything in his life – his apartment, his relationship with Kaitlin, and now, his new role as a father.

It was time for a change.

He needed to formulate some goals and take charge of his future. If Scientology had taught him anything, it had taught him that bouncing around randomly like he was inside some pinball machine was no way to live. He needed stability, and that began with a stable source of income. *He had a kid!* And it wasn't only about his two-month-old son. He needed money to pay for the Life Improvement courses that would take him to the next level.

It wasn't that bug hunting couldn't pay big. Finding a so-called zero-day vulnerability in a major software program that had already been released to customers – a vulnerability that had snuck past the software company's internal security team – could earn you ten grand in one day. Unfortunately, such hits were rare in the bug hunting business. And there was another problem. It didn't feel good when you knew you were getting paid that ten grand so you would shut up and not publish your discovery to the world. Most of the companies Fallon sold information to had no intention of fixing the security holes he had discovered. They would rather put their customers at risk than spend the money to plug it and make their product safe.

Not for the first time, it crossed Fallon's mind that he was engaged in what amounted to institutionalized blackmail. The implicit threat was that without a payoff, he, like any of the thousands of other bug hunters out there, would publish the faulty code in the name of protecting consumers. The bug hunters would argue that there was no other way to force the offending companies to fix the code and make it safe. And they might very well be right. The corporate software vendors would argue that keeping bugs secret until they were fixed was a better approach, and they were willing to pay for that secrecy.

When you got down to it, the whole business was sketchy. It was time for a real job. But before he resigned himself to regular hours and a desk in a cubicle farm, he was going to negotiate one more deal. And it was going to be worth a lot more than ten grand.

He could hardly believe what he had discovered: a direct access path to a database used by some of the biggest corporations and government agencies in the world – even the I.R.S! It was a vulnerability he knew most bug hunters would be unlikely to discover, including the researches employed by the large Russian data theft organizations. But, if revealed, it could be exploited to devastating effect. Whoever could get to the screen he had hacked into could not only look at all the records in that database. He could change them. And he could block the real administrator from changing them back.

In the dim light of the basement office he rented for two hundred dollars a month, Fallon typed an instant message to a security administrator he knew could buy the bug. There was no need for anonymity. What he was doing was perfectly legal. Still, he used his online handle. He decided he would start the negotiation at a hundred thousand. By the end of the day, at least fifty would be in his bank account.

Kat was curled up against the early morning warmth of Stone's body in the small bed she had bought quite a while back, when the thought of sharing it had been far from her mind. Now, she wished it were bigger – wished her whole apartment were bigger, for that matter. It was okay for sex, but there wasn't really room for both of them to be comfortable and just hang out.

He was already getting restless. It was always like that. Like having her wasn't really enough. Like he still wasn't satisfied. That's how it seemed. But maybe he was just that way. It wasn't like she had slept with dozens of guys and knew exactly what to expect. Sometimes she wished she had had more experience. But then, he didn't seem like the type who would want a girl who had slept around a lot.

"I think we should get a place," she said, and as soon as she spoke she wished she hadn't. What was she thinking? The fact was, she hadn't been thinking. "I mean –"

"Where?" said Stone, to her astonishment.

She had no ready answer. "Somewhere that's convenient for you, I guess, so you could, you know, maybe spend the night?"

"I should stay with you sometimes, I know," said Stone, rolling over on his side and propping up his head with his hand. For a moment he looked much younger. She felt a pang. Things could only go so far with this man. He had already had a wife, a family, the whole show. But she did want them to go a little farther. No matter how close their bodies might get in bed, he still shut her out of his mind. She could almost never tell what he was thinking.

"This bed is too small," she said. "This apartment is too small. It's really only good for one thing." She hesitated. "Maybe that's all you want from me?"

Stone gave her a look of mock exasperation.

"I'd just like a place that's a little bigger. I mean, we wouldn't live there or anything," she added quickly, "We'd just rent it so you could, you know, come over and do some work and I'd cook us dinner. Just now and then. It wouldn't be gourmet. But it would be cooked with love." Love. She had never used the word with him before. With anybody. It hung in the air.

For once, she had actually caught him off guard. She could tell he didn't know what to say.

"We could split the rent," she said, veering away from the theme of love even though it was too late. "I've got a good job now. I can afford more than this."

Stone chuckled, then became serious. "What kind of a place do you have in mind? I was thinking maybe we could find a cottage near the lake somewhere. I've seen them for rent."

She could hardly believe her ears. She had blurted out a pipe dream that had randomly drifted into her mind and here he was, making it real. Just like that.

"It sounds awesome."

"We could rent a truck and spend a Saturday on Fourteenth Street," he said, referring to a couple of blocks in the old part of downtown where there were half a dozen so-called antique shops, although what they sold was really more like used furniture. "But I do think we should get a decent mattress if I'm going to have the honor of sleeping on it now and then. We could have that delivered."

That was Matt for you. He made things happen. He couldn't help it. He was as goal-focused as she was scattered. It was so sexy! Opposites attract, they said. Maybe it was true. And in fact, she wasn't so scattered these days. Something was changing.

Stone leaned over and gave her a kiss. "Duty calls," he said. "I've got a seven o'clock tomorrow."

"Is it going to be a twelver?"

Stone stared at her, eyes wide.

"What did I say? I just meant, are you going to work, like, until seven? I was thinking about a late run. I didn't mean to...."

"It's okay. Laura used to call a long day a twelver." He shook his head as though to clear it.

Kat touched his face. "You still miss her, huh?

Stone sighed. "Let me just say this. If she could look down and see us right now, she would be happy."

When Stone was gone, Kat got out of bed and took a quick shower. Then she pulled on a pair of jeans and a T-shirt and sat down at the little kitchen table. On her iPad, she made a list of the furniture they would need. Then she went onto Amazon and looked for a cookbook written for beginners.

Stone stopped by his house for a fresh set of clothes before he headed to the office. The kitchen seemed cold, and it wasn't only a matter of temperature. He was hardly ever here anymore. He had been forcing himself to spend a couple nights each week in what had been his and Laura's bed, but that was only because he couldn't bring himself to admit he and Kat were on the edge of a living together relationship. Actually renting the cottage they had found would be the final acknowledgement of this new reality.

During the hours and days they had spent together working or running trails or making love in her cramped apartment, the life had seeped out of his old home. Still, it shouldn't feel this cold. He wondered if he had left a window open somewhere.

Walking into the living room, he immediately saw the source of the problem. The front door was wide open. Stone fought a sense of panic. He had the only key to this house, and it was obvious that the door hadn't been forced. He had left it open. How could that happen? He thought for a moment. He had been at Kat's last night, and the night before. Which mean his house had been totally accessible, with no security, for almost three days.

He took a deep breath and then walked over to close and lock the door, making sure the deadbolt slid all the way home. Upstairs, before he got into the shower, he took a couple minutes to check the bedroom drawers, almost hoping to find his expensive watches stolen.

"Shit happens," he said out loud as he walked towards the bathroom, trying to shake off the fear that the "ambiguous" situation deep within his brain was turning into a problem.

Driving along the familiar route he had taken to Numerica every weekday for almost twenty years finally calmed him down. He could clearly picture the shape of his day, although he had to admit his sense of commitment to the company he had built wasn't what it used to be. He was constantly distracted by thoughts about what it would take to mount a crippling attack on the IRS. The people who were capable of such an attack wouldn't be easy to find, nor to control once he found them. Who could he trust in the shadowy world of the Dark Web?

Entering the lobby he walked straight to the front desk where Connie sat with her perfect posture and perfect hair.

"Good morning, Captain," she said with a smile.

He returned her smile. "I've got a job for you," he said in a low voice. He handed her a slip of paper with the address of the cottage he and Kat had found, along with the owner's contact information. "I think we need one more guest apartment."

Like many larger businesses, Numerica rented a number of apartments for visiting customers, some of which were almost within walking distance of the factory, and a couple of which, reserved for Army brass, were "discrete." These were located far from Numerica, and featured well-stocked bars as well as other amenities Stone chose not to think about.

Connie looked up with a forced smile. "I'm happy," she said, "but I have to admit part of me wishes it could have been us."

Stone sighed and nodded. Shacking up with Connie would have probably been a lot smarter, but his life was no longer governed by what was smart.

"I take it you want this to be discrete." This meant that the rent and any other expenses would be paid via a small slush fund Connie managed and therefore kept off the books. The money could no doubt be traced back to Numerica, but it would take time and determination.

"Yes," said Stone, "but all you need to do is pay the rent. No liquor or anything."

"I'm on it," she said. "One top secret safe house comin' up."

"Thanks," he said. There were days where he felt that Connie was the only person in the company he could really trust, and he realized to his chagrin that those days were becoming more and more frequent. As he walked passed the busy cubicles of the engineering department on the way to his office he tried without success to focus his thoughts on the teleconference coming up in less than an hour. Why had he decided on this clandestine rental arrangement? Hiring a woman you were sleeping with as a consultant was shaky, true enough, but he could demonstrate substantial ROI from her efforts. Paying for her apartment out of a secret company slush fund was over the line. He certainly had the money to pay the rent himself. But an inner voice had told him he might need a place to hide. His inner terrorist.

Stone entered his office, where his secretary Chase was waiting for him with some Excel print-outs for the teleconference. It was about cost overruns involving a major supplier. They could be justified, but he felt it was time to put his foot down and let everybody know the CEO of Numerica was running a tight ship. After all, it was the taxpayers' money they were spending. Yes, he would use that line.

Kat had realized that it was possible to put together a meal that was pretty fancy without cooking a thing. There was a deli called Ralph's on Nicole Street where you could get a Caesar salad, a couple different kinds of salami, some cheese and a French baguette, and with a bottle of red wine, you had dinner. The wine, she realized, was important, and she was clueless about wine. In restaurants she always picked the most expensive glass on the list, white with chicken and fish, red with everything else. That was the sum total of her knowledge, but Ralph was educating her, and Matt seemed happy with the choices she brought home. *Home.* That was how she was starting to think about the cottage, and she knew that was a dangerous thought. The whole thing with Matt could blow up any day.

She wished he weren't so secretive. She could never get him to talk about work beyond the narrow limits of the IT department, except that one time at Lily's. She wondered if he had ever talked about work with his wife. Probably so, but it was different if you were the wife. Kat was something else, and part of what he wanted from her was distraction from work. At least that's how it seemed. Sometimes she wanted to help him out with the problems that were on his mind, but what did she really have to offer?

Tonight, she had a simple dinner to offer. Hot dogs, potato salad and a local pale ale. She knew he would like it, maybe after a Jack Daniels with a little soda. He didn't want something exotic every night. It was the same way with sex. Although she constantly worried about it, he seemed to be happy with anything. He had actually said, "I don't care what we do so long as I get to do it with you." Could he mean that?

Kat pulled her iPhone out of her pocket to check the time. Almost six thirty. He would be home soon. *Home.* There was that word again. Well, it *was* homey, in a romantic sort of way. The cottage was basically one big room with a stone fireplace, a cooking area with an old-fashioned stove, a refrigerator and a sink, a little bathroom with a small, claw foot tub, and a loft for sleeping where they had put a futon instead of a conventional bed. Kat had become fanatical about keeping it neat and clean, which wasn't all that difficult.

She heard the sound of tires on the gravel two-track road that led up the hill to their door, followed by the close rumble of his car announcing his arrival. She went to the door and opened it to welcome him. It felt so good when he put his arms around her it sometimes scared her. She wanted this man in her life. And there was no doubt. He wanted her.

While Stone shed his jacket and took of his tie she set out the dinner and put a bottle of ale at each of their places. It felt more rustic that way, drinking out of the bottle. She asked him how the day had gone for him, and as usual, he was noncommittal.

Trying to draw him out a little, she told him of the progress she had made researching security for mobile devices. That was the new frontier of security. There were millions of them, and employees wanted to use them to access corporate data, resulting in a whole new world of opportunities for hackers.

When she saw that his bottle was empty she brought him a second, and as she handed to him she heard herself say, "What ever happened with that security clearance you mentioned? Am I going to get one?"

He raised his eyebrows. "You thinking about spying on me?"

She thought, *How could I have said that?* She said, "No, it's just, well, isn't what I do almost classified anyway?"

"Are you serious?"

"I guess not. It's just that... Matt, I just wish you would talk about what's on your mind. I don't want to know government secrets. I want to know *your* secrets. You're so preoccupied sometimes. I get worried. I worry that things are blowing up at work. I worry that you're sick and won't tell me. I worry I've done something to upset you."

"You haven't done anything to upset me." He leaned back and took a swig of ale. "Okay. My first meeting this morning was a teleconference with the head of compliance for the medical group and a guy in Washington from a department called MHRA that regulates artificial joints. They've issued new preliminary guidelines – "

"Stop!" she said, half amused but half annoyed. "That's not what I mean and you know it. I just wish we could share important things."

He gestured with his free hand, to indicate the cottage. "This is very, very important to me, Kat."

"I know it is."

"I thought I'd be alone for the rest of my life, and now I'm not."

She though, *How could I ask for more?* But later, in bed, she couldn't keep herself from resting her fingers on his temple and whispering, "Please tell me what's going on in there one of these days."

Kat had spent the whole day wondering what to wear for this... date? Is that what it was?

She had run into Selena a week ago in the little snack room off the corridor that separated the engineering department from IT. She tried not to eat junk food but sometimes she needed the sugar rush to help her think. She had just bought a granola bar, the healthiest option the machines there offered, and was headed out the door as Selena entered. They had literally bumped into one another, Selena in her expensive executive clothes, Kat in old jeans and a hoody. It made her feel like a janitor who had come into the boardroom to vacuum while some big meeting was still going on. Selena had stepped back and politely excused herself with that French accent of hers. Then her eyes fell on the name tag clipped to the right pocket of Kat's jeans.

"Oh," she said, "You're the one Matt hired to spy on me!"

Kat didn't know what to say. It seemed like Selena was joking, but she wasn't sure. The woman had extended her hand and as Kat shook it Selena had put her hand on top, like they were old friends. Or maybe that was a French custom. She didn't know.

"I'm not a spy," she said, but the accusation, if that's what it was, made Kat feel guilty.

"Of course you aren't," said Selena, and again, Kat couldn't read her. Was she stating a fact, or just being sarcastic? The whole situation was awkward.

"I have to get back to my desk," she had said, maybe a little too quickly.

"Me too," said Selena. "A pleasure to meet you."

Kat forced a smile and walked away, feeling like Selena was staring at her from behind. She wasn't happy about her walk. She wished it could be more feminine, but when you walked like that guys constantly hit on you, or said things you didn't want to hear.

The invitation had been tucked into her keyboard at work the next morning.

Let's meet for a drink. I think we have a lot in common. There's great place in Ann Arbor called McNally's. Are you free Friday night? I could meet you at 6:00.

Selena

And here she was on her way to McNally's, following the instructions of her iPhone's synthesized feminine voice.

The parking lot was full of expensive cars. Well, they weren't exactly expensive, but they were clean and polished, like cars owned by people who cared about themselves. Hers still looked clunky – a holdover from what she was coming to think of as her old life – and she had consciously decided to leave it that way. Why spend your time and energy on a car of all things?

She parked in the far corner of the lot. The sky was a clear, cobalt blue and there was a chill wind, heralding the cold front that was descending from Canada. Kat hugged her arms across her chest as she walked to the entrance. She had chosen to wear a dressy fitted skirt and a silk blouse her sister had given her as a Christmas present. The gift had made her feel bad at the time because it was an obvious hint that she should dress better, but now she was glad she had it in her closet. She didn't want to look weird next to Selena or embarrass her. But that was silly, she told herself. She actually looked pretty good with the little bit of lipstick she had put on.

The bar was busy but not too crowded, a typical Irish pub with high wooden stools upholstered in black leather running along the length of the bar and more than a dozen beers on tap. Kat had imagined McNally's would be full of students, but the crowd here was a little older and more dressed up. Selena greeted her in front of a booth she had staked out.

"This is how we do it in France," she said, putting her hands on Kat's shoulders and then kissing her lightly on both cheeks. "Actually, we hug," she added, "but I didn't want to scare you."

"Why would that scare me?"

"Am I wrong?"

"No," said Kat. "You're right. I'm kind of shy."

"I am too," said Selena, "but I feel we have a connection. So we can just relax and have fun."

They sat down and soon Kat was sipping a glass of red wine just like Selena, the woman whose digital defenses she had been spending eight or more hours a day trying to penetrate. How could this be fun?

"Okay," she said, after a long silence. "What's this about? Why am I really here?"

"We're just a couple of girls having a drink after a long week at the job. I don't know, maybe we can pick up some guys to buy us a free dinner. The food here is amazingly good for America." She delivered this line with a crooked smile.

"I've never done anything like that."

"Neither have I. Well, maybe once or twice." She paused. "I thought you were the kind of girl who's always ready for something new."

"Sometimes," said Kat – but she was certainly not ready for dinner with some horny engineer. This was going to a business dinner.

Selena raised her glass. "Here's to sometimes."

Kat could feel her inhibitions melting with each sip. She had to be careful about alcohol. But, on the other hand, sometimes it could help you cut through the clutter. Sometimes. "Selena," she said, "We're not just a couple of girls, okay? We have a special connection." Oh my God, she thought. Would this woman take that the wrong way? She lowered her voice to a whisper. "Numerica, I mean."

"I know what you mean."

"I'm just saying, if we're going to be friends, we have to be straight with each other. You invited me here for a reason. Just tell me what it is, okay"

"Darling, we girls have to stick together, that's all. I just want us to not be strangers. We're a little bit enemies at work, but... well, listen. I want to tell you that whatever you do, I won't hold it against you."

"I just write code. I'm not your enemy."

"Isn't it your job to find holes in my security system?"

"I guess I don't think of the firewall and all that as belonging to you."

"I am the one who gets blamed if anything goes wrong."

"Wow! That makes me feel great."

Selena shrugged. "It's just how things are. We didn't make the world, right? We just live in it." She looked over at the bar, which had become crowded as they talked. "Those two look interesting," she said, nodding at two academic types sipping red wine. "Do you want to try to pick them up? They would be easy. I know it."

"Not really," said Kat. *I'm taken*, said a voice in her mind, although it was interesting to see who Selena had chosen:

not the best looking, but the smartest looking. And red wine drinkers. She seemed to have a thing about that.

"Let's just hang out," said Kat.

"I love American slang."

Somehow, the brief exchange about men relaxed the tension that had been growing between them. They soon signaled the waiter for menus. Kat ordered a cheeseburger and for once felt comfortable doing so. Selena ordered some sort of Irish crêpes. Over the dinner and a second glass of red, Kat learned that Selena's family owned a restaurant in Paris not far from the famous Champs-Élysées, which her two brothers now operated. She had been a bit of a black sheep, with no interest in participating in the restaurant business. As she put it. "I prefer to be served rather than serve."

She had spent a year in America as a high school exchange student, although her father had disapproved, and when she returned to Paris she found she could no longer fit in to the narrow and highly constrained paths French society offered in life. Everything seemed too rigid and bureaucratic.

"So here I am," said Selena, finishing her story, "a big shot in a fancy American corporation at thirty-one. Not bad. But it can be lonely."

Kat thought, *You don't have to be a big shot in a fancy American corporation to be lonely*, but she didn't say it out loud.

Selena put her hand on Kat's. I have a proposition for you, maybe."

Kat tensed, wanting to withdraw her hand.

"Relax," said Selena. "It's no big deal. I've been thinking, my defenses are getting better and better. It's like we have been playing a chess game, except pretty soon you're going to run out of moves. I wouldn't say this to just anyone, and maybe it's the wine a little, but our company's defenses weren't what they should have been. I focused too much on making a splash in other ways. But now they are they are strong at every level. Next week I'll have automated log monitoring in place, so we can detect anything that – How do you say it? – Gets through the cracks, right?

She patted Kat's hand. "My point is, you will soon be out of a job. And I was wondering if you'd like to help me with some mobile apps. If it doesn't interfere with anything else you're doing for Matt, of course."

Kat thought, What does she know? The answer had to be nothing. Kat was off the grid so far as Numerica was concerned, literally operating on a different set of physical wires when she was online, so none of her activity could possibly be monitored. But Selena was right in suggesting that she was running out of things to do in the security department. Kat knew nothing about writing apps, but it couldn't be that difficult. She was no Dark Dante, but she was good. For years, she had felt like coding was her only good point. And maybe there was a time when that had been true.

"I'll talk to him. I don't know what he'll say."

That, she reflected, was the trouble with her and Matt. She never knew what he would say. What went on inside his head was still a total mystery.

If he says no, it's no problem," said Selena. "I can hire someone. I thought it would be a way for us to know each other a little better." Again, she patted Kat's hand. "It's a good thing to have a friend who knows Paris well. You might need some tips about good restaurants some day," she added, laughing.

Needing tips about good restaurants in Paris was a situation Kat had never in her life imagined.

Selena seemed to read Kat's mind and added, "You never know."

Stone stared at the report on his desk from his medical division, unable to glean meaning from it. The Medicines and Healthcare Products Regulatory Agency, which regulated "medical devices" ranging from X-ray machines to condoms to the artificial hip and shoulder joints manufactured by Numerica, had issued new guidelines, and Numerica needed to respond. There were several options, each with its own plusses and minuses, and each with its own spreadsheet. It was simple math, but Stone couldn't get his mind to make sense of the numbers.

All he could think about was hacking the IRS. It did not occur to most people that this could even be done. American citizens assumed their government maintained a level of security that just wasn't there, and it was an assumption that half an hour's research would prove false. According to an annual U.S. government study called the TIGTA report, the IRS computer systems embodied dangerous security risks.

The report revealed, for example, that the agency entrusted to collect the money that ran the most well-funded government in the world didn't even have an accurate inventory of all its computers. As a result, security patches to eliminate vulnerabilities could only be installed in a hit-and-miss fashion. Of the servers that were on the record, sixty-three percent had recently failed a security patch audit. There were also many instances of "default or blank" passwords which meant, so far as Stone could gather, that many of the systems really had no passwords at all. You could just type in "default" and you were in, if you had to type in anything at all.

Strike at what is weak!

Stone's problem was that he didn't know how to get started, much less where to strike. What was he supposed to do, run an ad on some tech recruiting site? "Hacker sought to crash IRS computer systems, salary commensurate with experience?" In fact, that was exactly what he should do, only with some subtlety. He knew there must be a way to search the web, sneak into its dark corners and make contact with somebody who could do the job. The person who could help him was Kat. But he couldn't involve her, much as he would like to. It wasn't fair, and it would dishonor the connection they were building. It would feel like he was using her. But then again, maybe not telling her was just as bad.

From the sound of the approaching car, Kat could tell that the man she had fallen in love with was upset. His moods weren't extreme, but they each had their own character, like the weather, and for the first time in her life she found she could accept these changes without freaking out, blaming herself and wondering what was wrong. As he went through his routine – closing and locking the car, popping the trunk and retrieving the protective cover he threw over the car at night – she poured some deli spaghetti out of its paper carton into a pan and set it on the stove over a low flame. The salad was already done, and the wine was uncorked and ready. She wondered if he would want a martini tonight. She could not join him if he did. Drinking pure alcohol like that was a disaster. But wine she could do.

The door opened and there he was in his perfect suit and striped tie. She sidled over and loosened the tie like a character in some old black and white movie. He liked things like that. She knew she could never take care of him like his wife had done, but he seemed happy. No, wrong. He *was* happy. At least when he was with her. She was less sure about the nights when he went to his house and slept alone.

"Martini?" she asked.

"You read my mind," he said, taking off his coat and hanging it over one of the cottage's two straight backed chairs.

She made the drink as he had taught her, poured herself some red wine and sat down across from him at the small kitchen table that doubled as her desk when he wasn't around. The Drink After Work. It was a cliché from her grandparents time, but then, maybe they knew something she didn't. It felt good.

"Are you going to tell me? Or is the problem classified?

Stone laughed. "You can see right through me."

"Well?"

Now his face darkened.

"It's about us."

Kate stiffened. In the back of her mind, she had thought all along this was too good to be true. She braced herself.

"I've been holding back about myself. There are some things I haven't told you, and they're things you ought to know. But, if I tell you, you'll be in danger."

"You can tell me anything."

"That's easy to say."

"I know. I just said it. Want me to say it again?" She kicked his shin playfully, but it didn't make him smile.

Stone took a sip of his drink. She studied him. He was very stressed.

"I'm a big girl, Matt. Look at me. I'm drug-free, I have totally put all that ADHD shit behind me, I make eighty thousand dollars a year as a security consultant for a pretty hot company and I'm dating the captain of the high school football team." She reached out and put her hand on his thigh. "Trust me."

"It's not about trust."

"Hey, wherever we started out, we've gone a long way. I'm your girl, okay? No matter what."

Stone nodded. "You *are* my girl. I can't believe how lucky I am."

She stared at him, incredulous. There were tears in his eyes.

"Matt, what's wrong? Are you sick?"

He shook his head. "No. I'm fine."

"Then what is it?" Now Kat was truly alarmed. She had never seen him in this state.

"Okay," he said, "Here it is." He paused and coughed, as though the words were literally stuck in his throat. Finally, he spoke. "I've decided to take down the IRS. Temporarily. To force some changes that will put permanent limits on their power."

Kat had been prepared for something big, but not this big. *Holy shit!* The idea sounded crazy, but at the same time it sent a thrill through her body.

"Is this about your friend?"

"At first it was. But it's more than that now. It's about the giving American citizens the government they deserve. It's about ordinary people not living in fear."

Kat felt a wave of relief. This wasn't about saying good-bye!

"Do you know how you're going to pull this off?"

"Yes. You gave me the idea. It's going to be a computer-based attack. That's where the IRS is weak."

Kat struggled to take this in. Whatever he was planning was beyond illegal. It was... there was no word for it. If he got caught, it would mean jail for life. That much was certain. But it wasn't certain that he would be caught. In fact, in the shadowy world of the Dark Web there were plenty of places to hide.

"You think you can do this?" She asked.

"Not alone. But with the right team, yes."

"Are you going to let me be on the team?"

"Kat, this is going to be very dangerous."

"It will be a lot more dangerous for you if I'm not on the team. You know that. It's like you're an explorer in a jungle for the first time. But I *live* there." She caught herself. It sounded like a reference to Vietnam, not what she had meant.

"You're right, of course. But I don't want you to think...."

"To think what?"

"That I'm using you."

Just then, the pan on the stove started to sizzle. Kat jumped up to take it off the burner.

"Just in time," she said. "No harm done to our gourmet spaghetti." She sat back down. "You wouldn't be using me."

"It's not your cause."

"I've never had a cause. Maybe I need one."

"This isn't a game, Kat."

"I know that."

The two stared at one another across the table. The wind had come up, prefiguring a storm.

"Do you have an escape plan?" she asked

"Not yet."

"I hope you weren't planning a suicide mission."

Her comment had obviously hit home. He reached out and took her hands in his. "Before you, I didn't care. Now I do."

Now Kat's eyes were damp. "We need an escape plan. Fake passports, fake personal histories, money, all that."

Kat could see the wheels turning in his head. Practical Matt. She had just added a whole new column to his to-do list.

"Money's not a problem. We can work on the rest of it."

We. He said "we."

"You understand that I can't just break in to the IRS databases like I did at Numerica. We'll need some serious help. Some Russian genius or something."

"I understand. It took me awhile to figure out this could even be done. There's a lot to think about. And, well, I've told you, sometimes I feel like I'm not thinking as clearly as I could."

"Did you eat lunch today?"

"No."

"Matt! You know what that can do to your blood sugar. You're not a twenty-something guy anymore, like it or not."

She stood up and put the spaghetti back on the stove. "Let's just eat and go to bed and not try to think about this when we're tired." She said to herself, *I'm starting to sound like my sister.*

"Okay," he said. He looked both relieved and exhausted. Kate thought, *What have I gotten myself into?* She said, "I'll start reaching out tomorrow. And we need some better computer security for ourselves pronto."

Rajesh Gupta's expression radiated calm, but inside, his thoughts and emotions were racing. The magnitude of the vulnerability this freelance bug hunter had discovered in his company's new release was enormous. Any hacker who managed to gain access to a corporate network and log on could wreak havoc. He had a feeling he wouldn't have the authority to meet the bug hunter's price, but it was his opinion that it ought to be met, whatever it was.

"How much do you want?" he asked over the encrypted voice connection he had established for negotiations like this.

"One hundred thousand."

"You know I can't authorize that," he lied. In fact, that was exactly how much he was authorized to pay without going to his boss.

"Find somebody who *can* authorize it then. This could hurt your company big time."

"I won't argue with you there. But I can't say yes right now. Give me two hours."

"Sounds like a plan. I'll be here in exactly two hours. And no games, okay? I've got a wife and a kid now. I need this money. And it's going to be our last deal. I'm going straight."

"I'll do what I can."

Gupta pulled the earphones and speaker off his head, set them on his desk and studied the code one last time. This would not be easy to patch. The vulnerability itself, yes. But changing one line of code in an application as complex as this one could have unintended consequences that could crash all the customers who installed the patch. Testing it to avoid that eventuality might take months.

He wondered for a moment if he could appeal to the bug hunter's altruism and convince him not to publish the bug for the greater good of the millions of consumers whose credit card and social security numbers would be at risk. Not a chance. The kid had no sense of the bigger picture, the amount of time an effort it took to fix what looked like a problem with half a dozen lines of code, the corporate politics involved. He would perceive any delays as foot-dragging, if not corporate duplicity.

In this case he would be right. There was no way his company was going to fix this until the next rev, which was nine months out. Gupta would have to pay the kid's price and then pray to God that nothing happened.

Kat sat in the window of a small student café not far from the University of Michigan campus, watching the snowflakes drifting downward to the pavement and checking the time every couple of minutes, trying to decide whether or not the only friend she had ever made at LightSpeed Software would show up. He was erratic, which meant he might change his mind, or simply forget. But he was also Ukrainian, so the fact that he was already fifteen minutes late didn't mean much. She used to be late all the time, she reminded herself.

When he did arrive, Kat stood up, and Sasha Plaksly hugged her warmly. "Are you coming back?" he asked with a grin. "Have they finally realized your value?"

Sasha actually looked presentable, and he smelled presentable as well. When he had first arrived at the shop, he had needed a lot of coaching on America's accepted hygiene norms, and that job had fallen to Kat. It wasn't an easy task. "I here to write code, not be movie star," he had said more than once. But since Kat shared a lot of his feelings about the b.s. that revolved around work, she was able win him over and ultimately communicate that it was important to bathe every day, brush your teeth, and wear clean clothes. He had obviously listened and learned. The week that Kat was fired, he had even signed up for some English tutoring to Americanize himself even further. Now, only a trace of his once thick accent remained. With his tousled but neatly cut hair, his *clean* graphic T and friendly blue eyes, he was almost attractive.

They gossiped, coder-style. In response to her questions, she learned that Ruby-on-Rails was replacing JavaScript as the language of choice in the shop. There had been a hardware upgrade to a Dell cluster with one hundred percent solid-state drives to test big data projects. The vending machines now accepted Google Wallet, so you could pay with your phone.

Kat suddenly realized that Sasha was never going to ask her what *she* was up to. Maybe he thought she was still working at the café, which he would see as an embarrassment. Maybe his social skills were better than she thought.

"I'm working as a security consultant," she finally volunteered.

Sasha raised his dark eyebrows, which contrasted sharply with his fair skin.

"Actually, that's why I'm here," she continued. "I'm hoping you can help me."

"You know I will. You taught me a lot. I'm leading a team now because of you."

Kat felt herself blush. She paused to sip her cappuccino. It was second rate compared to the ones she had learned to make. Could she *really, really* trust Sasha? The fact was, she didn't have a choice.

"I'm looking for a genius hacker. I need somebody to test my defenses, and maybe set up some encryption protocols."

Sasha smirked.

"Okay, I admit it. I thought you might have a cousin somewhere who could help me. Come on. Your country is the world capital of black hats." She waited. Had she insulted him?

After an uncomfortable pause, Sasha burst out laughing. Reverting to his thick accent of the past, he said, "I help you, for a price," and laughed again. Then, speaking normally, he asked about the nature of the project.

"I need someone who can devise threats against big databases. That means infiltrating a network and figuring out how to steal the data," she paused, "or maybe just modify it. My company has classified government contracts, and we've got a big target painted on our back."

"Are you telling me everything?" asked Sasha.

Kat smiled. "No. I'm telling you as much as I can."

"Of course. And I think I know someone. My cousin has done business with him. It's true. I do have a cousin who wears the black hat. But this guy he does business with is all black."

"I don't understand."

"He's African American. He lives in Detroit—what he calls the Real Detroit. He is extremely cautious. I suppose that doesn't matter to you, since everything you're doing is legal, of course."

Kat thought, *I'm no good at this. He can read me like a book.* She said, "What's that supposed to mean?"

"He has a businesses doing websites and promotions for rappers. He's not engaged in the Dark Web directly, but he has connections."

Kat started to speak but he cut her off. "Listen, Katia, the people who can do these things you want, they are not always – I know the word! They are not always Boy Scouts." He beamed, but only briefly. "You do not want to deal with these people directly, believe me."

"Why not?"

Sasha once again slipped into his old accent. "'When the chickens have been stolen, do not walk with the fox.' Is old saying my mother taught me."

"Really."

"No, I made it up. But you see what I'm saying. You don't want these people on your vendor list. Believe me. Particularly if you're doing government work."

"How do I contact him."

"I will do it for you. Then you will hear from him. Probably by snail mail."

"You're kidding."

"Snail mail leaves no digital traces, Katia."

Wednesday had been "hump day" in every office where Stone had ever worked his entire life. He had always disliked the term, with its implication that the work week was something to be endured. But today, at five fifteen, he was glad to have the day – and more than half the week – behind him. Unfortunately for his mood, Kat was meeting with an old co-worker for dinner as part of her intensive search for "coders who don't have resumés," so his first choice for the evening – to spirit her off to the Roadhouse – wasn't in the cards.

Pulling on his jacket, his mind drifted to Ginny. Their regular Wednesday night dinners had become a thing of the past, but they still texted almost every day and exchanged long phone calls once or twice a week, often on the subject of his relationship with Kat. Ginny's progress in getting her life back together was amazing. She was turning her new QuickBooks skills into a business, and already had two clients plus the Blackhawks, for whom she had taken over managing the books. He had to admire Herb's old friends, rag-tag as they were. What they lacked in sophistication they made up for in loyalty, and giving Ginny a few hours of work every week was an example. They took care of their own.

On a whim, he texted Ginny to see if she was in the mood to share a drink somewhere. She didn't respond. In fact, his iPhone showed that the message hadn't been delivered much less read, and maybe that was for the best. Her offer to give him "what was missing in his life" was definitely no longer on the table and she was hardly flirtatious when they talked, but there were moments when he still felt a lingering attraction, and he was sure she felt the same way.

He would drink alone – but only a couple. He had three short internal proposals to review and he would take them along. Then he would go over to the cottage to be there when Kat arrived and see what she had learned.

The old two-lane highway that led to the Roadhouse passed by the turn off to Herb and Ginny's neighborhood, and when he reached it he decided to drop by. She had probably forgotten to charge her phone, although that wasn't like her.

As he turned onto the street he could see that her lights were on, but there was a surprise: a large silver pick-up truck parked in the driveway. The license plate read

BLKHWK 1

Stone was hit by a flash of jealousy. He knew he had no business having feelings like that, but there they were. He speeded up, and headed for the Roadhouse.

He tried reaching Ginny on the drive back to the cottage, and she picked up on the first ring.

"Hi, stranger."

"Hi yourself. I actually came by your place earlier, but it looked like you had company."

"Oh, you should have come it. It was just Mark. You know, Mark Stetson, with the Blackhawks. He's been really sweet to me."

"I didn't want to interrupt anything."

"Matt! There was nothing to interrupt! I just asked him over for dinner to thank him for all he's done." She paused. "I mean, there might be something to interrupt one of these days. He *is* a handsome man. In fact, he looks a lot like you. You two could be brothers. And he doesn't have a girlfriend who's about half his age, like some handsome men I know."

Stone was at a loss for words. "One day at a time," he said lamely.

"I think we're beyond that stuff, Matt. My life is moving forward now. But, you know, with Mark I do worry a little about this Blackhawk stuff. For Herb, it was mainly a chance to get into the woods and think about something besides work. But for Mark... He's really angry. He talks about Herb's death a lot. Too much, I think."

"I think about Herb every day."

"It's not the same."

Stone had the strong impression that there was a subtext to this conversation that he was missing, but he was almost to the cottage and didn't really have time to probe.

"Let's get together soon," he said. "We can talk some more."

"Sleep tight," she said.

Stone turned into the road that led to the cottage. Kat's car was already there. He parked and walked quickly to the door. Would she have positive news?

When the corporal behind the glass window had handed Stone his discharge papers and his last pay envelope, he believed he would never again fire a weapon, and for several years he hadn't. Then, one Saturday, after endless entreaties, he had accompanied Herb to the old Blackhawk range. It was primitive then, hardly more than a vacant lot at the edge of town with unsheltered shooting stands and targets on a clothesline strung in front of a bulldozed earthen berm.

Stone had to borrow one of Herb's clunky hunting rifles, but he found to his surprise that he enjoyed the experience, so long as the targets were bull's eyes and not men.

And here he was again.

Visiting the range had been on his mind ever since Herb's funeral, but he had put it off, much as he had put off cleaning out Laura's office. He didn't want an in-your-face reminder that Herb was dead. But Herb *was* dead, and given the mission of reparation Stone had taken on, he felt a need to refresh his combat skills, *just in case*. It was an irrational thought. He wasn't going to shoot anybody. Nonetheless, the urge to visit the range kept nagging him, and after a restless Friday night alone in his own bedroom, he decided the next morning there was only one way to get it out of his system.

The rifle he had checked out from the Blackhawk armory was unfamiliar to him, but that didn't matter. A good rifle helped, but at its root, marksmanship was about the battle with your own body. Lying in the familiar prone position and with a heavy jacket against the cold, Stone was winning that battle, staying still and calm and getting consistently good groups, with no bullet hole more than three inches from any other. If he had been shooting at agent Chan instead of a black silhouette, the man would have been dead a dozen times over.

Two other men were on the range down at the far end. Blackhawks, he assumed. They exchanged polite nods but didn't speak. He did, however, speak to the range master when he checked his rifle back in, a man who looked to be in his mid-thirties and wore a cowboy hat that shadowed his eyes.

"We get discounts if you're considering buying your own rifle, Mr. Stone," the man said. "Here's one that looks about right for you." He handed Stone a brochure. It was for an assassin's rifle, one of the new ultra light-weight models you could disassemble into small pieces.

Stone looked at the man, a sense of alarm flooding his body. It was as though this stranger had peeked in on the dark fantasies that had passed through Stone's mind as he fired at the targets.

"Now what use would I have for a thing like that?" said Stone with a forced laugh. "I've got plenty of ways to take out my competitors already."

"Just thought you might be interested. It's a precision tool, and we could give you a good price. And, well, I know you can afford it."

"Not today," said Stone. He gave the man a quick smile and headed for the front door, rattled. Nobody had to die for him to get his point across! But there was no question somebody *deserved* to die. He couldn't get that thought out of his head. Maybe he should be visiting the range more often. With enough visits, he might eventually rid himself of these murderous thoughts.

Kat sometimes pictured her world as the circular Yin/Yang symbol in which the darkness represented the anonymity and safety of the digital world, and the light stood for the real world, with all its uncertainties and trouble. In the digital world, you didn't have a body that required attention and care. You didn't have feelings that could run wild. And you could hide.

The man she and Matt were about to meet, known only as The Drummer, had turned this symbolism inside out. The way he saw things, the safety of the digital world had been compromised, due in large measure to the efforts of the NSA, which was everywhere now, not only inside Google and Facebook and all the other social networks, but even in some pockets of TOR. His own social world, built on trusts established since childhood, and set in one of the most dangerous cities in the world, was truly an impenetrable maze.

The Drummer would not communicate with his customers over wires or satellite connections. He knew that, as amateurs, they couldn't be trusted to take the meticulous precautions that hiding in cyberspace now required. Thus, Kat and Stone found themselves at Baker's Keyboard Lounge on 8 Mile Road, about one mile north of the Renaissance Center, the only Detroit landmark with which she was at all familiar.

The club featured a circular bar painted like a giant piano keyboard, strong drinks, and some of the best jazz musicians still playing gigs. The band was in full swing when they arrived, and The Drummer was waiting for them at a noisy table. He wore wraparound sunglasses, and held his head at a tilt which, along with his coffee-and-cream complexion and dreadlocks, reminded her of Stevie Wonder. Was The

Drummer blind? No, he spotted them as they approached his table and gestured at two empty seats waiting for them.

Kat glanced at Stone, wondering what his take on this eccentric man might be. His expression gave no clue. The Drummer was certainly not lacking in social skills. He talked easily about the history of Baker's, the African roots of jazz and of his handle. It was a reference to the drumming networks of Africa, which prefigured the Internet by centuries, or so he said. Kat winced at that statement, but Stone seemed favorably impressed.

"My understanding is that you didn't want to discuss business until we were face to face," said Stone. "So here we are. We've come to you. Let me explain what we're looking for."

With that, he described The Project in stark terms. Although she couldn't see The Drummer's eyes, his body language told her he didn't expect a project of this scope and boldness.

"I need a credible, demonstrable threat," said Stone. "The less damage we do, the better. The goal is control, not destruction. Can you do that?"

"Allow me to educate you," said The Drummer. "An exploit on the scale you are contemplating isn't achieved by one single individual. It requires coordination. There are the researchers, who will seek out vulnerabilities in the target software application. There are the farmers, who manage the botnets we will use for the attack."

"Botnets?" said Stone.

"Botnets are computer networks created from computers that have been infected with a remote control virus unbeknownst to their owners. These computers are known as zombies. They can be temporarily taken over by a farmer to enable someone to execute a specific attack. Basically, farmers rent them out.

"In addition to researchers and farmers, there are dealers, which is the class I belong to. We are the commanders who plan and orchestrate the attacks. We also provide the resources, and sometimes choose the targets. But of course, you already have a target in mind."

Stone nodded. "Yes, and as I said, we need to evoke fear, not create damage."

"The best thing of all is to take the enemy's country whole and intact."

Stone recognized the quote immediately. "Sun-Tzu. I'm impressed."

"In my environment, a knowledge of war is essential."

Kat wasn't sure whether he was referring to inner city Detroit or the Internet. Perhaps both. She could see that Stone liked what he heard, and it made her feel good, even though she knew that depending on a man's approval for happiness was unhealthy. And with this man, it wasn't like that. She just cared about him.

"Given the parameters we've discussed, what are my options?" Stone was saying.

"My rate is five thousand dollars per day."

"That's not a problem. I can give you ten in cash right now. Will that be enough to get started?"

Now it was The Drummer's turn to be impressed, although Kat could see he was trying to hide it.

"How many days are we looking at?" asked Stone.

"Only two or three," said The Drummer. "You've selected an easy target."

Stone finished his drink with one swallow. He was ready to go, but Kat put her hand on his arm to restrain him.

"One other thing," she said. "Do you ever deal in documentation?"

"What sort of documentation? You mean manuals?"

"No. Personal documentation. Passports. Credit cards. Things like that."

"I don't," said The Drummer with a smile, "But I have a source."

The location of the second meet with The Drummer was as seedy as the first was elegant: The Imperial, a neighborhood bar in one of the most dangerous districts in Detroit. Stone and Kat had driven into the city in Kat's Ford, seeing it as a less likely target for a break-in or outright theft than Stone's Crossfire. He had stashed his old service revolver in the glove compartment, but they had managed to park almost directly in front of their destination, so he had left it there.

The Drummer met them at the door as they entered. The bar was very dark, illuminated mostly by neon, but he was nonetheless wearing his wrap-arounds. He escorted them past a long row of empty stools to a back room that was a little more brightly lit. The walls were painted a garish green and decorated with old boxing posters that were faded and curled at the edges. In the center of the room was a card table with three metal folding chairs.

The Drummer gestured that they should seat themselves. "Sometimes," he said, "It's best to avoid exterior evidence of wealth. But please be assured that you are safe here. And thank you for arriving in such an unobtrusive vehicle."

Stone wondered how he had gathered that piece of information, but said nothing.

"You have my fee?" asked The Drummer.

Kat handed him the paper grocery bag she had carried from the car, which contained another ten thousand dollars in cash.

"Thank you," he said with a smile. "I appreciate the business."

"Now what?" asked Stone.

"We have developed the threat software you requested. I think you will be pleased. It is a form of ransomware.

The Drummer obviously read the concern on Stone's face. No way were hostages going to be part of this project!

"Let me explain. It's not a literal term. We will begin the attack by taking control of thirty-three servers on the IRS network – computers that have not been active for at least one year. This virtually guarantees that the network administrators will not be aware of their existence, if they ever were. So we can do whatever we want with them. And what we will do is selectively encrypt taxpayer files on a region-by-region basis. The files will remain within the system. They will not be damaged in any way. But they will be inaccessible without a key, which only you, Mr. Stone, will possess.":

"In other words," said Stone, "If somebody calls up and asks a question about what he owes or what he's paid, they won't be able to find that information?"

"It goes far beyond that. In fact, *they* won't be able to do anything. They won't be able to determine if an individual even exists in their system. They won't b able to send out bills, or refunds, or routine correspondence. Any region you choose to attack will fall into a state of total paralysis within a few minutes."

Stone could hardly believe what he was hearing. He looked over at Kat. Her eyes were shining.

The Drummer reached into the pocket of his jacket and pulled out an iPhone and put it into Stone's hand.

Stone gave him a questioning look.

"It's been somewhat modified," he explained. "Tap the Encrypt icon."

Stone studied the screen. Among the familiar icons – the telephone hand set, the compass, the clock and so on – was an African drum, ochre and red against a black background. Underneath it was the word ENCRYPT. He tapped it, and a map of the United States appeared. It was broken into geographical regions, each consisting of half a dozen contiguous states. Kat leaned over so she could see what was going on.

"Now tap on one of the regions," said The Drummer.

Stone did as he was told. A message appeared:

Do you want to attack the Delaware Maryland Region?

Below it were two buttons. One was marked ATTACK, the other, CANCEL.

"Hit Cancel for now," said The Drummer.

Stone hit the CANCEL button. "That's it?"

"We pride ourselves on developing intuitive interfaces," said The Drummer. "You can use this device at any Wi-Fi hotspot. It has no GPS locator, and it cannot be traced."

Stone continued to study the map. It was, he realized, a map of the various administrative districts of the IRS. He had seen one like it before, maybe on the IRS site itself.

"When a region is under attack," The Drummer explained, "it is displayed in red. That means that all the data related to taxpayers in that region is encrypted and inaccessible. To end the attack, tap that region again and it will revert to its previous color. That's all there is to it. For any given region, the attack will begin or end in less than an hour after you enter your command, and often in a matter of minutes."

The Drummer watched the two with a mixture of pride and amusement. "Only use your powers for the good of humanity," he said with a laugh.

Stone glowered at him but said nothing. Kat had warned him about The Drummer's smart mouth, but she insisted it was a small price to pay for his connections, and he had a reputation for delivering the goods. He looked over at Kat, who couldn't hide the smile on her face.

"We can give you this capability because we've uncovered a vulnerability in the IRS database that the vendor has chosen not to fix," said The Drummer. "It allows us to modify any file we choose. However, there is still one bridge to be crossed. We need to get onto their network.

"How hard is that?" asked Stone.

"It won't be simple. The IRS is using two factor identification for its mission-critical systems now, and we know the second factor is a physical device. My people are working on a way to simulate that device in software, but it may take a little time."

"How much time?" asked Stone.

"If I knew, I would tell you," said The Drummer.

"Days?" said Stone. "Weeks?"

The Drummer leaned forward ever so slightly. "Mr. Stone, I often assume the style of a thug, but I am a man of honor. I simply cannot make a promise I may be unable to keep."

Silence. The moment had the feeling of a standoff. Then Kat spoke. "What if your team had one of those devices in their possession? Or, say I had access to one for a few hours. Would that make a difference?"

"The team on this project could most likely hack the network in less than an hour."

"We'll get back to you," said Kat, taking charge of the interaction in a way Stone had never seen before. She clearly had something in mind, and she obviously wasn't comfortable talking about it in front of The Drummer. They could discuss it once they were in the car. At the moment, now that business was over, Stone's primary concern was getting to that car in one piece.

The Drummer seemed to sense his concern. He pulled his smart phone out of his jacket, tapped it twice, and then displayed an image of the street outside the bar to Stone and Kat. It was deserted. Not good.

"Would you like an escort to your car?" asked The Drummer.

"Yes," said Stone without hesitation.

The Drummer once again tapped his phone. "They'll be waiting at the front door," he said after a moment.

The three stood up. For the first time, Stone saw that The Drummer was actually quite thin, somebody who, lacking muscle, had learned early on to live by his wits in this tough neighborhood. Stone stared at his own reflection in The Drummer's wrap-arounds, wishing he could look him in the eye.

"Do we have a product I can trust?" asked Stone. "Because if there are *any* doubts about whether or not this is going to work, I need to know now. There's a lot riding on this."

"There is no doubt in my mind. The database is built on a commercial software application. That application has a fatal vulnerability for which no patch exists. The team that designed the ransomware tested it live, on operational systems in three major corporations. This weapon works."

This weapon, thought Stone, feeling its weight in his hand. *My sword.*

IV.

No Corresponding File

Kat felt like she had gotten involved in some YouTube video that was sliding out of control. The whole thing with Matt had started out as an adventure. It was thrilling to be with a guy like him who was so powerful and in control. And for all his drive, he was never in a rush when they were in bed. Sometimes, actually, she wished he'd hurry up a little. What was most important was that she always felt safe with him. But that feeling of safety was starting to fade. The fact of the matter was, she was about to commit a crime for him.

Okay, it wasn't that simple. In fact, if everything worked out, most of the people in the country would probably see Matt as a hero, like Snowden when he published all that stuff about government surveillance. Still, hero or not, Matt would go to jail if he got caught, and she'd go with him.

Maybe that fear was part of the rush.

She had never felt so alive, and it wasn't a bipolar thing. It was like when you were on a roll when you were coding, staying up all night, seeing the whole structure in your mind and typing as fast as you could. But this was so much healthier. She was running every day, she was getting enough caffeine but not too much, her diet was wholesome and she was actually gaining weight.

It made her a little uncomfortable that Matt was pretty much supporting her. Now that her status was consultant instead of employee, she wasn't doing any work that had anything to do with Numerica at all. It was all about alternatives for getting into the IRS network. Sometimes she had moments of amazement that a company could pay five thousand dollars a month for no visible work and no one would question it or ask to see some results. But there it was, paying her rent, her phone bills, everything, and all because Matt signed off on her invoices. She might as well be married!

Kat quickly put that thought out of her mind. That was the last thing she should be thinking about. She studied herself in the oversized mirror that dominated one wall of her four star hotel room. The new jeans and light sweater outfit she had chosen, finished off by retro All Star sneakers, would make her look respectable without scaring off the guys she was stalking tonight. She thought about calling Matt. Not a good idea. It would just make him nervous. Better to wait until she could report success. She tucked the plastic card key in her pocket and set out.

On the plane from Detroit she had made a list of the attributes she would use to rate bars likely to attract the types she was looking for. Skeeball was worth one point. Real pinball machines were worth two, three if they were pre-1960. Pool was a two, billiards a three. So much for rating schemes. The bar that was her destination rated zero, yet she had been assured by two girls about her age that The Mecklenburg Inn in Shepherdstown – "The Meck," as it was known to the locals – was The Place To Be.

It was amazing the way strangers would help you out. She didn't know how trustworthy their advice would turn out to be, but The Meck couldn't be worse than the

Starbucks near the local airport where she had hung out earlier. That place was filled with creepy businessmen who never looked up from the proposals for government contracts on their laptops.

Seen from the wrong angle, this whole trip was a little creepy. Matt hadn't really wanted her to go. He wouldn't say it, but he was afraid she would end up sleeping with somebody to get the information they needed. How could he have such a thought? And, *would* she? What if it was the only way that would work?

Kat found a parking space for her rented white Kia behind a picturesque chapel just down the street from the bar. The air was unseasonably warm, as though summer had arrived three months early, and it felt like the people on the street were all tourists looking for a place to eat dinner, not locals employed by the IRS or one of the many consulting firms that agency relied on to solve its more complex problems. But she had to start somewhere.

According to the sign over the front door, the bar dated back to 1793. Inside, it did have an old school men's club feel, or what she imagined such a club would be like: dark wood, lots of brass, a gilded mirror behind the bar, glass shelves laden with bottles of expensive alcohol.

Kat approached the bar uncertainly. Ultimately, this was a game of chance. She chose a stool next to a management type in his early thirties wearing a starched shirt and a tie, which he had loosened. He looked like he might be an interesting man. He also looked worn out.

She studied the array of beer tap handles, each with its own elaborate label. When the harried bartender showed up, she ordered a Cold Trail Ale and asked for a bar menu. No drinking on an empty stomach.

"Good choice," said the man. "It's a local microbrewery."

"I'm new around here," she said. "Looking for work."

"I could tell you're not a tourist. What kind of work?"

"I'm a coder. A computer programmer," she added, realizing that most people didn't know what a coder was.

He looked a little surprised at her answer, as though he had always thought this was a job only men could handle.

"I'm trying to meet people who can help me network. You can only go so far online."

"I've heard some people go pretty far."

Kat shrugged, ignoring the innuendo. "What sort of work do you do?" she asked.

"I can't say. You know, it's that old 'If I told you I'd have to kill you' thing."

Kat stood up, beer in hand." Nice talking to you."

Now where?

She walked along the bar, which now offered standing room only, and then through a set of oak doors that opened onto a large patio with tables you could share. She looked around for a place to sit but saw no obvious options.

She heard someone call, "You can join us if you want," and then saw a couple of twenty-something guys waving at her at a table with a pitcher of beer and a bowl of wings. One of them wore a hoody – a good sign, she thought – and the other had a graphic T-shirt from a band she had never heard of. She wasn't sure whether that was a good sign or not. She was feeling old lately.

The two of them both had longish hair, but neither was scruffy. Two or three years out of college at best. They were the types who got hired at D.C. area firms. They were not high school geniuses who could figure everything out on their own. Those guys went to Google or started their own companies. These two, she imagined, had followed the straight and narrow path, majored in computer science, interned at a local firm, and gotten hired right after graduation. But what did she know? They could just as well be ambulance drivers or baristas. She doubted they would have to kill her if they told her about their jobs.

She sat down on one of the table's curved stone benches and introduced herself, Samantha Rose, Java coder. They understood what she was talking about. Java, an established norm and yesterday's news in the private sector, was the hot computer language at the IRS under the guidance of a new Chief Technical Officer. Knowing Java would be a big plus, they assured her.

As Kat's glass emptied she became more relaxed. Like many coders, these guys loved to talk about their work, even more when the listener was a girl, and one who could actually understand them at that. They worked at a company called DataTech whose only customer was the IRS. She could not believe her good luck. They were going to give her what she needed.

DataTech employed about sixty people, and almost all of them were working on a project called CADE 2, the main processing engine for the 1040s that millions of people submitted every year. The project was behind schedule and over budget. Dave, who was blond and muscular and the more talkative of the two, encouraged her to apply for a job. Frankly, we need more bodies."

"He means we need more quick minds," said his friend Nate, who looked more like a traditional geek, thin and a bit pale. She reflected that Dave would probably be promoted first, and might end up as Nate's boss. Would their friendship survive that?

"Do you have to get a security clearance and walk through metal detectors every morning?" ask Kat.

"It's not like that," said Dave. "The security is just like anywhere, which means hardly any, right?"

"We do have two-factor authentication," said Nate. "So you have to have a designated cell phone where they can send you a code to type in after you've put in your email address and your password. But the company pays for the phone. In fact they pay for your whole data plan, and you can use it for whatever you want."

As they chatted, Kat made mental notes. The air conditioning failure last week, the upcoming quarterly "Super Sunday" picnic at Rock Creek, wherever that was, the gossip about a new Treasury Department project that wouldn't involve the IRS, the company president's new Tesla. The Drummer had told her to focus on tidbits that couldn't be learned from a company's official website. It was all about what the hackers called "social engineering," the aspect of hacking that depended not on technology but rather on human frailty: the tendency to use obvious passwords, and even share them with strangers. She didn't know how The Drummer would use these random bits of information, but use them he would. His credentials were flawless.

When the pitcher the two coders had bought was empty, Dave excused himself to go to the men's room and Nate followed him. Kat was to guard the table. They would return with a fresh pitcher. In fact, only Nate returned. He sat down facing her. He seemed a little nervous.

"Here's the situation," he said. "Dave and I are both in love with you. We flipped a coin and I won, so I get to invite you over to the 311 for dinner. It's only a block away so we can walk. If you turn me down, you can go with him. If you turn us both down we have a suicide pact to jump into the Potomac at midnight."

Kat couldn't help but laugh, and without really thinking about it accepted his offer. Nate had delivered his speech with a winning, dry style. She was hungry. And with luck, he would talk about data structures over dinner.

He didn't talk about data structures. He talked about his family, the music he liked, and his plan to walk part of the Appalachian Trail during his vacation. He was, she realized, an interesting guy, and really not that young. In a different universe, they might have gotten together. Instead, when he went to the men's room at the 311 and left his cell phone on the table, she considered stealing it. She could stick it in her pocket. When he noticed it was missing, she'd suggest he left it at The Meck. They'd go back. It wouldn't be there... and then they'd say goodnight.

It would take him a couple of hours to get around to shutting down his service. If he was feeling buzzed and sleepy, he might put it off until morning.

She'd immediately connect with The Drummer, and if he could mobilize the resources to launch a brute force attack on Nate's password, they could get halfway there in less than an hour. Nate's phone would receive a text message with the code, she'd send it to The Drummer, and they'd be into the company network in stealth mode in a couple of hours. There would be evidence that "Nate" had logged into the network, but maybe The Drummer could erase that. The next morning, she would go over to Tech Data with his phone and some lame excuse that he might or might not buy. There were a lot of uncertainties in this plan, but life was full of uncertainties. Life *was* an uncertainty. When Nate returned to the table, his phone was in her purse.

"Nice to have you back," she said.

The night ended with Nate standing very close to her in the lot behind the chapel where she had parked. On impulse, she gave him a real kiss, then gently pushed him away. "I'm sorry. I'm kinda taken. I shouldn't have kissed you. But I did."

Kat drove home full of guilt – for being willing to steal this nice guy's phone, for kissing him, for drinking too much and getting into the manic state she was in, which she knew would be followed by a crash. But there was no going back. There never was.

When she got to the hotel, she logged on to TOR immediately and transmitted the news of her successful theft to The Drummer. Then she took off her clothes, got into the bed and stared at the ceiling with the phone next to her ear. waiting a ping from him... or a knock on the door from the local police. Manic confidence told her she could talk her way out of any trouble.

Exhausted but not able to sleep, Stone picked up his watch from the bedside table and stared at its glowing dial. Three fifteen, and still no word from Kat. What could she be doing?

He reminded himself once again that they had agreed not to communicate except via TOR, and then only if truly necessary. Nonetheless, he had half expected at least a brief note. Perhaps it was in his encrypted message queue right now, but he didn't quite have the energy to trundle down the stairs to his office where he had left the only laptop in the house that could decrypt it.

How was this all going to end? Assuming Kat got her hands on the physical device they needed and they managed to penetrate an internal IRS network, then what?

At first, he had thought it was going to be more or less like a hostage negotiation with a few twists. But that model had problems. With hostages, you met the demands and got live human beings in return, human beings who could be transported to safety and never retaken. When the "hostages" were data files, there was no knowing whether or not they were really safe. The people he was going to be dealing with wouldn't be satisfied with a decryption key alone. They would want the code to the ransomware as well, and they would want to know about the vulnerability that allowed their database to be breached in the first place. In short, they would want to know everything they needed to know to prevent another attack.

Once they were in possession of that knowledge, Stone's leverage would be zero, and the IRS could quickly return to the old path of threats and intimidation Stone had vowed to block. He had been over this ground many times, usually in the middle of the night, and as yet had not been able to formulate a viable strategy. His first inclination was to reach out to Bobby, to call him right now in the middle of the night, but with Bobby he couldn't go beyond hypotheticals, and he was far beyond that point now. So instead, he turned on his bedside lamp, got up and went over to the closet where he retrieved a cloth bag he kept tucked away on the top-most shelf where no one would ever find it unless they were looking. It contained three brass divination coins inscribed with Chinese characters on both faces: *I Ching* coins. A similar set had saved his life during the war. On the advice of an old woman who had thrown them for him, he and eleven of his men had avoided walking into an ambush that would have surely resulted in their deaths, or capture, which was perhaps worse. His mind had told him it was coincidence, but on a battlefield you don't dare argue with events like that. Maybe the experiences of the war had made him a little crazy by that time. Nonetheless, from that day forward, he had taken every opportunity to seek out *I Ching* fortune tellers both in the villages and in Saigon, and had actually committed the divination system's hexagrams to memory. When he returned home, the *I Ching* had become a hippie fad, which in his view cheapened the coins and drained from them what had seemed to be a magical power.

He had put them away, along with a lot of other memories from Vietnam, but once every few years, in moments of uncertainty, he took them out.

Now, sitting cross-legged on his bed, he threw the coins onto the covers six times. The resultant hexagram was called Heaven over Wind: Hexagram number forty-four, *Go to Meeting*. As was always the case, this guidance was oblique at best. But he knew that if he held it in his mind, he might get some help from a source he would never understand, but could always trust.

What could the hexagram mean? That the end, represented by Heaven, justified the means, the "Wind?" Or were the coins simply telling him to seek out an ally? *Go to Meeting*.

Stone had never in his life followed a path so far with no clear plan. Without Kat, he wouldn't even have an escape route. At least those details were handled. All he lacked, he thought ruefully, was a battle plan for the main thrust of the mission. And to figure it out, he was sitting half-naked on top of his bed throwing fortune telling coins.

It was time to act. The virus The Drummer's team had devised would soon be in place on multiple servers inside the IRS firewall, awaiting the command that would awaken it. In fact, if Kat succeeded all would be ready in a matter of days.

If she succeeded. What if something had gone wrong? She had a knack for making things happen, but no one could completely escape failure, and when you were trying to steal the keys to a government database, the consequences of failure could be grave.

He was letting his imagination run away with him, an indulgence a warrior could not afford. He put the coins back into their bag and stood up. He needed to give some attention to Numerica, and since sleep was impossible he would get an early start on the numbers. He had a secure link to the office – an actual physical cable he leased from AT&T with no connection to the internet – so he could review classified project without fear of compromising company security. After he went through his morning routine, that's exactly what he would do.

She's okay, he told himself. Holding that thought, he headed for the shower.

Kat awoke fully dressed and disoriented, with a pounding headache and Nate's cell phone still clutched in her hand. Her eyes searched for a clock and found one on the bed stand. Four thirty. Her heart was pounding. *I will get through this*, she told herself, stripping off her clothes and heading for the shower.

Why hadn't The Drummer responded? He knew she was here, and what she was up to. And she had come through, damn it!

No. She hadn't come through. In fact, as things stood, she had fucked up royally. She had in her possession a cell phone that was one half of a two-factor authentication system used to access what was arguably the most sensitive data in America short of the nuclear codes. A cell phone she had stolen!

The shower calmed her a little, and when she threw on fresh clothes she felt almost normal. If the police were after her, they would have found her by now. *I will make this okay!* She packed her things, took the elevator to the underground parking lot, climbed into her rental car and headed for DataTech, stopping only for a three shot latte on the way.

By seven thirty she was in the parking lot. At eight fifteen, Nate showed up in a vintage Jeep. In another life, she thought once again, they might have gotten together.

She walked towards the Jeep, holding his phone in front of her like a peace offering. "You forgot something last night," she called. She could tell he was glad to see her, and felt another pang of guilt as she handed him the phone.

"Did you freak out?" she asked. "I didn't know how to contact you."

"Well, I did have to do a complete remote wipe, including photos of my new-born nephew and my trip to Egypt last summer."

"Oh no!"

"It's okay," he said. "Everything is still in the cloud. And I made up the stuff about Egypt and my nephew."

"Still...."

"A kiss from you is worth a little hassle."

She found herself blushing.

Nate stuck the phone in the front pocket of his jeans. There was an awkward silence.

"So," he said, "How did my phone end up in your hotel room last night?

She had been prepared for this. "I've never stolen somebody's phone before. I wanted to know what it would feel like."

"Kat – "

"When I got in my car I realized that I left my purse in the restaurant. When I went back for it, they gave me your phone as well. I guess they figured it was safe with me."

Nate gave her a long look. "We had a lot of alcohol last night."

She thought, He wants to believe me. She said, "The kiss wasn't about the alcohol, Nate."

Nate took a theatrical deep breath. "Okay. Are you here to drop off a résumé?"

"Not today. But I might. Will you put in a good word for me?"

"I don't know, Kat. If we were co-workers I couldn't ask you out."

Kat punched his shoulder playfully, and then instantly regretted the gesture. Her business with this guy was done.

There was another awkward silence. Kat looked over at DataTech's squat, square building. "Well, I know how to get in touch," she said. With that, she turned and walked back towards her car, leaving Nate to stare at her ass.

Kat maneuvered her car through the traffic on Gaviot Avenue towards The Drummer's storefront, wondering what it would take to get the project back on track. It was a depressing drive. Half demolished buildings alternated with open lots sprouting weeds, abandoned stores, and occasional fast food chain outlets whose fresh paint and signage only served to emphasize by contrast the once-proud thoroughfare's decay. The need to drive into Detroit annoyed her, although she appreciated the security value of face-to-face meetings. And it was a mid-morning meeting, which made the neighborhood less scary.

The Drummer's legitimate business occupied a well-maintained building on a block that seemed to be holding its own, with a couple of old-style cafes with counters and stools, a lock smith, an auto parts store and a small market. She parked a couple of doors down from the entrance and locked the car, painfully aware that hers was the only white face to be seen on the street.

Putting that thought aside, she pushed open the heavy glass door, wondering if it might be bullet proof. Inside, a thin, light-skinned woman about her age wearing a headset with a curved speaker tube sat behind a counter that reminded Kat of the reception area at Numerica, only on a smaller scale. The receptionist was dressed in an expensive-looking pastel summer suit with a pearl-colored silk blouse that made Kat feel shabby in her jeans and long-sleeved T-shirt. On the wall behind the counter there was a stylized map of the world done in shades of black and dark blue, over which a spidery network of golden lines had been inscribed: a map of the Internet, and a reminder that with the right technology, no one could be excluded from the global economy.

"May I help you?" said the receptionist.

"I'm here to see...." Kat hesitated, realizing that she didn't know the name of the man she and Stone had already paid twenty thousand dollars, only his Internet handle.

"The Drummer? We all call him that. He prefers it."

The woman offered Kat a gentle smile. At that moment, a door to the left of the counter opened and The Drummer appeared, dressed in a dark suit, a blue, open collar shirt, and no sunglasses. He seemed to enjoy her surprise.

"Welcome to my domain," he said, making eye contact for the first time. "Let's go back to my office."

They walked by a dozen cubicles occupied by busy coders all equipped with conspicuously up-to-date gear, unlike the IT departments Kat had known, which always seemed to be two or three years behind the curve. The Drummer's office was windowless, with a large flat panel display on one wall that broadcast a beach scene. He closed the door and offered her a seat on one end of a black leather couch. He sat at the opposite end.

"I live a double life," he said. He went on to explain how Computer Courage worked, providing computer repairs and general consulting plus low-cost web design and maintenance to a community that could not otherwise gain a foothold in the digital economy. These activities were funded by his Dark Web exploits. Apparently he saw himself as a latter day Robin Hood, which he was, but with dark overtones. After all was said and done, she reflected, not all his victims could afford to be robbed. That thought was followed by another that was even more troubling. *Am I one of his victims?*

Kat only half listened as The Drummer shared one of his success stories that had to do with a web site selling imported African crafts. She was here to get the project moving, not listen to him brag.

"Look," she said finally. "I admire what you're doing here. I really do. But I'm here on serious business, and when I take a significant risk like I did in D.C. I expect some kind of acknowledgement, like 'Got it, we're on it' or whatever. You didn't even respond to my email."

The Drummer nodded, and then provided the one response Kat didn't expect.

"I'm sorry," he said. "We were able to determine that the phone in question was already deactivated by the time we received your message. I should have informed you. You must understand that I teach my brothers and sisters to be overcautious, and I need to set an example. In this case, my judgment was less than perfect."

Kat was disarmed. She had been braced for an argument, and there was none to be had. The Drummer knew how to keep people off balance. That was one of his skills. *He goes through life like a boxer*, she thought. But boxer or not, they needed to work together.

"Okay," she said, "So what do we do now?"

"We'll employ deception. We'll trick someone who's already on the network to download our code. Whoever takes our bait will probably realize very quickly what's happened, but it will be too late. We'll be in, and well-hidden.

He stood up and picked up a tablet from the top of his desk. Resting it on one knee, he tapped the glass for a moment and then handed it to her. The screen was blank save for the image of a keyboard. "Put yourself in the position of an employee at DataTech. Let us say it's one week from today. Construct a couple of email messages making reference to past events that will enable us to include an attachment. A photo would be best."

Kat didn't like the way The Drummer was ordering her around like some flunky, but she was here to get a job done, not prove a point about who was in charge.

Hey, she began after thinking a moment, *Wasn't the picnic at Rock Creek great?*

In less than twenty minutes, she and The Drummer had crafted a couple dozen messages revolving around the same theme, each with a high enough percentage of differentiation from the others that the DataTech spam filters would perceive them as a communication from one individual to another, not a mass dissemination. As an extra measure of safety, they would all arrive from different internet addresses, with delivery times several minutes apart. If even one of the recipients clicked the bogus link to the photo that was offered, the payload would be delivered.

She stood up, her work complete. The Drummer escorted her to the front door, where they shook hands innocuously, as though she had just approved the design of a web site for small restaurant or a shoe boutique.

Behind the wheel of Stone's Crossfire, she couldn't help marvel that a multi-billion-dollar government agency would be content to protect its assets with a single point of entry that was the cyber equivalent of a wooden gate in a fence around some pasture. A single point of failure. Anyone who had taken an engineering class knew you didn't design important systems with a single point of failure. But the people in charge probably weren't engineers. They were bureaucrats reporting to politicians. No wonder everything was so fucked up.

As she proceeded down Gaviot Avenue the words *single point of failure* kept cycling through her mind, like in the old OCPD days. But this wasn't obsession. There was something important about these words. There was a thought lingering just at the edge of her mind. And then it appeared.

Our plan has a single point of failure... and it's Matt. He was used to trusting himself, and why not? He was smart. He was determined. He had built a hugely successful company almost from scratch. He had fought in a war. Why shouldn't he trust himself to mount a successful attack on the IRS? He had the weapon in his hands, and once The Drummer worked his magic, the IRS's defenses would be useless. But what if something went wrong? What if Matt... failed? They had worked so hard and spent so much money and made such perfect escape plans. They were less than a month away from the day they would get on an Air France 747 headed for Paris.

What if he got caught in spite of all their precautions? What if one of those awful things that sometimes happened to guys his age happened to him? A stroke. A heart attack. It wasn't impossible, and they didn't have a plan for anything like that. But it wouldn't be hard to put one together. She could do it.

She pulled over and parked the car in front of a large open field separated from the sidewalk by a chain link fence.

She glanced around. It seemed safe. She took her cell phone out of her pocket and punched in her sister's number. It was ten after twelve, which meant she was probably home eating lunch at her kitchen table.

Her sister picked up immediately, her voice full of familiar worry. "Are you alright?" she asked.

"I'm fine. But I need some help. You know that money you told me about. The money in the secret account?"

"It's still there. Why? Do you need it? Are you in trouble? Are you having problems with this Matt?"

"No, but I need some money. Like, now."

"How much?"

"Five." *That ought to be enough*, thought Kat. The Drummer wasn't greedy. "Can you just wire it to my account if I give you the number?

"Kat, what on Earth...."

"Don't ask, okay? I'm not working right now, and I just don't want Matt to know about something. I can pay you back in a couple of months."

"That's not the issue. Just tell me you're okay."

"I know it sounds like the old Kat, but trust me, I'm not going back there."

There was a pause, then, "I believe you. And I would do this even if I didn't believe you."

Kat felt a lump in her throat. "I do love you, Sis."

"What's your account number? I can transfer money with my phone now."

Kat provided her with the number, and then said good-bye, with a promise to meet for dinner on the following Wednesday. Then she headed back to The

Drummer's offices. She and Matt needed a Plan B – one that, for Matt's own good, she would keep to herself.

After nine months in management at DataTech, Jim Gunderson was finally getting used to the idea that sitting through endless meetings and dealing with vacation schedules was real work, just like writing code. It hadn't been an easy transition. He had never thought of himself as a manipulative guy, and that was what management was all about, right? Getting people to do what you want. At least getting them to show up on time. But on this Wednesday morning, settling in at his desk with a cup of coffee on one side of the keyboard and a free doughnut on the other, he was ready for work.

DataTech was a government contractor with one customer: the IRS. It was not glamorous work, but on the other hand, you were not expected to reinvent the world every six months like they did out in California. For all the IRS talk about modernization, good, solid code built with proven, time-tested methodologies was the goal. Even the modernization program that had gotten so much press a while back was based on ideas that were old hat, like service-oriented architecture, which was about as up to date as Mario Brothers. The bottom line was, you didn't have to make up the rules as you went along. He liked that.

The other thing he liked about DataTech was that there were no products, so you weren't constantly in competition with four or five other companies to get the Next Big Thing out the door before they did. You got to do things right, and you got to know the people you worked with as people, because they weren't constantly bent over their keyboards racing against a deadline.

In the fast lane, all-nighters weren't that uncommon. Here, he left his office before six o'clock almost every day, and the only weekend time he spent with the company was at the quarterly "Super Sundays." The last one had just taken place, at Rock Creek Park right in DC. His kids had loved it, and from a work perspective, his whole team had showed up, which made the day a work success as well as a family success, something that was impossible at his last job. As a bonus, he had been able to spend some time with Mary Clark, the sociable data integration specialist who was a candidate to join his team.

Gunderson logged into the system and scanned his e-mail. There was a message from Mary, and it wasn't about work. Instead, it was about the last Super Sunday.

> Got some pics of your wife and kids from Super Sunday at Rock Creek. Click on the link.

This was a good sign. He had just finished reading a book about team building, and one of the key principles was getting people to communicate with one another on subjects other than work. And here she was, sending him a non-work email before she had even joined the team! He clicked on the link she had provided, but it sent him to a blank screen. At that moment, his phone rang. It was his boss. Somebody at Treasury was complaining about the documentation related to data calls. That was trouble, because data calls affected what thousands of employees at the IRS did all day long: look up people's files. This deserved a team meeting, and quick.

Gunderson had completely forgotten about the bad link in Mary Clark's email until he ran into her two days later in the company cafeteria. When he mentioned it, she gave him a blank stare.

"I didn't take any pictures at Rock Creek," she said. "I deliberately didn't bring my phone so I wouldn't be distracted."

"You sure you didn't send me an email with a link to some photos?"

"Absolutely"

"Shit!" He spun around and ran towards the door. He had to get onto the network immediately. "Don't delete anything from your computer," he yelled over his shoulder. "I think we've been hacked."

Four frantic hours later, Gunderson and his team members began to relax a little. There was no evidence of an intrusion into their network that they could find. No alarm bells had gone off at the IRS either. Of course, given the notoriously lax security procedures that prevailed over there, that didn't mean much. There was nothing more to be done. But Gunderson left work that day knowing it was entirely possible a virus had snuck by him and was now hiding somewhere among the thousands of IRS servers to which DataTech had access, just waiting to be activated.

Stone had felt like he was inside a bubble for the last twenty-four hours, a bubble that admitted light and sound, but only after applying a filter to these inputs that made the outside world seem remote. While he wrote emails, drank a coffee, met with engineering teams and executed all the other routine tasks of his life, he could only think of the virus, insinuating itself into the internal data networks of the IRS, snaking along the wires that comprised its physical infrastructure, infecting server after server and then moving on, while erasing all traces of its presence from the activity logs. Now that the silent invasion was complete, it was time to put those servers to work.

Unable to concentrate at work, he had driven over to Kat's old café, having told his secretary there was a dentist appointment he had forgotten to put on the schedule. Chase knew he was lying – he had lied about quite a few absences over the past few weeks – but he couldn't allow himself to worry about it. On his one-to-ten loyalty scale she was at least an eight, which was good enough to get him through the next few weeks.

Sitting in the sunshine on the nearly empty terrace, he cradled the weaponized iPhone in his hand, contemplating the reality of its power, and the difficult dilemma of how to wield that power effectively. A frontal attack with all the trappings of cyber terrorism would never work. "We don't negotiate with terrorists," would be the response. And in any case, he wanted guarantees that were written into law, not a capitulation that could be undone as fast as it was put into effect. He had come to the conclusion that the only path to long-term success was to get a law passed. But getting Congress to do something – anything – seemed an impossible task, even if a total government shutdown was at risk. How would he get it right?

Ever since the night with the *I Ching*, the idea of an ally had been on his mind. He needed one who valued power above all else and was willing to bend the rules and accept Stone's shady "help" to achieve it. At minimum, he could provide that ally with the means of embarrassing the current administration beyond anything that had ever happened in political history. Who would want to do that? Who would take the risk? Who could be trusted? When would he strike with the digital sword he held in his hand? Did he need a few lines buried in an appropriations bill, or would a high profile bill be better. He didn't know. He needed help.

Stone had connections in Washington, but none in the upper echelons. In fact, he didn't really know his way around the political scene in the capitol anymore, only the military side. He needed someone who could move Congress to action, and it would help if it that someone could be influenced with money. Dollars for access – that was a formula that always worked in D.C. Could Stone modify that formula a little? Dollars for *action*? And could he find a member of Congress with ideals that were congruent with his, and could believe in his cause? That would help. For sure, he was looking for a person he could trust. That last requirement might be the toughest one of all.

No names came to mind. He would have to approach this methodically. He got out a yellow pad and carefully drew a matrix. Then he got out his laptop and signed on to *Politico*.

The image on Stone's computer screen flickered slightly, like a real hologram, and then steadied. He saw himself dressed in the blue coat and golden tights of a Continental Army officer. To avoid standing out in the simulation, Congressman Samuel Hawthorne was similarly dressed, and, to the extent Stone could gather, he seemed quite uncomfortable. The faux holographic images to some degree reflected the body language and facial expressions of the players in the online roll playing game Kat had suggested as an anonymous venue for a meeting, but with nothing like the precision of an actual video conference. On screen, the two were seated in a historical tavern that had been razed more than two centuries ago. Tankards of ale rested on the rough wooden table they shared. Every so often, a buxom bar maid passed by, her broken tooth and unkempt hair adding a touch of realism to the scene.

Congressman Hawthorne began the conversation without hesitation. "May I know whom I'm speaking with?" he asked, "and why we're meeting like this?" His voice, familiar to millions, was substantially distorted by the system, and would be unrecognizable both to humans and digital snoopers, as would Stone's.

"Trust me," said Stone. "You don't want to know who I am."

"I think we should terminate this conversation right now."

"I am a patriot. And a ten thousand dollar contributor to your campaign."

"I'm aware of your contribution."

"Yes. It's perfectly legal, and will stand up to scrutiny if necessary. You're doing good work, Congressman. I want to further the cause. I want to accelerate it."

"I represent the government of the United States of America, soldier," he said with more than a touch of irony. "I cannot and will not involve myself in secret online encounters like this. If you really mean business, and can outline a serious agenda, I'll consider a face-to-face meeting. Ten grand gets my attention, but it doesn't buy me. Do you understand what I'm saying?"

"A face-to-face meeting might create problems over time, Congressman. But if those are your terms, I accept. Here's the agenda. A flat tax in eighteen months and your hat in the ring for Presidency in the next election cycle."

Hawthorne was clearly taken aback. "Laudable objectives," he said after a long pause, "but hardly achievable in the time frame you suggest."

"That depends on how far you're willing to go to achieve them."

"This is a democracy. We achieve our objectives one vote at a time. Things don't happen overnight."

Stone had the strong impression Hawthorne was directing half of his remarks to a recording system. He had obtained good evidence that the man was without scruples, and would do anything to achieve his goals. But the appearance of propriety was essential in Washington these days.

"Things can happen very quickly when there's a crisis," said Stone.

"I'm terminating this conversation."

"I'll send a letter to the Bricker Court address to suggest times and places for a face-to-face."

"What Bricker Court address?" said Hawthorne, but with just enough hesitation to let Stone know that the reference to Hawthorne's secret girlfriend had hit home.

"I repeat," said Stone, "I am a patriot and I support your goals. I assure you, I have no interest in your personal life. But I'm a man of action, and I do what it takes to get things done."

"Including threats and innuendo, it would seem."

"Congressman, I think we're natural allies, but we've clearly gotten off on the wrong foot. Please, let me take a step back. In fact, let me quote you. Stone looked down from the screen to a transcript Chase had copied off Hawthorne's web site for him. '*We have become a society of makers and takers. Government has become The Great Enabler of this shameful state of affairs, and it's wrong. The transfer of wealth from the makers to the takers is not the government's business. The creation of give-away programs that remove every incentive for these takers to get a job and support their own is not the government's business. And the use of Gestapo tactics to intimidate the creators of wealth to give up their hard earned dollars to fund these programs is most certainly not the government's business.*'

"I couldn't agree more with those words, Congressman. We need to put a stop to this. And we can. But to do so may involve unorthodox tactics you would most probably want to disavow, at least publicly. If we meet, even once, you put yourself at risk. And you have a lot to lose. But here in this simulation, it's safe. There are no security cameras, no GPS trackers, and no private detectives hired by your enemies to uncover something that could compromise your reputation."

"You forgot to mention that you can record every word I say," Hawthorne shot back. "This conversation could be in chat rooms all over the world tomorrow."

Stone thought with dismay, *I'm an amateur here.* He had believed the money would be enough to at least open a frank discussion. Wrong. He had thought that meeting in an online simulation would impress this Congressman with his concern for privacy. Wrong. Hawthorne was playing this whole encounter like a sting.

Stone sighed. "Of course you're right. So let's meet face-to-face, but with caution. I think you'll be interested in what I have to say. And if you're not, I'll give you enough personal information so we'll have mutually assured destruction. It's not trust, but it's a start."

Hawthorne chuckled, a weird sound when distorted by the simulation. "Sounds like you're ready for a career in politics."

Stone thought, *He must have turned off the recording system.* He said, "Not me. I'm not cut out for compromise. I have ideals."

"So do I, believe it or not," said Hawthorne. "That's why we're still talking."

Stone's paranoia increased with every step as he approached the restaurant Hawthorne had chosen for their meet. Only yesterday, Kat had sent him a blog post from *Security Week* about drop cameras. They were small enough to fit in the palm of your hand and could provide a continuous video stream to anyone who had an Internet connection, or any *thing*, for that matter, including a facial recognition system. Since the stream was digital, it was possible to archive thousands of hours of images for future review. You could defeat those systems by tilting your head fifteen degrees or more while you walked by, but that in itself could single you out for more attention based on your clothes, the initials on your briefcase and half a dozen other tell tales that most people never thought about.

What if there were such a camera at the entrance to Bartolino's? How could Hawthorne be so cavalier? They shouldn't be meeting like this at all, and certainly not in D.C. But Stone didn't have any choice.

He gave his name to the maître d' as Paul Revere, an obvious pseudonym that caused the man to smirk, and was led to a table in the rear of the restaurant that was far out of earshot from the others. The room was dimly lit with a low ceiling that created a sense of slightly claustrophobic intimacy. It crossed his mind that the whole meeting could be a set-up, but that was a risk he had to take.

Hawthorne rose as Stone approached. The Congressman was shorter in person than he appeared on TV. He offered Stone a firm handshake and a steady gaze. "I wasn't sure you'd show," he said.

"The feeling is mutual," said Stone, coaxing the hint of a smile from the man.

They both sat down and Stone pulled out two small recording devices Kat had recommended he buy. They were designed to pick up ordinary conversation in environments like this. He handed one to Hawthorne. "We both record the whole meeting, which means we each have enough ammo to sink the other."

"Agreed," said Hawthorne. They had settled on this plan in advance.

"It's a pleasure to meet you, Congressman Hawthorne," said Stone.

"Likewise. I've always admired Numerica, and as the CEO, you deserve a lot of credit."

They were both speaking for the record to identify themselves, but soon they would get down to business. That part of the conversation, Stone reminded himself, would also be on the record, for better or for worse. *Mutually assured destruction.*

Hawthorne ordered an expensive bourbon and Stone joined him. He sometimes wondered if any business ever got done in Washington without the help of alcohol. He had come to think that government would function a lot more effectively if there were open bars on the floor of the House and Senate. But that was an idea for a different, simpler century. *Focus!* he commanded himself.

They both ordered steak sandwiches. Hawthorne consumed his with a second bourbon. He seemed relaxed, if distant, and more likable than Stone had imagined. But then, when all was said and done, wasn't politics ultimately about being liked? It certainly wasn't about ideals and principles, no matter what Hawthorne asserted.

After the waiter had removed their plates and brought coffee, Hawthorne folded his hands on the table. "Talk to me," he said.

Think of this as just another sales pitch, Stone said to himself. *You've done this a thousand times.*

"We both agree that government has become too powerful and too intrusive in our private lives," he began, "and it's my opinion that the IRS is at the center of the problem. If there's going to be change, it has to begin there."

"Hold it," said Hawthorne, raising both hands, "Nobody fucks with the IRS. They're too powerful."

"Exactly."

"If this is about taking on the IRS, we've got a non-starter here."

"Just hear me out."

Hawthorne leaned back and crossed his arms across his chest, a bad sign. But Stone held to his script.

"Let's say, hypothetically, that someone had the ability to blow up the whole system."

"Do you mean literally?" said Hawthorne with a note of alarm in his voice. Had he sat down to break bread with a terrorist?

"Poor choice of words," said Stone with an easy smile. "Let's say, 'render inoperative.' Make it so the IRS couldn't collect taxes. Couldn't send out bills. Couldn't recognize revenue. Couldn't look up peoples' names. Couldn't do what it does now to terrorize innocent citizens."

"Holy shit! You're not kidding."

Stone nodded. "Think about how much leverage a person who had control over the power of taxation would have in this town, how simple it would be to discredit a chain of command that had allowed a successful attack on the IRS. Hypothetically, of course."

"That's quite a hypothetical," said Hawthorne. "How would it be accomplished?"

"We can talk about that," said Stone. "But the more important question is, would you like to be the person who has that power?"

Stone could see that Hawthorne was having trouble processing this question.

"Let me help you out. What I'm telling you is that there's a way to shut down the system without destroying it. So we're not talking about an all or nothing option here. We're talking about temporary paralysis. That's the beauty of it."

"So I'm supposed to threaten a government shutdown if I don't get the new bridge I want in my district? I already know how to shut down the government. I don't need your help. But... could this threat apply to individuals?"

Stone was suddenly flooded with alarm. It was so obvious! Individual threats were all he needed. Not the cyber equivalent of nuclear war. He should have figured that out. But this clearly wasn't his kind of game. It never had been.

When he first started doing business with the government, he had thought he could win on excellence or, failing that, the lowest bid. The government sales consultant he finally hired taught him how things really worked. You made friends with whoever it was that wrote the request for quote, and offered to "help." In fact, you wrote it yourself, and the end result was an RFQ that only your company could fulfill. Right now, Stone had the wrong product for Hawthorne's RFQ. And even if he had the capability to tamper with individual accounts, he had no wish to give a man like Hawthorne that kind of power. But did he have a choice?

Probably not. That was reality, and that was why he was sitting across from a scoundrel, a man whom Stone could never control. How had he gotten himself into this position? He experienced an awful moment of doubt. Could he even pull this off?

It was time for a gut-based decision. He would go back to The Drummer and get the control over individual tax accounts Hawthorne was asking for. He had to believe that was possible. "I want the Fair Taxation Act written into law," he said, slapping the table firmly with the palm of his hand, "and I will do whatever it takes to make that happen."

"The Fair Taxation Act?"

"That's what I call it, but the name doesn't matter. The law I want makes the same rules that apply to police departments apply to the IRS. Right now, what they do amounts to illegal search and seizure. I don't care what the Sixteenth Amendment says. Citizens who can't pay their taxes haven't committed a crime, and they shouldn't be treated like criminals. Look, I'm no politician, but I think this is a winning issue."

"You understand that what you're talking about isn't exactly a popular cause among legislators."

"Of course not. It's too risky. Who wants an audit? But here's what's different this time. You can make tax records disappear. Or make them public, for that matter."

Hawthorne drained the last of his second bourbon and signaled for a third. His body language was still negative, but at least he was willing to listen.

"So I'm supposed to associate myself with a group of cyber terrorists?" he asked.

"Sam... May I call you Sam?"

Hawthorne nodded, a good sign. First names worked wonders in some negotiations.

"Sam, no one is going to associate you with anything. One of your colleagues refuses to play ball and he gets an audit notice a couple days later. Somebody on the fence comes over to your side and gets a surprise refund." Stone was ad-libbing dangerously now. He had no idea what The Drummer could actually do.

"Word gets around," he went on. "They'll just think you've got special friends in the agency. And if the IRS starts asking questions, well, you've got a pretty big stick to wield."

"Stone, if I'm implying to my colleagues that if they don't vote for my bill the wrath of the IRS will come down on their heads...." He shook his head. "It sure sounds like extortion to me. How am I any different from the kid who wants twenty bucks to protect your car from getting scratched in the parking lot while you're at the ball game?"

"You have a cause. You have ideals." Would Hawthorne swallow that line along with his third drink?

"This takes hardball politics to a whole new level," said the congressman. "But what I don't understand is why you want to get involved in all this. What's in it for you?"

"The IRS killed one of my best friends."

Hawthorne's eyes widened.

"Not with bullets," said Stone. "I'll tell you the story."

When he had finished, Hawthorne seemed touched, although Stone knew he might be acting. At least he seemed more interested in carrying the conversation forward.

"Your plan has a lot of holes in it," said Hawthorne."

"Hey," said Stone. "I'm just the weapons designer. You're the one who figures out where to point it. I am ready to give you a weapon of enormous power and all I'm asking for is justice. Beyond that, I don't care how you use it."

"If I can point that weapon at single individuals, we might have a deal. That line I have about democracy working one vote at a time isn't just bullshit for campaign speeches. That's actually the way things work in the House and Senate."

The two men eyed one another, each trying to read the other's thoughts. Stone could see in Hawthorne's eyes that he was winning him over now.

"I hear you," said Stone at last. "You give me the names, and I'll do the rest."

The meeting was over. Stone handed Hawthorne the Dark Net cheat sheet Kat had prepared for him. From now on, their communications would be anonymous. Hawthorne picked up what appeared to be an extremely heavy briefcase and they headed for the entrance. Stone opened the door for him and watched him as he trudged away in the mid-afternoon sunlight. Only later did it dawn on Stone that Hawthorne's head had been tilted more than fifteen degrees the whole time he was in camera range of the restaurant.

Stone thought, *I've got a lot to learn*. But at the moment, he had to get back to Detroit, and to The Drummer. And before that, he had to figure out a way to come up with some cash.

Congressman Samuel Hawthorne's body was humming as he entered The Dubliner, one of the most prestigious hang-outs in the Capitol. He had realized early on that power was what life was all about. His dad was a proud union man and a Democrat to the core, but for all his beliefs in the rights of the working class and the dignity of human labor, the fact was that the bastards who ran the plant where he worked held all the cards. When push came to shove and the union contracts got too fat for their liking, they had simply shut the plant down, putting half the people in the town out of work in one day.

That was when Hawthorne, age twelve at the time, decided that when he grew up he wanted to be one of those bastards. The willingness of Jim Bradley to meet him here – be *seen* with him here – was proof that he had achieved his goal. And more power was in his reach than ever before. He was about to arm wrestle with the chairman of the House Ways and Means Committee. And he was determined to win.

Hawthorne secured a booth, sank into the leather and ordered a whiskey. He scanned the crowd and nodded at a couple of senior White House staffers conferring at the bar. The younger people couldn't afford to frequent these dark oak confines on a regular basis now that lobbyists were no longer allowed to buy their drinks.

Bradley arrived a few minutes late, as Hawthorne expected. This man couldn't be seen alone at a table waiting for someone. Not here! But he did show up. Bradley was a heavy set man in his mid-fifties whose solid frame and physical bulk seemed to add to his political power. A twelve term veteran from New Mexico, he could pass for Hispanic, and proudly claimed a great grandfather who had fought in the Mexican revolution. The waiter brought him a tall beer without even asking for his order.

"Nice to see you, Nick," he said, opening with a lie. "How are you faring these days?" This was a clearly a reference to his loss of Laura.

Hawthorne quickly concocted a story about his daughter's success out in California as a Silicon Valley physical trainer. Bradley had two kids, both in college and both pursuing liberal arts degrees that would be worth very little in today's job market. *What use is this information?* thought Hawthorn, but he played the small talk game as they sipped their drinks, each waiting for the other's opening gambit. To Hawthorne's surprise, Bradley spoke first.

"I suppose you're here to talk about that cockamamie tax bill of yours. I think you know there's nothing I can do for you. I'm personally sympathetic. But if you go ahead and introduce it there's just no way I'll be able to line up enough votes to get it out of committee. And I wouldn't even want to bring it up for a vote. The price would be too high."

Hawthorne nodded sympathetically. "It's a sad story when nobody can vote his conscience anymore. I'll bet every member of Ways and Means would say the same thing. They believe in limiting the power of the IRS. It's always, they'd like to help me, but."

Bradley looked annoyed, as though Hawthorne were questioning his ethics. "You know as well as I do that not every member of the house is a choir boy. Nobody in my committee wants to go on record voting against the IRS. It's like asking for an audit, or worse."

"They're all scared. The fact is, nobody has the balls to stand up to the IRS."

"Those are strong words, congressman."

"But factually accurate."

The two men stared at one another.

"I've been looking into the IRS lately," said Hawthorne. "That new computer system," said, shaking his head. "It's like the Wild West. The records aren't necessarily tamper-proof. They even admit it themselves. Anybody could be hacked."

"Just what exactly are you saying?"

Hawthorne realized he was now the object of the committee chair's famous "power glower." Then, his expression changed, and Hawthorne could see that Bradley had connected the dots, or at least the ones he was aware of.

"Then rumors are true," said Bradley, shaking his head incredulously.

"What rumors?"

"Nick, don't play games with me. You do not want me as an enemy."

"No, I certainly don't. That's why I'm here. We've got a lot of common ground. Forget my bill for a minute. Forget the IRS. The bigger picture is that *you* want the party to move away from all these divisive social issues and focus on the economy, and I want a government that stays out of people's lives in every way, financially and otherwise. I frankly don't give a damn what they do under the table at gay bars, and I don't think the U.S. government should either."

"The point being?"

"I have a national audience now. I can help steer things in the right direction for the party, with your guidance."

"Do you have personal knowledge of the tax problems that Jim Brisbane and Arthur Green are having?"

"I can't talk about that."

Bradley glared at him once again.

"Jim," said Hawthorne, "All I'm saying is there are people out there who could hack the IRS and wreak havoc with somebody's tax returns. Zap them. Change the numbers. Initiate an audit. Anything."

"Is that supposed to be some kind of threat?"

Hawthorne thought, *Of course it is.* He said, "I am sharing sensitive information to which you would otherwise have no access. I'm probably breaking the law."

Bradley was obviously angry. "Thanks for sharing," he said mockingly.

"The point is, any person or group who is pissed at the IRS is going to love my bill. Anybody who's perceived as trying to block it could be in serious trouble with the voters.

I'm just stating a fact. And I have to introduce that bill now or my credibility is shot."

"Do your worst. This discussion is over."

Hawthorne ignored this. "I don't see why you can't support a bill that puts reasonable, transparent legal controls on an agency everybody hates and makes you look like the only person in Washington who can put together a bipartisan coalition."

Bradley raised his eyebrows. "You're not going to give up, are you? Well, you've got *cahones*, I'll grant you that." The big man lifted his beer to his lips and drank deeply, then set the mug down on the table as though it were a gavel. "I'll think about this. And I *would* very much like to find a cause that could change the direction of our party a bit. But understand, if I join you, it's as a full partner, with full access to all the information at your disposal. And I'm not getting involved in falsifying government records."

"Understood."

Bradley stood up and offered his beefy hand, a good sign. "You be careful, congressman. We've got a saying in New Mexico. It actually comes from the other side of the border. *Quien se acuesta con perros se levanta con pulgas.*"

"Which means?"

"If you go to bed with dogs, you wake up with fleas."

"Yes," said Hawthorne. "But we're dealing with wolves."

Hawthorne drove along Democracy Parkway under a gray sky, his windshield wipers pushing away the flakes of a late season snowfall. His destination was Bethesda's Cabin John Park, where he was to meet Chairman Bradley at the head of a naturally surfaced trail that ran along the creek that gave the park its name. He pulled into the lot in front of the outdoor tennis courts and stepped out into the cold, dry air, his boots crunching on the new snow.

He was heading into this meeting carrying a weapon with only one bullet: Stone's promise to expose more of the committee members' tax records if asked. The good news was that Stone had come through with two test cases. He had refused to make alterations – he was too much of a Boy Scout for that – but the threat of exposure would be enough. No politician wanted his tax records in the public domain any more.

Bradley was waiting for him, a bulky figure dressed in a black top coat and scarf against the cold. He nodded a greeting and then gestured with his head towards the trail. They trudged in silence through the monotone landscape. The park was virtually deserted due to the bad weather. Finally, Hawthorne spoke.

"You asked for a meeting. I'm here."

Bradley gave him a long look. "If you have serious political ambitions, you have to get yourself back within the bounds of the law."

Hawthorne said nothing.

"It appears that somehow you've figured out a way to put the credibility of the United States government at risk. That's not acceptable, and I'm not going to let it happen. When that threat is neutralized, which I believe you can do, I'm prepared to make a deal. You give my experts the source code – that's what they say they need to see – and I'll help you out with your bill. If we're going to work together, that's how it's going to work."

Hawthorne's heart leapt. *If we're going to work together!*

They were now on a path that followed the course of the creek, which was still half frozen over. The water had slowed to a trickle. *Like our government*, thought Hawthorne. There might be a line for his next speech in there somewhere. But right now he had to get Bradley on board. If not, he could end up giving speeches to local Rotary Clubs for the rest of his life. How in Hell was he going to get Stone to hand over the only asset that gave him any leverage?

Hawthorne came to the icy realization that he was overmatched here. Bradley had gotten to where he was for a reason. The man was two moves ahead of him at every turn. Now, he could see no other option but honesty.

"I'm not sure I can get any code. I don't have that level of control."

Bradley stopped walking and stared at him, his face ruddy from the cold. "Jesus Christ! What have you done? Did you hire a team of North Koreans?"

"No foreign nationals are involved in this."

"Who, then?"

Hawthorne spread his hands in a gesture of helplessness. The two men regarded one another, their breath visible in the cold air.

"Help me pass this bill. It's a good bill, and you know it. Within five minutes of passage, you'll have your source code and everything the IRS needs to get rid of the infection."

"And if I say no?"

Hawthorne sensed that this was the moment to kiss the ring. "If you say no, I'll follow your guidance, including turning myself in to the FBI."

Bradley closed his eyes for a long moment, then shook his head. "There's no way to put this genie back into the bottle, is there?"

"I believe a confrontation would lead to chaos."

"Agreed. Go ahead and introduce your bill. I'll help you. Who knows? Maybe some day you'll be in a position to help me. You've got the ambition, that's for sure. And you're smart enough. But Congressman, we are a nation of laws, and you need to respect that. Do you understand me?"

"Yes, sir, I do." With that, they shook hands and then headed back to the warmth of their cars.

Within an hour, Hawthorne was on the secure line Stone had set up for him. "Good news," he said, "It looks like we're in business. I only need eight names. Some of them aren't on the committee, but they'll help down the road. Have you got a pencil?"

Ted Bruder, Numerica's chief financial officer, was a stocky, round-faced man with blonde hair and blue eyes that reflected his Swiss heritage. He came from generations of bankers. When anyone described him, the words "nice guy" and "easy going" would always come up, but when it came to money, he could be tight fisted and stubborn. Stone had deliberately hired a risk averse CFO to balance his own tendency to take chances on potentially lucrative deals and put too low a priority on regulatory compliance. Today, he was paying for that decision.

They were sitting on opposite ends of Stone's black leather office couch, Bruder in a dark blue pin-striped suit, Stone in shirt sleeves with his tie loosened. The CFO had accepted Stone's offer of tea, and seemed to be taking forever to deal with the bag and add precisely the right amount of cream and sugar. He was stalling. Stone was sure of it.

"Matt," said the CFO at last, "We have a little problem, or actually, I'd call it a mid-sized problem. In the last month you have spent fifty-five thousand dollars that's unaccounted for. Now I understand that we have some sensitive contracts where you have discretionary spending and where we can't have public audit trails an enemy could follow to gain military intelligence, but fifty-five is too much for me to sweep under the rug."

Stone had known this was coming. He had prepared an eyes-only memo on where the money should be attributed, with no chunk exceeding the ten thousand dollar level that would attract attention. He stood up to get the memo, which was on his desk. As he did so, he looked down and saw a spider on his shirt not three inches from his face.

Involuntarily he yelled as he brushed it away, but it clung to his shirt. It took him a moment to realize it was the polo logo, not an insect.

Bruder was alarmed. "Are you all right?" he asked.

Matt did his best to laugh. His heart was racing. "I thought I had a spider on my shirt. Sorry."

Bruder seemed to be making a calculation in his head, a common occurrence. There were times when he would think for two or three minutes before answering a question in a meeting. It drove people crazy, but his thoroughness often kept the company out of trouble.

"Matt, off the record, is there something you need to talk about? We're not close friends, but you have to admit I can offer a different point of view from yours on just about anything. So, if there's something weighing on you and you need a new perspective...."

Stone experienced a moment of pride at the team he had built. They worked together well and, without being intrusive, they all cared about one another's lives as a whole. Unfortunately, that was the last thing he needed right now. He was obviously broadcasting signals. Cotter, his chief engineer, and now Bruder. They had both picked up something. He was slipping. He was hearing voices when he visited his old house and now he was seeing spiders on his shirt... and occasionally missing meetings because he simply forgot about them, in spite of daily reminders from Chase.

"Well, the offer's there," said Bruder, when Stone failed to respond.

"Thank you. It means a lot. The thing is, the bigger the company gets, the more there is to worry about. When we started out, there was no such thing as a carbon footprint. Now, we have to report it every quarter or get on a list of bad guys. And this classified stuff. I'll tell you the truth, Ted. Sometimes they make up the rules as they go along."

Bruder raised his eyebrows.

"Nothing you want to know about, I promise you," said Stone. "You'd have ulcers in a month."

"Do you have ulcers?"

"No," said Stone. He walked over to his desk and got the memo. "Take a look," he said, handing it to Bruder.

While Stone stood over him the CFO read Stone's memo, re-read it, and then nodded. "I think this will fly."

"Then we're good."

Bruder stood. "Have you got a folder for this? I don't want to walk around with an unprotected sensitive document."

"Chase will have what you need."

Bruder paused before opening the door. "I shouldn't say this, but you know, there's nothing like some between-the-sheets time to relieve tension. Laura wouldn't want you to be stoic. You take care, Matt."

Stone was astonished. Bruder had just stepped way out of character. The man was genuinely worried about him. So was Cotter. Who else? He didn't think his external behavior had changed, but he was obviously wrong. Eventually, his lieutenants were going to start talking to one another – if they weren't already. He had to get his act together!

As soon as he felt sure that Bruder was gone, Stone buzzed Chase on the old-fashioned intercom he still used and told her to reschedule his afternoon appointments. It had been four days since The Drummer's team set to work modifying the original program so it could target individual accounts, and that revision could be ready today. A drive into Detroit was the only way to find out. He would take his own car this time. So what if a window got smashed? He was only going to be using it for a few more weeks.

When Stone arrived at the cottage Kat wasn't there, but a bag of groceries was sitting on the table, which told him she had gotten his message, shopped, and then most probably gone for a run. He truly admired her physical discipline.

"If I don't keep my chemistry balanced, you'll pay for it more than me," she had said, only half joking. In fact, he had never seen any of the behavior that belonged to her "fucked up past," as she characterized it. In fact, her past such as he knew about it had been relatively unremarkable. Early on she had felt the need to tell him that she was disease free, which took him by surprise, but he had attributed that reassurance to something that simply belonged to her generation and not his.

Tonight, he had the feeling she would be a lot steadier than he was. He was about to cross into territory from which there would be no return. Simply inserting the virus The Drummer had engineered for him into a government network would surely violate a few laws, even if he didn't activate it. Actually *stealing* data, and stealing was the word, was unambiguously a crime, one that could easily put him in prison for the rest of his life, particularly when the victim was the U.S. government

In a fire fight, you didn't have time to think about the consequences of your actions. You just acted. In the war he was waging now, there was too much time to think. Would the new malware really work? Would its built-in safeguards succeed in protecting his anonymity? Did Hawthorne have the skill to steer the Fair Taxation bill through the House and Senate? Would the Congressman try to betray him once he had possession of his enemies' tax returns? If so, Hawthorne would pay dearly.

Stone glanced at the old dresser where he had stashed the thumb drive that stored the recording of his initial face-to-face conversation with Hawthorne. There was a second copy back at his house, although at the moment he couldn't remember where he had put it. *Fuck!* He took a couple of deep breaths to calm himself. One copy was enough. That wasn't the problem. It was his damned memory. Kat kept telling him he was under too much stress, and that everything would be fine once they were in Italy. *Maybe.*

Just then, he heard her light footsteps as she trotted up the path to the cottage. The door opened and there she was, smiling at him in her blue running shorts and white T-shirt, a light sheen of perspiration on her face. There were moments when, at least to his eyes, she looked like a teenager.

"Uh oh," she said. "I know that look. What's up?" She came closer and put her hands on his shoulders. She smelled of fresh sweat.

"The moment of truth," he said, with more gravity than he had intended. "The software mods are in place. All I have to do is enter the names on your phone. Then with one tap we're in business."

"I am so proud of you, Matt. This is the right thing to do."

He put his hands on her waist and pulled her closer, feeling her hot body against his. "I wish I could have done this on my own. I have a bad feeling about this Hawthorne."

"You could do it on your own," she said, looking up at him. "But this is the best way. I mean, what could be better than a law?" She released herself from his grip. "I need a shower. Don't tap that button 'till I come back, okay? It'll only take a couple of minutes."

When she came back, barefoot in jeans and an old sweatshirt, she sat down on the floor next to him with one arm on his thigh. The weaponized iPhone rested next to him, sitting on top of a sheet of lined yellow paper with a hand-written list of names. Two had stars. The proof-of-concept names that would demonstrate conclusively to Hawthorne that the system really worked.

"We should burn that list after you type the names in," she said, "and share a glass of wine. We should celebrate."

"There's no going back, you know."

"There was no going back from the first time we met at the lake, Matt. Start typing. You're the man of action here. I'm the one who's supposed to think too much."

Stone tapped the drum icon. It now presented two options: a map, which would allow him to selectively shut down IRS districts across the country, and a spy glass that would select individual returns for inspection. He tapped the spyglass. A screen appeared with an empty fill-in box. He typed in the name of the first congressman Hawthorne had targeted. Then he hesitated, his finger hovering over the SEND button – the button that, when tapped, would make him a criminal, at least according to the laws of the land. But there were higher laws, and by their measure he was no criminal. *They* were the criminals. He tapped the button. Almost instantly the words SUBMISSION RECEIVED appeared on the screen. He reflected that he had just put the private tax returns of an innocent lawmaker, one Thomas H. Bender, into the hands of a man he could not trust. It was messy. But there were no other easy options to achieve his goal. *When among wolves, howl like a wolf.* He repeated the process seven more times.

The deed was done. Now it was Hawthorne's turn to step up to the plate. Stone would have no direct communication with him. Instead, he would follow the legislative process on Politico. If Hawthorne kept his word, IRS excesses would be the lead story for several weeks to come.

Kat gently squeezed his leg. "Let's light a fire."

Hawthorne glanced at his notes one last time as his car approached the home of Mr. and Mrs. James Seward, major contributors to his campaign and major benefactors of an earmark he had inserted into the Airport and Airway Extension Act of 2017. It was just after five o'clock and a little muggy, the perfect time for a couple of frosty mint juleps, heavy on the bourbon. Not tonight though. This cocktail party, whose well-to-do attendees could afford box seats at the Kentucky Derby held in nearby Louisville, was what the marketing people referred to as a "soft launch." It was a low-visibility test of how well the focus group results would play out in the real world with real contributors as he began his campaign to win a spot on the Republican Presidential ticket.

One of the keys to success was using plain language that framed issues in ways people could relate to. Hawthorne had wanted the launch to revolve around the Bill of Rights and the Fourth Amendment in particular, a strategy he thought would tie him back to the roots of democracy and the wisdom of the Founding Fathers. When a survey revealed that almost half of all adult Americans didn't even know that Bill of Rights was part of the Constitution, he was forced to take a different tack. That was how he came to focus on the phrase "unreasonable search and seizure," which rang a lot of bells. The assertion by a candidate that he would stand up to the IRS rang even more bells, and it tied into the "get things done" theme he was also testing.

Preparing for today's modest meet-and-greet had been a grind. If you wanted to play at this level, you couldn't just buy your way into the game with a combination of favors and actual cash. You had to have a real story to tell, with plenty of facts and figures thrown in to back it up. Sarah Palin had learned this lesson the hard way. Hers was a path he had no wish to follow.

He also had no wish to run afoul of the IRS. In spite of Stone's promise that he would be safe, Hawthorne had hired a team of tax experts to comb through his returns for the past seven years, looking for anything that would appear even slightly questionable. Digging up – or fabricating – the documentation they said he needed had been time-consuming and difficult. Of course, he didn't have a choice. He was well aware that the Mafia had been taken down by the IRS, and he was not eager to follow them.

Hawthorne stuffed his note cards into his pocket and straightened his tie. They had passed through the gate and were now on the circular driveway that led to the entrance of the Seward's ornately columned mansion.

Ellen Seward herself opened the door when he rang the bell and gave him the obligatory hug, with air kisses to both cheeks. Her husband stood behind her and offered a firm hand shake once Hawthorne had untangled himself from the man's wife. She was actually quite attractive for her age, with a figure that implied regular aerobics, artfully colored ash blonde hair, and striking blue eyes that radiated sincerity and commitment. Hawthorne idly wondered what she might be like in bed, but immediately put the thought aside. He was here to secure votes and extract money from this crowd of moderate conservatives, not fuck the host's wife.

After a half hour of hand shaking and small talk, during which he limited his drinking to a single glass of white wine, the guests seated themselves in the folding chairs rented for the occasion and Hawthorne took his place behind the impromptu podium.

"I am a patriot," he began, "And I have to tell you, it breaks my heart to see what America has come to." He paused for effect. "In healthcare, the United States of America ranks number thirty-seven in the world. We're not only behind developed countries like Canada and Sweden. We're behind Costa Rica, Morocco and Saudi Arabia.

"In broadband distribution, we do a little better. We're number thirty-five. But that's still good enough to leave us behind countries like South Korea, Romania and – are you ready for this? – Latvia.

"The economies of Taiwan, Singapore, Korea, India and even Ireland have grown twice as fast as ours over the past twenty years, and China's economy has grown almost six times as fast.

"That's not acceptable to me, and I don't think it's acceptable to you either. The fact is, our government isn't helping us in any of these areas. It's getting in the way." Hawthorne scanned his audience and saw plenty of nods. The numbers his staff had dug up were shocking. He had the room's attention. The us vs. them theme was working.

The second theme he tested was us vs. us. It revolved around the decline of the manufacturing sector, and in this room it didn't do so well. While the figures were in their own way equally shocking, he could see that audiences like this would rather hear a message of hope on the topic of manufacturing. He would have to get some different statistics, and a list of manufacturing companies with success stories. He could single them out as companies that were doing well *in spite of our government*. He closed by repeating what he hoped would become an applause line for larger audiences. "Once again, our government isn't helping us. It's getting in the way!" Now was the time to move on and test unreasonable search and seizure.

"The thing that's most troubling to me doesn't have anything to do with technology or economic growth. It's the fact that too many people in our government hold the U.S. Constitution in contempt. In the America where I grew up, you didn't pick up the phone and wonder if your call was going to be recorded. You weren't concerned that the GPS device embedded in your car was broadcasting your every move to strangers. And you didn't worry whether the money in your savings account was safe from the IRS if you got a little behind in your taxes.

"Friends, I have a story to tell you. It's about a man named Herb – I'm not going to reveal his last name – who owned a small business in central Michigan that employed twenty-four people. Now Herb was no mathematician, but he was a good leader and he knew how to take care of his customers, prime contractors for General Motors and Chrysler. As the result of hard work and perseverance, Herb managed to keep his doors open for twenty one years, carrying on a family business that dated back to the end of World War II. And then, for no other reason than the fact that he couldn't quite pay all his taxes on time, the IRS padlocked those doors and seized all his assets.

"Herb was heart broken. He didn't have the means to fight back. So he took the only way out he felt was left. He killed himself."

Hawthorne heard several gasps in the audience. *This was good stuff!* He saw no reason not to stretch the facts just a little.

"Herb, ladies and gentlemen, was a Viet Nam veteran. But he wasn't killed by an enemy bullet. He was killed by his own government. And if Herb's story isn't an example of unreasonable search and seizure, I don't know what is. The fact of the matter is, the IRS could go after anybody in this room. And even if you've paid every dime you owe, they can still cost you thousands of dollars in attorneys' fees defending yourself."

Once again, he was getting lots of nods. He stepped out from behind the podium and walked back and forth in front of his audience.

"I want to be clear here. We need a government. Not the big, bloated one we have, but we do need government. And we all have an obligation to take on our fair share of the tax burden. But to arbitrarily and automatically treat people who have a problem paying their taxes like criminals is just plain wrong. As a matter of fact, suspected criminals have more rights in our system of justice than people who get in trouble with the IRS. They are – and all of us here in this room *could be* – subjected to a level of unreasonable search and seizure that's blatantly unconstitutional.

"I'm not saying we should dismantle the IRS. I'll grant you, it would feel good." He paused for chuckles from the audience, then moved to his conclusion. "We shouldn't take down the IRS, but we have to get it under control. If you're a criminal and the police want to search your house, they have to get a warrant from a judge. The same process should apply to the IRS. It's as simple as that.

"I will soon be introducing legislation to put legal curbs on the IRS. Somebody has to stand up to them, and that somebody is standing up right here in front of you."

His politician's sense of timing told him that the moment to close had come. He nodded his head in a gesture of conclusion. "Thank you," he said, "and God Bless America."

The group responded with a standing ovation.

Now, he thought, *time to pass the collection plate.*

For the first time in years, Stone found himself in the somewhat cramped confines of a business class seat. There was something chummy about first class, at least on some flights. It could feel more like a friendly bar than a passenger service, and on this flight he wanted to be alone. As the plane took off, it occurred to him that this round trip to San Francisco might be his last. He would not need a return ticket from Rome. He was going to do anything in his power to realize Kat's fantasy: the two of them in a small village in Southern Italy where life was calm, no one asked questions and any problem that came up could be handled with a bribe. After they got their feet on the ground, maybe they would open a little café bar. The other night they had had a semi-serious conversation about faking their deaths before they left so no one would look for them when they vanished.

Fake deaths or not, if Hawthorne came through they would have more than enough time to make a smooth transition – to disappear gracefully, as he thought of it. If anything went wrong, his alternate identity documents were safe in the carry-on he had stowed in the bin directly over his head. He brought them with him everywhere now, plus the credit cards and the cash he would need to make a run for it in the worst case scenario. So far, everything was going smoothly. Hawthorne was making all the right public moves, and presumably he was doing the same behind the scenes. But you never knew. That's why he wanted to see his daughter Kimmie one last time right now. He wouldn't have that option as a renegade on the run.

The Boeing 767 shuddered as it left the runway and took flight. Automatically, Stone's mind began to analyze whether that unsteady moment was the result of some component that was out of spec, one that Numerica could do a better job of manufacturing. But those times were gone. More than gone. It was as though they had been lived by some other man. Lately, Stone had come to see his whole life as a series of islands in a broad river: childhood with Mom and Dad in control, high school and football, college with Laura, 'Nam, the early days of Numerica when it was still called Stone Custom Manufacturing and he personally supervised his employees, the later years of long hours as the company grew and grew while Laura stayed home to take care of Kimmie... and now this. It wasn't a smooth continuum. It was a loosely connected archipelago that led inexorably from one separate life to another, and ultimately to death – but not for awhile. He was a fortunate man. Fate had dealt him a hand that allowed him to do something important before it was all over

Stone settled back into his seat and closed his eyes. In a few hours he would see his daughter for the first time in more years than he cared to count. Somehow, in the months after her graduation from art school, something had happened that set her adrift. She lost her job at the art gallery where she had worked on and off for several years. She had a falling out with her roommate, and began sleeping on whatever couch was available. She was suddenly unavailable for the Sunday evening telephone calls that had been part of their family life since her freshman year.

After a while, their only communication was through email, and almost all the messages had to do with money. They were alarming. She needed thirty-seven dollars and sixteen cents to pay the utility bill. She needed "ten or fifteen dollars" for new socks. To Stone, these messages reflected a life that had gone off the rails. He couldn't bring himself to say it aloud, but he feared she was surviving through prostitution.

It was almost a year after she left Michigan before he discovered that she had qualified for California ATD, Aid to the Totally Disabled, with a diagnosis of borderline schizophrenia. She had gotten help from a vaguely Christian commune in Berkeley, to which she contributed her monthly welfare check. Stone had wanted to organize a rescue mission and get her into a hospital where she could get real medical treatment for whatever was wrong with her, but Kimmie, who had now taken the name Bethany, would have none of it. It was Laura who had finally convinced him to let go. "She has a roof over her head and she's safe," said his wife. "We need to accept that it's enough." Soon, he would find out if his wife had gotten it right.

For all his experience with rifles and hand guns, the shooter had never travelled with a firearm before. As he made his way to the ticket counter he tried to affect a casual stroll in spite of his limp, hoping he would project an image of calm.

Nervousness was the prime emotion that the TSA spotters roaming the terminal were trained to recognize. When he reached the counter he produced a smile for the ticket agent, a no-nonsense Asian woman in her early thirties. He displayed the boarding pass he had printed out and then, after putting his bag on the scale and letting go of it, said the magic words. "I have an unloaded firearm to declare."

He had expected some sort of reaction – raised eyebrows at the least – but she had merely reached into a drawer underneath the counter, pulled out a small orange tag and instructed him to print his name and address on it and sign underneath a paragraph that stated the firearm was in a locked, hard container and not loaded. That done, she had opened his bag, tied the tag to the handle of the gun case, checked to verify that the case was in fact locked and asked to see the keys, which he was carrying in is pocket.

"You're good to go," she said with a professional smile. "Have a good flight."

That was the moment when he was finally able to relax. This was nothing more than a business trip. That was the way to look at it. And it was a type of business in which he was well schooled.

He actually dozed on the flight, which landed at San Francisco International Airport just a few minutes after eleven a.m., right on schedule. He made good time down I-99 in his blue rental Chevy, and arrived at the outer limits of Fresno with plenty of time to grab a cheeseburger at an air conditioned eatery just off the freeway. He was wearing his desert camo gear by that time, but no one seemed to notice. He paid in cash and left a good tip for the waitress, who looked to him like she was too old to be waiting tables. Then, after stopping at the bathroom to pee, he climbed back into the rental and drove over to the town of Sanger, where the new IRS complex was located. He parked at the base of a large hill that overlooked the half dozen modern, two-story buildings, where literally thousands of transactions were processed every minute. He would have preferred a site closer to Detroit, but here his chances of a successful mission were much higher.

He followed a deer trail up the hill with some difficulty, in spite of the fact that he worked out regularly and led simulated combat missions once a month like clockwork. He could not fully attribute the hesitancy in his gait to the small piece of shrapnel lodged in his left thigh. Was it the nature of the task at hand? He chided himself. This was no time to lose his nerve.

He reached the crest of the hill and abandoned the trail, low crawling to a position where he could see the sprawling complex from which his target – a randomly chosen stranger – would emerge into the parking lot. It wasn't exactly fair, but it was the fairest solution he could find, and somebody had to pay. From his small day pack he removed and assembled his rifle, a miracle of hypervelocity design at 5.25 pounds, with a flat trajectory that was reliable for a shock-and-drop shot at 500 yards. Locked and loaded, he assumed the familiar prone position and waited. He had determined that the target would be the first individual to exit from the main door after 4:30 p.m.

He didn't know how he would feel after he had completed this mission, or what his next move would be. If it felt right, he would drive north, ditching components of his weapon here and there, but only after wiping off any finger prints and giving each component a solid spray of ERASE to neutralize any DNA. Then, he would continue north to the airport and catch the redeye home. If it felt wrong, well, he didn't think it was going to feel wrong. And if it did, he would do what he needed to do.

Stone's plane touched down just before noon, and by one thirty he had found the restaurant café where he was to meet his daughter at two: Café Gratitude, an artfully rundown spot in what was known in Berkeley as the Gourmet Ghetto. Even in khakis and a polo shirt, Stone felt over-dressed in this "ghetto." He walked over to the famous Telegraph Avenue, where he bought a T-shirt that didn't look too ridiculous from a street vendor and a pair of canvas sneakers. There were enough barriers between him and Kimmie. He didn't want to make his clothes yet another.

At one forty-five he was back in front of Café Gratitude. He knew there was a good chance she simply wouldn't show up, and then he would have to face the possibility of leaving the country, most likely forever, without having said good bye. Of course, the reality was that Kimmie had said good bye to him years ago, and to Laura as well. It was almost as if they didn't exist for her. Still, he wanted to see her one last time.

Kimmie arrived on time, a miracle considering how she had acted during their last days of communication. When their eyes met, she nodded her head in recognition, as though he were a co-worker or someone she knew from riding the same train to work every day. With that gesture she made it clear that they were not going to embrace, or even touch.

"Hi, Dad," she said in the soft, flutey voice he remembered so well. It sounded strange coming from this woman who was almost forty, with too many wrinkles for her age. He didn't really know how much time she had spent on the streets, on the edge of homelessness, but her skin had suffered. The clothes she was wearing today, a long, straight skirt and a black, long sleeved T-shirt, looked like they had come from a thrift store.

"I don't even know what to call you," said Stone.

"My name is Bethany."

"I guess I did know that," said Stone. "Let's go inside, Beth."

The décor was intentionally rustic, and the waitresses were dressed in the same style as Kimmie, a throw-back to the 'sixties but without the bright colors. Café Gratitude served only raw vegetables and vegan baked goods. Stone realized he had hoped for a glass of wine. He settled for chamomile tea and a slice of carrot cake. The forty-year-old woman who was his daughter ordered a drink called *I am Pure.*

"Are you out here for business?" she asked.

"No. I came to see you."

She nodded. "Your timing was good. I'm leaving next week."

"You mean you're moving?"

"It's an extended retreat."

"Where?"

"In the wilderness."

"I hope you're not going alone," said Stone, unable to reign in his parental habits, even after all these years.

"I won't be alone," she replied.

They sat in uncomfortable silence until the waitress returned and set the carrot cake between them, along with two forks. Kimmie gently pushed the plate towards Stone. "I can't handle sugar," she said.

Stone took a couple of perfunctory bites. Why was he here? What had he expected? He had certainly *not* expected her to fly into his arms and beg forgiveness for being such a bad daughter, one who had even declined to attend her own mother's funeral. But she was so aloof!

"I'm thinking of going away myself," he said.

"To France?"

"I'm not sure." Stone now realized why he was there. It was not just that he wanted to see her one last time. He wanted to tell her what he had engineered. He wanted her just for one hour to see things his way, to understand that he had found a goal worthy of a man's life. But he dare not share his plans, for her own safety. Beyond that, Kimmie, now Beth, was not a woman who could be trusted. Better to stick to the script.

"Beth, if my plane crashes, which it won't, but.... Listen, there will always be money for you. Just go to Numerica. Even if I'm not there."

"I don't need money."

"You never know. You might need new socks one of these days," he said, forcing a smile to which he received no response.

"I'm sorry Mom was taken from you," she said out of the blue. "I know how hard that must have been."

Stone thought, *What has happened to my daughter?* Once again, she was talking to him almost like a stranger, some casual acquaintance who had endured a sad event. He said, "I do miss her." It sounded inane, but he could find no better words.

She had finished her weird drink, and his teapot was empty. Stone realized that whatever happened in the weeks to come, neither his actions nor their consequences would touch her, any more than anything he said or did right now.

He put a twenty dollar bill on the table, more than enough to cover the bill, and then they both stood up without saying a word and walked out into the sunlight. Stone noticed for the first time that Kimmie had a few strands of gray in her hair. For some reason, this brought tears to his eyes.

"It's okay, Dad. Everything is okay. I'll call you when I get back. I promise."

That was it. She walked away and Stone went back to his rental car. He had done everything he could.

A day of empty hours lay ahead, and on impulse, when he reached the freeway on ramp he headed north. He could be in the Napa Valley in less than an hour, the wine country where he and Laura and little Kimmie had spent several vacations before they could afford the trips to France. Soon he was on the old highway, with turn-offs every couple of miles leading to tasting rooms where you could sip and buy some of the best wine in the world. He wasn't in the mood for alcohol, but when he saw the sign for Laura's Winery he took the turn off. Then it struck him that there couldn't be a Laura's Winery. That was crazy. He drove a little farther and saw that he was approaching the tasting room of Lumara's Winery. He pulled into the small parking lot in a state of panic. *I only misread a sign*, he told himself. *Anybody could do that*. But how many other mistakes had he made? Had he typed in the names on Hawthorne's list correctly? Had he fucked up logging into TOR and created a path to his identity?

Thank goodness April 15 had arrived. Hawthorne had scheduled a major speech and, according to Politico, the Fair Taxation Act would be introduced tomorrow. It was the beginning of the end. He would quietly sell the house, set up a trust for Kimmie, get his body into better shape. Then, one night instead of going to bed, he would drive to Detroit Metro with Kat and get on a plane to Rome. Everything was going to be okay.

Stone got out of his car and went into the dim, somewhat cramped tasting room. There was a small bar with stools. The walls were lined with bottles of wine. Had he been on vacation, he probably would have bought a couple and had them shipped home, but those days were over – at least until he was safe in Italy – *if* he made it. Instead of making any purchases, he browsed the collection for a few nostalgic moments and then he headed back to his hotel for a late check-in.

Stone awoke from a confused nightmare to the sound of an alarm buzzing on the nightstand next to his oversized hotel bed. He blinked the alarm into focus. Its glowing numerals told him it was a little after four a.m. That couldn't be right. He had set it to go off at six. For a frightening moment it seemed that the confusion of the dream had leaked into reality. He was losing control. Then, after a long moment, he realized that the source of the sound wasn't the alarm clock, but an incoming call on his business iPhone. A call from an unknown number.

He hesitated a moment, then tapped the phone to accept the call.

"Stone? It's Hawthorne. What the fuck is going on?"

Stone sat up, instantly clear-headed. "This isn't a secure line."

"I'm on a burner phone."

"That doesn't matter. If –"

"Have you seen the news?"

"Sam, it's four a.m. out here."

"Well, I suggest you get your ass out of bed and turn on CNN. You're a wacko Stone. I wish to Christ we'd never made a deal, but we did and I'm not going to rat you out."

Stone struggled to understand what was going on. Of course Hawthorne wouldn't expose him. There was enough information on the recording Stone had made of their initial conversation to sink Hawthorne's ship in ten minutes. But why was he calling? Stone picked up the remote with his free hand and turned on the TV.

"What exactly am I looking for?" he asked.

"An alibi, for starters." With that, Hawthorne broke the connection.

Stone flipped on the lights and clicked through the unfamiliar channels until he found CNN. After three commercials and a story about yet another devastating tornado in Oklahoma, he saw why Hawthorne had called. CNN was now broadcasting a police artist's sketch that could have easily been Stone himself. The caption read

IRS MURDER SUSPECT.

The sketch was replaced by footage of the IRS facility in Fresno, California, where one of the agents who worked there had been shot in the late afternoon, apparently the random victim of a sniper with a grudge against the agency. Shortly after the shooting, two hikers had encountered a man wearing desert fatigues with a small pack. At this point in time, the man in fatigues, who apparently bore a remarkable resemblance to Stone, was a "person of interest."

Stone silenced the television with a click of the remote. *Hawthorne thinks I was the shooter!* Sitting on the edge of the bed, he buried his face in his hands and contemplated the avalanche of problems this would create. The deal with Hawthorne was dead, and the congressman was furious – an enemy now, and a formidable one at that. He might even risk revealing their recorded conversations proactively, fingering Stone as a terrorist and saying that he was playing along to get more information before going to the FBI or whoever it was that had jurisdiction in terrorism cases.

Terrorism cases. The situation was rapidly spinning out of control. Operating within the system was no longer an option. That flanking maneuver, as he saw it, would have to be replaced by a frontal attack. A terrorist attack.

Meet our demands and we'll unlock your system. We'll give you the source code so you can see how we did it. Even if we lie, your own experts can find ways to ransom-proof your data. We won't be able to come back again and again. It was still a deal that reasonable men could buy into. But not if it was perceived as being offered by some paramilitary extremist.

Stone struggled to think clearly. He had booked a mid-morning flight back to Detroit. Should he risk going to the airport? Could he get through airport security? The image of his look-alike was everywhere. There was a high probability he would be detained. Or was there? The fact was, thousands of upper middle class white guys about his height and weight with blue eyes and graying hair passed through San Francisco International every day. Why should he be singled out? And so what if they question him? The facts were on his side. Worst case, they detained him, he missed his flight and had to book another.

Was that really the worst case? Stone made himself a cup of instant coffee from the hotel machine . It would taste awful, but it would give him some much-needed caffeine. He sat back on the edge of the bed, plastic cup in hand.

Right now, he was safe. However, if he became linked to the murder of an IRS agent, even as a remote and unlikely suspect, everything would change. His long-term friendship with Herb, a man who killed himself because of IRS problems, would surface. So would his relationship with Kat, a data security expert. With that kind of information floating around, he could not risk a direct cyber attack while continuing to live his daily life as Mathew Stone, manufacturing executive. The U.S. government had enormous resources, and although its investigative agents were notorious for bungling important cases, time and numbers were on their side. They might not be able to trace a hack back to him through the tangled digital paths of the Internet, but they could find him the old fashioned way. He had means and motive, which meant that before he started knocking out administrative districts he would have to go underground.

He *could* go underground right now. He could rent a second car under his new identity, drive east as far from California as he could and hope the clerk at the motel where he finally landed hadn't seen the police sketch on the news. He would need some rest after a marathon like that, but within thirty-six hours he could be on a plane to Rome, where Kat would be waiting for him. Or maybe it would be wise to delay flying for a few days until the image of his face had faded from the memories of the airport security cadres.

He didn't like this underground option. There were too many loose ends he would leave behind, not to mention the two million dollars the sale of his house would bring. Besides that, he was innocent, and having to run because of a crime he didn't commit pissed him off. It was another example of how America was turning into a police state. He was not going to let himself be pushed around just because he happened to look a little like some criminal. He would go to the airport and act normal. If questioned, he would tell the truth. There was nothing incriminating in his luggage, no weapon, no map of Fresno, no cache of extremist literature. Well, the presence of a false passport in his carry-on could be a problem. There was no easy way to explain that away. But it was well concealed under a false bottom panel, and they would have to rip his luggage apart to find it. He was almost certain they wouldn't do that. Not without cause.

Stone quickly showered and dressed in the polo shirt and khakis he had worn on the flight out of Detroit. The sky through the window was a dull blue. His flight was hours away. On impulse, he changed into the running gear he always brought with him when he travelled. He had plenty of time for a run, and running might help clear his head. Beyond that, he had no wish to hang around San Francisco International any longer than necessary.

He ran from his hotel down to the harbor and then along the water past bars and restaurants, which soon gave way to a grassy park. He was alone in the cold air at first, but as the sun rose he began to encounter other runners. He couldn't shake the thought that one of them would spot him and call the police, but those who were not oblivious to him simply nodded and smiled. On the way back he stopped at an espresso café for a muffin and more coffee, which to his surprise calmed him down a little. Then he returned to the hotel, showered for a second time and packed.

Driving down 101 to the airport and reviewing his movements on Saturday, he realized that if questioned, it might not be all that easy to substantiate the truth of his story. He had arrived a little after noon, and was behind the wheel of his rental car by twelve thirty. Eight hours later, he had checked into his hotel. But there was no record of how he had spent those hours. He hadn't used his credit card all day. The one person who could identify him, his daughter, had disappeared into the wilderness and wouldn't be easy to find. Stone wasn't sure how far away the town of Fresno was, but he was pretty sure that you could drive down there, ambush an IRS agent and get back to San Francisco by eight-thirty.

There was another issue he hadn't thought of. Would the weaponized iPhone stand up to scrutiny? It was supposed to look and work like an ordinary iPhone, and it had gotten through security once already, but he knew that the circuit board inside it had been extensively modified and those modifications would be obvious to anyone with the right technical background.

He dropped off his car at the Hertz parking lot, grateful for the automated systems that involved no human interaction. Then he took the shuttle to the terminal and checked in at a kiosk, again with no human interaction. It was time to face security.

He didn't even make it to the line. The two men who approached him were polite but firm, and probably armed. He had no choice but to obey their instructions.

Ginny had just sat down to a low-carb breakfast of scrambled eggs and bacon when she heard the familiar rhythmic knock on the door. It was Mark. She felt an instant flash of desire between her thighs, along with a pang of guilt. It still didn't feel quite right to be sleeping with a man she wasn't married to. If her sister found out she would never hear the end of it. As a matter of fact, after more than two months no one knew, and that also troubled her a little. Maybe she was thinking too much like a high school girl, but she didn't want a relationship that was only about sex.

It's not only about sex, she told herself as she went to the door, pulling her robe around her a little more tightly, a sense of foreboding growing in her chest. They weren't exactly in love, but they cared about one another. And unlike Herb, he did share what was on his mind, the physical problems of a tree surgeon approaching sixty, the constant practical challenges he faced as the leader of the Blackhawks, his anger at the government. That anger was actually a little scary. She liked to feel she was a calming influence in his life.

The man she opened the door to receive was anything but calm. Mark looked haggard, with dark circles under his eyes, as though he had been up all night. He was carrying a small suitcase. What was up?

"Come in," she said, closing the door behind him and hugging him tightly. His body felt stiff and unresponsive.

She took his hand and led him towards the kitchen. "Do you want some coffee? You look like you need *something*. A little brandy? What's wrong, Mark?"

"I'd like some coffee," he said, taking a chair at the kitchen table where her food sat uneaten.

"Are you hungry? Do you want some breakfast?"

"I'm fine," he said, although it was obvious he was anything but fine.

She made a quick pot of fresh coffee and poured him a mug, black and a little stronger than she preferred. Then she sat down opposite and put on what she thought of as her serious face.

"Talk to me," she said.

He took a sip of coffee and set the mug down gently. "I've done something, Ginny."

He didn't have to say what. She already knew. She had known last night when she watched the news, although she had tried to convince herself she was just inventing reasons to be nervous.

"Some deeds cannot be forgiven," he said. "What they did to Herb is one of those deeds. Ginny, as a man and as a patriot I couldn't let that stand. They had to pay. And last night, flying home on the plane, I realized I had to own up to what I did. Anything less would be cowardice."

Ginny burst into tears. Where did all these ideas about honor and cowardice come from? She had always admired men who stood up for what they believed in, but it could be so stupid! And now she was going to lose Mark before they even really got started.

She looked at him through her tears. "You shot him."

He nodded.

"You didn't have to do that."

"Yes I did."

She reached across the table and grabbed his hands.

"I'm on my way to the police station, Ginny. I just wanted to say good bye."

Her thoughts flew in a dozen directions. Would they just arrest him then and there? What about bail? She didn't know anything about how these things worked. Did he need some clean clothes?

"Shouldn't you get a lawyer?"

"I did what I had to do and I'm willing to accept the consequences. If I need a lawyer I can get one."

He stood up and walked around the table to embrace her. "I'll miss you." She spoke the words softly, almost in a whisper.

He loosened his hold but she pulled him back.

"Just promise me one thing," she said.

"If I can."

"Don't crash your car into a tree on the way to the police station."

Stone wasn't claustrophobic, but the small room with its white walls and harsh fluorescent lighting was starting to get on his nerves. He knew from his army training years ago that letting captives stew in their own juice for awhile before an interrogation was a standard tactic. That didn't mean he had to like it.

He was sitting on a metal chair on one side of a utilitarian table with a white plastic top stained with pale rings from coffee cups. The two identical chairs on the opposite side of the table had now been empty for almost two hours. His captors – that's how he thought of them – had taken both his carry-on and his phone before they parked him in this room. That was the real worry. If they didn't find the passport, he would be free to go pretty soon.

If they did, it was a different story. He would be in jail for at least a couple of days, and after that he would have a whole new set of problems to deal with, including a probable prison term. He slammed his fist on the table in frustration.

Fifteen minutes later, the hold room's flimsy door opened and one his captors appeared, a young man in his thirties who had maintained an air of cool professionalism during the initial questioning.

"You're free to go, Mr. Stone," he said. "I apologize for the inconvenience."

Stone did his best to disguise the wave of elation that flowed through him. "You're just doing your job," he said, choosing words that would help this TSA agent feel Stone was on his side. *Not so long ago, I would have meant it*, he thought. "Where do I get my bag and my phone?"

"They're here." The agent held the door open for him. His carry-on was right outside the door, with the weaponized phone sitting on the zipper between the two hand grips. Stone wondered whether a handshake was appropriate and decided against it. He also wondered why he was being released, but he knew if he asked he wouldn't get an answer. These agents were like cops. Withholding information was an instinct.

"Have a safe trip," said the agent with a perfunctory smile.

"Thanks," said Stone. In fact, nothing about this airport felt safe to him now.

He walked down a makeshift corridor lined with doors identical to the one he had just exited until he reached the main terminal hall, where he was once again surrounded by the familiar sights and sounds of a busy airport. In less than minute, he passed one of the ubiquitous television monitors mounted everywhere on the airport walls and learned why he had been summarily released. The shooter had turned himself in. It was Stetson, the Blackhawk commander. The screen showed a head shot in which he was wearing a black beret. The crawl under the photo read

Former Vietnam hero has no regrets, bail ruled out.

There but for fortune go I, thought Stone. How many nights had he drifted off to sleep with thoughts of pulling the trigger on agent Chan in his mind? The morning light of reason had held him back, and now he was in a position of much greater power than he ever imagined. The time had come to wield that power.

There was only one way to understand the events of the last few hours. They were a warning, a reminder of how easily things could go wrong. If he wanted to launch an alternate plan - if he wanted to be *sure* the virus was going to be activated - he had to take immediate action. The mistaken identity fiasco was bad enough. Who knew what other obstacles fate would put in his path?

Stone assessed his situation. He was in a secure part of the terminal, one out of thousands of anonymous travelers who would pass through the airport in the next few hours. More importantly, no one was looking for him, at least for now. He couldn't be sure how long that would last. For all he knew, Hawthorne was plotting revenge at the very moment. That was irrational to say the least. Stone had fulfilled his end of the bargain to the letter, and he certainly couldn't help it if a man who physically resembled him decided to take the law into his own hands. But none of that mattered. Hawthorne felt Stone had dragged him into a confrontation with the IRS that was now on shaky ground, and he was pissed. This was a serious problem. If he wanted to get at Stone, he would find a way. The congressman was deceptively clever.

Stone looked around for a place where he could sit down. All he had to do was to log onto the Internet using the weaponized phone's TOR app and launch an attack. Afterward he could re-book his return flight. He would have to go back out to the unsecured part of the airport where the ticket counters were, and then pass through security a second time. He wasn't worried. His carry-on had been inspected multiple times already. The chances of anyone finding the hidden passport this time around were very low, and if they did, it would be too late to stop the attack he had initiated.

Stone hesitated as he passed a crowded restaurant bar. It was past two in the afternoon, and his stomach told him he should eat. He moved on until he found a Starbucks, where he ordered what amounted to a coffee-flavored milk shake. Then he reached into the inside pocket of his jacket where he kept the weaponized iPhone – next to his heart. Anyone observing him would see a senior executive checking his email before he finished his coffee and headed to his gate. Not a terrorist.

Terrorist. One who employs the systematic use of terror, especially as a means of coercion. He had looked it up in an online dictionary last night. He wasn't sure he fit the definition, but he was sure as Hell going to scare the shit out of some very important people in the U.S. government today. It felt good. And, as Kat had said a while back, those government types were the real terrorists. They were the ones who sent the intimidating letters, broke into people's bank accounts, confiscated their money, threatened them with jail.. and sometimes drove them to suicide. Now it was going to be their turn to know what it was like to live in fear.

He had chosen the Delaware/Maryland district as his target because of its proximity to D.C. He had considered taking out Michigan, and therefore the office that had put Herb on the path to suicide, but he was concerned that an attack on Michigan might somehow point investigators in his direction. He needed to minimize that risk if he was going to see this through to the end. He would be powerless behind bars.

Stone picked up the weaponized iPhone and tapped the drum icon. A familiar United States map appeared, the states color-coded like a child's puzzle, but modified slightly to reflect the IRS districts, of which there were thirty-three, not forty-eight. Spreading his thumb and forefinger apart on the glass, he zoomed in on Maryland. Again, he tapped, and a message appeared.

Do you want to attack the Delaware Maryland Region?

Did he indeed? There would be no turning back once he tapped the **ATTACK** button. And he was not only putting himself at risk, but Kat as well. He knew that no matter how much thinking and preparation had gone into this decision, things would be different once he tapped the button. It would be like the day Laura died. He knew it was coming, but when it really happened, everything changed. Forever. This time, though, the change couldn't happen soon enough.

He tapped the button.

Now the clock was ticking. According to the drummer, the first take-down could take several hours, but after that when he pressed the button the effect would be almost instantaneous. Restoration, when the time came, would also take only a few seconds.

For now he needed to vanish. He could continue the attacks from anywhere in the world where the Internet was available, and he believed that included plenty of small villages in southern Italy. When he got what he wanted – an executive order was his new goal – he would restore all the encrypted files and life would go on for the IRS as if nothing had happened so long as its agents continued to behave. With the internet it would be easy to keep an eye out for abuses, and they would be met with punishment. That was to be his new life's work.

He would compose a message communicating his demands on his redeye flight and send it in the morning to the private cell phone whose number he had obtained through a TOR site for a mere thousand dollars. But before thinking about any of that, he needed to communicate with Kat. She wasn't safe under these new conditions, and the sooner she got on a plane, the lower her risk. She might balk, but he would insist, and beg if necessary. The thought of her spending ten or twenty years in prison was intolerable, and that was now a real possibility.

Kat had just arrived back at the cottage after a quick shopping trip to Ralph's for wine and a large carton of spaghetti bolonese when her iPhone hummed with the unique sound of the encrypted voice app. It could only be Matt. She dug the phone out of her jeans pocket, sure that something had gone wrong.

"It's time to go. Right now." She could hear the strain in his voice through the distortion imposed by the app. "Don't take more than a few hours, and only use your new identity from now on." She glanced over at the book shelf where the Euros, credit cards, passport and other papers that documented her false identity were stored in one of those innocuous-looking accordion folders you could buy in any stationery store.

She felt the floor swaying under her, like it felt when one of her old panic attacks was on its way. "What happened? Where are you."

"Still in California. I had to do an emergency launch."

"Oh my God! Are you all right?"

"I'm fine. And if all goes well I'll join you in a week or less where we agreed. I can't wait to see you."

She could tell he was trying to calm her down, and it was working. "I guess I should hang up. I need to sterilize this place."

"It wouldn't hurt. Just don't take too long." She stared at the phone's small screen, wishing they were on Skype so she could see his face.

"Matt, there's one other thing," she said. "I love you." As she spoke, she realized she had never said these words to anyone outside her family in her entire life.

"I love you too." With that, the line went dead.

She stuck the phone back in her pocket and looked around the cottage that had been her first real home since high school. Sadness welled up in her chest, but also a sense of power. She could do this. They had made a plan, and now she was ready to execute it. At top speed.

Kat added a few more changes of socks and underwear to the carry-on she had pre-packed. Then she went online and used her new identity to book a round trip to Rome, which was less suspicious than a one-way ticket. She glanced at her watch. Two fifteen. In about six hours she would be in the air, probably before anyone was even chasing her, maybe even before her and Matt's exploit had even been discovered.

She wasn't sure why Matt wasn't getting on a plane tonight from San Francisco. Maybe he wanted to be here when the first districts went down, even though it wouldn't exactly be a public event he could celebrate. Maybe he just wanted to come back to Michigan and say good-bye to the place where he grew up. Why not? It was safe enough. The chances that anyone could trace the exploit back to him were zero. Well, almost zero.

Elisa Parker sat in her cubicle at the IRS office in Baltimore full of Wednesday morning energy. It was hump day – not that she didn't like her job. Some of her friends thought working for the government's most despised agency was a strange career choice, but they didn't understand how much freedom and responsibility they gave you. Her decisions affected people's lives, and she took pride in the way she balanced compliance with compassion in her audits. Instead of crushing tax payers who had gotten behind, she helped them get back on their feet. But when they cheated, she made them pay.

There was another reason for choosing the IRS which she normally didn't mention. It was a place where being a black woman could actually be an advantage. It certainly didn't hold you back.

Sipping from a cup of chamomile tea, and particularly happy to have arrived in the office before her group manager, she booted up her computer and typed in the social security number of her first client of the day. The screen displayed an error message:

NO CORRESPONDING FILE

She tried again, this time watching her fingers tap the numbers to make sure she didn't make a mistake. Again, the machine responded:

NO CORRESPONDING FILE

This was not a common occurrence, but it had happened before. She slid the client's thick file into the middle section of her old-fashioned wire mesh in-and-out box, and set to work on the next case.

Again, her computer wouldn't cooperate. She tried a third case with yet again the same result. Seemingly blocked, she got up from her desk and walked towards her boss's glass-walled office, where the light was now on, indicating she had arrived.

Elisa tapped on the door and stuck her head in. Her group manager, Loretta Washington, was in the process of hanging her coat on the coat hanger. She was a sturdy, dark-skinned woman who carried what Elisa guessed to be at least a hundred and sixty pounds with relative grace. "I know you just got here," she said, "but do you know if the network's down?"

"I haven't heard, but as you so perceptively noted, I just got here. And without my coffee, I don't know up from down."

"You sure you don't want to try some of my chamomile tea this morning?"

"With no caffeine? No thanks."

"It soothes your nerves."

Washington turned to face her. "Next thing, you're going to want to put me on a diet." She sat down behind her desk and clasped her hands together. "What's the problem, Elisa?" she said, sighing. "I might as well dive right in."

"I can't call up any files. It just says "no corresponding file."

At that moment there was a tap on the door. It was one of the new members of the group, a young white guy named Clark. "Is there a problem with the network?" he asked.

"Hey, it's not just me," said Parker.

"I'll call IT and let you know what's up," said Washington, picking up the phone as she spoke.

Half an hour later, Washington emerged from her office and called an impromptu group meeting.

"As you may have noticed, our network is down, and IT tells me the fix is going to take the rest of the day at minimum. So if you can move any interviews to today to put the time to good use, please do so. If you've been looking for that free moment to catch up on training, we haven't lost our internet connection, so now's the time. I'll have an update at three o'clock. We may be looking at a one or two day furlough."

She smiled sympathetically at the groans. "Folks, it's out of my hands. We have computer problems all the time. I'm sure everything's going to be okay."

Parker was not among the groaners. As a single mom with a seven-year-old, she welcomed a little extra time to get things done around her apartment. But there was something in her group manager's tone of voice which made wonder if everything was really going to be okay.

V.

"I can't have you committing a crime

in front of my eyes."

Secretary of the Treasury Stanton Briggs was seated in the breakfast room of his spacious Bethesda mansion sipping a glass of fresh-squeezed orange juice and awaiting his poached egg on toast when the cell phone sitting next to his knife and fork unexpectedly buzzed. He carried the damned thing around with him everywhere. It was a necessary part of life in Washington now, but it also made endless interruptions a part of that life. The text message was from an unknown number, and that was ominous. So was the threat it carried.

> The Delaware Maryland district of the IRS has been incapacitated until further notice. This is only the beginning. Denver is next.
>
> The 1040 Strike Force

Was it possible? No one who had his private number would play a prank like this. He immediately linked to the department's online phone directory to find out who was in charge at the Maryland/Delaware district, and called the direct line to confirm that there was a problem. He had learned over the years that people at the higher levels of Washington bureaucracies rarely knew what was going on in the trenches, and whenever there was trouble he always sought information from the people who really did the work.

The news was not good. The computers over there were working, but all the files in the district were inaccessible. It was as though the memory banks had been wiped clean. Or, if the files were still there, no one could find them. At times like this, he felt a visceral hatred of computers. In the old days of paper files, this could never have happened. One file missing here or there, sure. But shelf after shelf after shelf? The only thing that could destroy all the files in a district was a genuine disaster – a fire or something like that – and even then you could go look at the smoking ruins and *see* what had happened. These data centers were like giant black boxes with no windows, and one of them had just turned into a black hole.

He put down the phone and took a few bites of his egg, which had cooled too much to be appetizing. He reconciled himself to a no-protein breakfast and thought about his next move while he consumed two thin slices of toast. If hackers had truly penetrated the IRS's defenses, the situation was grave. Anyone who read the Wall Street Journal on a regular basis knew how vulnerable today's computer systems had become, in both the public and private sector. And if this were the work of a nation state... he didn't even want to go there.

Briggs picked up the phone and called the private number of Charles Branson. An ex-department head known for his thoroughness and obsession with success, he was a cowboy of sorts. He played fast an loose with the government's money as well as its rules, but if anyone could deliver quick results in a situation like this, it was Branson.

The computer expert cum investigator picked up on the second ring.

"To what do I owe the honor of a seven a.m. telephone call, Mr. Secretary?"

Briggs outlined the situation, and as he spoke its seriousness began to sink in. Something like this could paralyze the government and send the economy into an instant tailspin. He tried to console himself with the thought that the IRS people surely had back-up systems for contingencies like this. Still, the department would take a significant credibility hit if things dragged on very long. So would he – and he wasn't ready to resign. What in Hell was the 1040 Strike Force?

He told Branson to get a handle on what was going on ASAP and schedule a late morning briefing.

"Charles," he said. "I want this cleaned up quickly and quietly. We have to keep the Department of the Treasury healthy. Don't forget, it is the tit from which you suck."

Christ, thought Briggs as he set the phone down. *It's the tit from which we all suck.* He didn't want to think about what could happen f this exploit wasn't quickly contained, but that was his job. He went upstairs to his home office and found a pad of yellow lined paper and a pen to make some notes about potential scenarios and outcomes. His hands had begun to tremble.

This must be what death is like, thought Stone as he walked through the house that had been his for some twenty-five years, coffee cup in hand. His footsteps seemed to echo as he crossed the kitchen, as though the furniture had already been carted away, which it would be at some point in time - by total strangers. Kimmie would never come back here. He wasn't even sure his lawyers would be able to track her down to let her know that she was a millionaire. She was happy, he told himself, if in her own strange way, and that was what mattered.

He sat down on the leather couch in the living room, clean and tidied by the maid he had kept on after Laura's death. He could still remember the day they bought that couch, and the days they had bought most of the other pieces of furniture in the room. Those purchases had always been a special occasion for Laura, even when there was enough money to buy expensive antiques on a whim.

He sighed. A new life awaited him. The last battle of this one was almost over. Briggs was in possession of the first communication. He had to be made to cave – and fast. Stone took out the weaponized iPhone, called up the map, and zapped Denver and then Omaha for good measure. Mid-morning he would hit another two districts and then send over his terms. By then, the sense of panic would be building.

He tapped out a quick message to Stanton Briggs.

Atlanta is next.

For now, Briggs could stew a little.

It was time for Stone to face the day. The plan was simple. He was going to buy a Lamborghini – for cash. At least that was the story he would be broadcasting. He was feeling a little down in the dumps, he thought a fancy new car would cheer him up, he could afford it, so why not? Cotter, his VP of engineering, would hear this story at the nine o'clock engineering budget review meeting. So would Bruder, his CFO, and at least a dozen other employees at various levels. At ten thirty he would duck out of the building and drive over to the dealership in Troy to test drive the vehicle he had in mind, a bright red Venetor Roadster. The purchase of this extremely expensive car was a cover – an excuse to explain large cash withdrawals from half a dozen accounts, money which he would in fact invest in Bitcoins. He had learned that they were always a somewhat risky buy, but even if the value of his holdings dropped ten or fifteen percent over the next few days he would have more than enough money to cover several years in a southern Italian town. The travel cash he and Kat had stowed wouldn't last more than two months.

Along with his goal of stashing money outside of normal banking channels, he wanted to create the impression, just for a day or two, that his sudden disappearance might involve foul play – a kidnapping, or worse. He had put down a thousand dollars at the dealership as a good-faith gesture in exchange for their promise to hold the car for him. Who would do that and then skip town? It was far better, he reasoned, to have the cops looking for a missing person than a fugitive. For starters, it meant they wouldn't be pouring over airport surveillance videos looking for him – at least not for awhile.

His plan was solid. He would drive to the nearby town of Troy were there was a cluster of car dealerships just off Highway 75. He would park his Crossfire inconspicuously on a side street a few blocks away and then go buy a cheap vehicle for cash, using his new identity. Then he would drive back to the Crossfire, collect his baggage and drive to the airport.

Stone stood up and walked back into the kitchen to rinse out his coffee cup and put it in the dishwasher, as though he would ever drink out of that cup again. Then he made sure the front door was locked, went into the garage and climbed into his Crossfire for the drive to work. In the driveway, he realized that he still hadn't purchased his ticket. He told himself it was okay. He could do it on his cell phone at Kat's old café. Once he was in Italy, absent-mindedness wouldn't matter. But for now he had to focus. He didn't want to show up at the airport and find the flight he wanted full.

One more day to get through.

Fired up by Treasury Secretary Briggs' early morning call, Charles Branson pushed open the conference room door at 1500 Pennsylvania Avenue with the sense of purpose and single mindedness that had driven him his whole career. Short and stocky, with sandy hair trimmed in an old-style military crew cut, his moves were those of a rugby player a little too old to take the field, but fit and ready nonetheless. In his early days, he had been known as La Machine for the long hours he put in as an IRS coder, team leader and eventually department head. Later, as a high-level trouble shooter for the entire Treasury Department, he had earned another nickname: Death Wish, after the title of the Charles *Bronson* movie where Bronson took the law into his own hands when he felt like it. In college Branson had majored in computer science, but minored in history, and he had been deeply influenced by Machiavelli. His favorite quote from The Prince was, "It is better to be feared than loved."

The five participants in the hastily called meeting were already seated at the dark, oval-shaped table. It was an all-male team and, as usual, represented an alphabet soup of titles. Two wore dark suits and ties: Ken Bourne, recently demoted Chief Information Officer, universally known as the CIO, and Branson's designated POC or point-of-contact for incidents like this, and Frank Townsend, whose title was SAISO, Senior Agency Information Security Officer. Two others, presumably with technical expertise in the matter at hand, were dressed in khakis and blue button-down shirts, and one - the youngest - had showed up in jeans and a hoody. He was probably the only one who would tell him the truth. As always, Branson mentally sorted the group into three mental columns: friends, enemies, and neutrals. Today, it was all neutrals.

"What do we have so far?" he said as he took his seat at the head of the table. Short, thick and balding, with a slight paunch, he was not an imposing figure. At fifty-five, he was already a grandfather, and beginning to look the part. His reputation was a different story.

Townsend, the taller of the two suits stood up and introduced himself to the others as head of the data security group. Branson had worked with Townsend before. He would put the best possible face on this disaster. That was at the top of his skill set. Managing a crisis was not.

"We've been hacked," said Townsend, wiping his brow with a white handkerchief. He was thin, in poor physical shape with a naturally pale complexion that was accentuated by his obvious nervousness. "The malware entered our network via an email message that was sent to a trusted primary contractor. It contained a malicious link and one of their people clicked on it. Since that individual's computer had access privileges to our internal network, the malware was able to enter and execute commands to modify the system."

"Do we have data at risk?" asked Branson.

"To our knowledge, no data has been stolen. And we would know."

"I asked you, is data at risk?" said Branson slowly enunciating each word in the question.

"That's... not the problem."

"So this time around, to the best of our knowledge the social security numbers of U.S. citizens and all the associated data are safe? Can I say that with confidence to Secretary Thornton, who might very well tell it to the President?"

Yes, sir," said Townsend, ignoring the veiled reference to earlier successful IRS hacks.

Branson smiled inwardly. Townsend outranked him, but still felt the need to tack a "sir" onto his response. *It is better to be feared.*

"Then, if our data is safe, what the Hell is the problem?"

"The data..." The head of the data security group paused, as though he couldn't bring himself to admit the problem. "The data is not available to us. When clerks ask for a file, the system doesn't respond. We can't assign payments. We can't send out routine notifications. Basically, we can't collect taxes. The good news is that the problem is confined to Delaware/Maryland – at least so far."

Branson recalled the hacker's chilling message, forwarded to him personally by the Secretary of the Treasury. *This is only the beginning.*

"And have we identified the problem?"

"It appears that all the files in the Delaware/Maryland district have been encrypted. It looks like a classic ransomware attack, but without the ransom request."

"All the files?" Branson hadn't expected this. Encryption required a substantial amount of computer power. He thought, *They're using our own servers against us.* It was the worst-case scenario.

"How could that happen?" he said, looking around the table, his gaze resting on each team member in turn. The kid in the hoody finally spoke.

"There's a service module that takes data requests from all our primary applications and passes them on to the central database. Then it retrieves the data and sends it back to the application that made the request in the first place. It looks like that module has been corrupted. When it retrieves the files, it encrypts them. And it's a bear of an encryption scheme. But like Mr. Townsend said, for now it's only affecting Delaware/Maryland."

The kid stood up and walked over to a white board on the rear wall of the conference room. "It's like this," he said, drawing a crude diagram with the infected service module in the center.

"How long will it take to crack the code?"

Townsend nodded to one of the men in khakis. He was in his late thirties, and like Townsend a bit pale. He looked like he had been up all night.

"Richard Hodes, Cryptology," he said, introducing himself to the group. "Unfortunately, this algorithm appears to come from an unknown source. It's not on the approved list, you might say. We don't have a skeleton key for it."

"Is that possible?" asked Branson, dreading the answer he was almost certain he would get. For years, as part of the War on Terror, the U.S. government had coerced technology companies to insert vulnerabilities and so-called "back doors" into their encryption products, leaving virtually any encrypted communication open to government inspection. In the post-Snowden era, this practice was common knowledge. It was inevitable that alternate encryption algorithms would appear on the black market.

"It's not only possible. It's happened." said the cryptologist.

"So what are our options?"

"The only approach we have is brute force. Basically, it amounts to trying one string of characters after another until we find the one that works."

"Thank you for that explanation," said Branson with more than a hint of sarcasm. "How long will a brute force approach take?"

"We don't have the internal resources to take that on. If we were running three or four Cray supercomputers in parallel it would take several hundred years," said Hodes.

Branson was stunned. "Obviously, that's unacceptable."

The cryptologist shrugged. He had obviously heard these words from higher-ups in the past.

"We're dealing with the laws of physics here."

"Can't we replace the corrupted module and do a re-start?"

"We think there's a high risk that replacing that module would crash the entire system."

"What about going straight to the central back-up and getting the files from there?"

Townsend shook his head. "The people who planned this knew what they were doing. They went after the one cog in the machine that can't be replaced."

"You mean to tell me..." Branson began, but then held his tongue. How could anyone with any brains sign off on a system this big with a single point of failure? That was engineering 101! But this was no time to debate design philosophy. He stood up and began to pace back and forth, hands behind his back, thinking. He had hoped there would be a technical fix. After more than a minute of silence, he surveyed the table.

"Do we know who we're dealing with?"

Townsend again shook his head. "We do not."

"Are we talking about state sponsored terrorism here? A prank? An inside job?"

Silence.

"Come on! We have to start somewhere. What kind of an organization would have the capabilities to do this?" Out of frustration he was asking questions he could answer himself. But it wasn't smart not to listen to your team, even the dim bulbs. Sometimes they had ideas you could use.

"Anybody could do it if they had an encryption algorithm like that." It was the kid. "To be honest, as a staff programmer, I can tell you that our security is a joke."

"That's a gross misstatement," said Townsend sharply.

Branson held up his hand to silence Townsend. It wasn't a misstatement. There had been numerous hacks in the past.

"Let's say you're right," said Branson to the programmer. "Our security isn't what it should be. Anybody could do it. Those were your words. But you're saying the encryption is a different story."

"That would take, like, a Russian genius."

"A Russian genius," Branson repeated.

"Russian, Israeli, Chinese, whatever. Somebody who gets off on cryptology."

"One person? Not a team?"

"Cryptologists are, um, secretive people?" said the programmer, responding to Branson's earlier sarcasm with some of this own. Branson liked that, but didn't show it.

"This is serious business," said Branson. "Do you understand me?"

The programmer nodded, but he didn't appear cowed. Branson made a mental note to pull the kid's file. He could always use an assistant with both brains and balls.

"What I'm trying to get at is whether or not we're dealing with a state-sponsored organization or potentially a lone wolf."

"It could be a lone wolf."

Branson looked over to the cryptologist, who nodded.

"I did a web search last night," said the kid. "There are two cryptology kits available on Silk Road 2.0 that claim to have the same 128-bit encryption as our web standard. There could be others that aren't for sale, like this one. I have to tell you, I know this world, and I think the only thing we can do is wait for the ransom note."

Branson thought, *If he only knew.* He considered sharing the hacker's initial communication with the group and decided to keep it to himself. Knowledge was power. Why share it?

Sitting in a beautifully upholstered leather chair and sipping his second coffee of the morning from a thin porcelain cup for which his fingers were a little too big, Branson couldn't help thinking about the chasm of privilege that separated the men who ran the government from the gears and wheels of the government itself. Secretary of the Treasury Stanton Briggs, whom he was about to brief, considered himself to be a public servant with a down-to-earth style. He didn't perch behind his huge colonial desk when he met with his subordinates. Rather, he sat with them at a low, round coffee table positioned next to one of his office windows overlooking Pennsylvania Avenue, so it felt like they were on an equal footing. It didn't cross his mind that the table was an eighteenth-century antique worth enough to feed a family of four for a year. You could call it public service, but the operative code of behavior in this building was, get what you can get while you can get it.

Branson had to admit that Briggs was effective. His efforts played a major role in keeping the world's largest economy on an even keel, and as far as Branson was concerned, Briggs deserved whatever he took. Also, the Secretary was smart. When he needed information, he sourced people who had their feet on the ground. That's why Branson was there.

"It's good to see you Charles," said Briggs, offering a toothy smile. With his rimless glasses and thinning gray hair, he looked a lot like FDR minus the cigarette holder. "Am I still going to feel this good after your briefing? Or am I going to want to shoot the messenger."

"It's a fluid situation," he responded, choosing his words carefully. "All the data in the Delaware/Maryland district has been encrypted by a computer virus. The virus falls into a category called ransomware. We've seen it around in one form or another for several years. Typically, you download a virus onto your PC by accident, your screen locks up, and then you get a message that if you send a hundred dollars to some PayPal account you'll get your data back. This exploit could be ransomware on a giant scale. Or it could be a prank. Or, it could be a probe by a foreign government. We can't rule that out, but I don't think it's likely. Right now, it seems like the only thing we *can* do is wait for further communication from the hacker.

Briggs' face reddened with anger. "Tell me how this could happen."

Branson knew the answer. It was because the contractors the government hired were fuck-ups, and so were people who supervised them. But that kind of negativity wouldn't fly with Briggs. He was the man in charge. He didn't want to hear that it was ultimately his own fault.

"The IRS computer infrastructure is like a building with a thousand doors," he said. "If you lock nine hundred and ninety-nine of them, somebody can still sneak in."

"That's unacceptable."

"When this is over, I'll look into it if you wish," said Branson.

Briggs didn't take the bait. "Is there a technology fix for this?" he asked.

"Unfortunately, there's not. The encryption algorithm isn't one of ours."

"And you have no idea where it came from?" He drummed his fingers on the table. "This could really be some thirteen-year-old?"

"Probably not. The encryption is very sophisticated. But it could be a lone hacker. I'm hoping there will be further communications that help us answer that question."

"How many people know about this?"

"Who knows it's a breach instead of some run-of-the-mill crash? Seven, counting you and me. The CTO over at the IRS will have to be informed, and I don't know whether he'll communicate with the Commissioner herself or not."

"We have to keep a lid on this. After that last Maryland fiasco, we're beginning to look as vulnerable as Target." Briggs was referring to the release of Governor Mitt Romney's 2010 tax returns during his Presidential campaign by a shadowy group of hackers known only as Anonymous. They had managed to hack their way into CADE2, the IRS's main database, and all efforts to track them down had failed.

"Do you want me to leak something? Some kind of red herring about a software glitch?" asked Branson.

"Not yet. But tell me, why are you so confident we're not dealing with an act of state-sponsored terrorism?"

"If you're China, why tip your hand and let us know what you can do? You lose the element of surprise."

"A test to see if the whole thing worked?"

"Stan," said Branson, deliberately addressing the secretary by his first name, "The whole IRS infrastructure is built from off-the-shelf software now, and that includes the database. Anybody could buy what the IRS has if they wanted to test something. Trust me. They wouldn't have to test it on us."

At that moment, a chime sounded, followed by the voice of Briggs' secretary. "It's Commissioner Brandeis. She says it's urgent."

In a low voice, Briggs said to Branson, "You're not here." Then, speaking normally, "Put her on speaker."

"Good morning, Sarah," said Briggs, addressing the IRS Commissioner in a casual tone of voice. "What's up?"

"Are you aware we've been hacked?" Briggs ignored her implication that he had spies over at the IRS. Of course he did. One of them was sitting in the room next to him. Everybody in D.C. had spies.

"Hacked?" he said.

"This could be a huge problem. They've managed to lock us out of our own data."

"Are we talking about a breach?"

"Not as yet. It's something else. But we may have to gear up for a rapid response. I'm just giving you a heads up. I'll have a POA over to you by mid-afternoon."

"No idea who's behind this?"

"Not yet. We're working on it.?

"I think we should involve Investigations in this," he said, winking at Branson. "Make sure and include them in your plan of action. In fact, I think they should take the lead."

"I agree, and, at this point I don't think we're ready to escalate." Escalating would mean informing the President, which could enormously complicate the picture.

"I won't say a thing, Sarah."

"This is not a goddamn surprise party we're talking about," she replied, reacting to what sounded like flippancy. "Somebody out there has figured out how to impair the most important function in the whole government."

"The Boss is going to learn about this no matter what we do. It's just a matter of time."

"I need all the time I can get."

"Let's talk again at four. Can you do that?"

"I will clear the decks. And I'll inform you immediately if there are important developments."

"Thank you, Sarah," said Briggs, signaling his secretary with a small electronic device he had in his pocket to terminate the call.

"Word is out," he said. "We have to get moving."

"I'm going to need some resources that are above my pay grade. We need to start developing leads, and we have to cast a wide net."

"You've got them. I'll have Cheryl get you a secure mobile link to my mobile on the way out. Just let me know what you need."

Branson thought, *What I need is a back door into The Onion Ring.* But that door didn't exist.

Stone smiled as he contemplated the earlier exchange of messages displayed on the screen of the weaponized iPhone. On the way to the dealership he had stopped at a Starbucks to zap Atlanta as promised. Then he had sent a message to Briggs' mobile, but this time with the response feature enabled.

> Five districts are now paralyzed. You have the power to make this stop.

*

> What do you want?

*

An executive order. No seizure of property by the IRS without judicial review. That includes financial instruments and savings accounts.

*

You must know that's impossible.

*

It's called due process.

*

I would like to handle this without involving the President of the United States.

*

I'm sure you would. Denver is next.

He could hardly believe he was negotiating directly with the Secretary of the Treasury instead of some intermediary who couldn't really make anything happen. But what, in fact, was going to happen? He had already decisively taken down three districts when that exchange of messages took place. It was surely clear to them what he could do. Right now, Briggs was playing for time, and no doubt frantically trying to trace the source of his transmission.

At four-thirty he had locked down Denver using the White Lake public library's WiFi system. Now, half an hour later, he was sitting in his living room, which had taken on a tomb-like quality in the dimming light of the late afternoon. It was not so easy to leave everything he had worked for behind, no matter what might lie ahead. He had known there would be sacrifices along the way, but he had grossly underestimated just how tough it would be. Walking through the Numerica lobby for the last time had been bad enough. This was worse.

There is only the mission, he told himself, repeating a line from a war novel he had read years ago. *Yes*, he thought, *and I am the commander*. He needed to think like a commander. In the business world he had been involved in situations like this dozens of times, and he sensed that Briggs was about to start haggling over details. He couldn't allow that. It would be like trench warfare, an endless exchange of shells with neither side advancing. Actually, that wasn't the best analogy. Stone *was* advancing, but not fast enough, or perhaps not towards the right objective. Briggs was obviously prepared to take heavy losses. Stone's attacks had not created the necessary level of terror. Maybe Briggs thought there was a technical fix. Maybe he thought his commandoes could get to Stone before the system was beyond repair. It didn't matter. Stone obviously needed to launch a new offensive to put even more pressure on his enemy. And he knew exactly where to attack.

He activated the weaponized iPhone and composed a new text to his adversary.

> Time is of the essence. The Executive Order must be issued by noon tomorrow. If not, this will become a public debate.

That would do it. This move was smarter than a massive strike, and it also had the element of surprise. The one thing Briggs held dear above all else was the government's credibility. If ordinary taxpayers came to believe their identities weren't safe with the IRS – not to mention their money – it would be a catastrophe. The tax collection system would devolve into something like Italy's, where people not only cheated, but prided themselves on doing so. With that threat, and the hacked district offices to back it up, Stone had Briggs by the balls.

He sipped the last of the stingy portion of scotch he had poured himself. Given the many hops his messages needed to take across the Internet to hide his identity and location, each back-and-forth included more lag time than he would have liked. He waited impatiently.

After several minutes, the phone clicked softly. A new message.

> This is the United States Government you are dealing with, not the local sheriff. I need a little time. I will contact you.

Stone could imagine the army of technicians now attempting to trace his signal. *Good luck*, he thought. He couldn't help taunting them with one last message.

> Noon is noon.

Branson glanced around the highly polished boardroom table at the senior officials the President's Chief of Staff had gathered to grapple with the disturbing problems created by The Hack, as it was coming to be called. He thought, *I am definitely in way over my pay grade,* and that was exactly the way he liked it. These were kind of situations where a win could ratchet you up the pay grade ladder. It was all about winning. His first wife, Stephanie, could never understand that. All she could see was a man who could make twice or maybe even three times as much money in private sector, and yet chose public service. And on the salary of a GS-12 she just couldn't find a way to be happy.

Margie, his second wife, was happy with what she had, even their somewhat rebellious teenage son. She hadn't managed to win over his daughter Melinda, his and Steph's child, and Melinda had gradually drifted out of the picture over time, even at Christmas. Well, that was life. People made their choices. The main thing was that Margie took care of things and didn't complain. None of this feminist bullshit that was so rampant in government these days. It crossed Branson's mind that he should give her a call and tell her he might not be home until late, and maybe not at all. She was used to that by now.

The table around which the chosen participants were assembled had recessed channels for electrical and network cabling, as well as a built-in projector that could be raised and lowered at the touch of a button for PowerPoint presentations and video. So could the wall screen upon which its images were projected. The gear, Branson noted, was about ten years out of date, which pretty much matched the thinking of this group. That, of course, was why he was here. And now, to his annoyance, he was being grilled. Nobody higher up seemed to really understand what was going on. The one who would, the Chief Technical Officer of the IRS, was en route to D.C., having interrupted a vacation in Bermuda.

"Isn't all this data backed up somewhere?" The questioner was Senator Edith Spellman, chair of the Senate Intelligence Committee.

"Yes, Senator, it is," said Branson. "The problem is, the agency can't access it. As soon as they call a file from back-up, it enters one of the infected operations programs and the virus instantly encrypts it. So the backup data is useless. We would have to build a whole new set of operations programs in order to actually make use of that data. We would also have to rebuild the network from scratch." Branson wondered how many more times he would have to go over this material.

"And how long would that take?"

"I can't speak to that with any authority, Senator. I'd be speculating."

"Please speculate."

"I believe the timeframe would be measured in months."

The Treasury Secretary, with whom Branson had met privately in the morning, now spoke, looking up over silver rimmed reading glasses. "I've talked to our key vendors. They confirmed that timeframe." He seemed to have aged five years in the last five hours.

Mark Creighton, Chief of Staff, summarized. He was in his early forties, tan and fit, with a short, military haircut like Branson's. He had a reputation for bluntness. "So, from a technology perspective, you're saying we have no options. We're fucked."

Edith Spellman cleared her throat and glared at him. "Thank you for speaking so colorfully, Mark"

"We're out of options. Whatever," he said with annoyance.

"That's the unanimous consensus, Sir," said Branson. "No short-term technology fixes."

"Alright," said Creighton, "Let's move on. How do we find out who's behind this and take them down?" For now, the working premise was that the attack was not backed by a nation state. Creighton had received assurances to this effect from high level officials in the countries that would normally be on the radar .

The room went silent, and Branson realized Creighton's question had been directed at him. He was on the biggest stage of his life now.

"We're conducting a two-pronged attack," he began. "Number one, we're looking at who has the *capability* to do something like this. Number two, we're looking at who has a *motive*.

"On the capability side, our target may be a brilliant individual who just loves encryption the way some people love crossword puzzles – the one who wants to climb the mountain because it's there. The other capability option is an individual who believes that current encryption protocols can't be fully trusted because of alleged government back doors. There are such people, and nothing would please them more than giving the government a slap in the face.

"The good news is, geniuses like this are not totally anonymous within the web community, and, perhaps more important, they know one another. Not personally on a face-to-face basis, but through chat rooms and bulletin boards. So this is one avenue of approach.

"The second group consists of disaffected current and former IRS employees, individual taxpayers who have a grievance against the IRS, and, on a broader scale, anti-government groups, libertarian extremists and so on. Again, these individuals and groups are not entirely unknown."

Creighton spoke. "I think what we all want to know is how long it's going to take to track down whoever is behind this. We can't cover this up forever, and if we give the public reason to mistrust the integrity of the IRS, well, that's simply unacceptable."

"Some would say they already have good reason," said the man sitting next to Senator Spellman, Calvin Trent. Also a senator and member of the intelligence committee, he had a reputation as a maverick, willing to make any alliance he needed to make in order to get things done. He spoke with a strong southern accent.

Creighton exploded. "God damn it!" he yelled. "We are not here to point fingers. I know what you're talking about and you know God damned well that every administration uses the IRS to harass its political enemies. People may not like it, but they accept it. But if our citizens start thinking the money they pay the government every April fifteenth isn't safe, that's a whole new ball game. This isn't fucking Mexico."

"Calm down, Mark," said the Senator in his soft drawl. "We're all on the same team here. I'm just suggesting that the tax code and the way it's enforced may have contributed to this situation."

"What are you proposing? That we rewrite the tax code over the weekend so more people like it?"

"I'm just wondering if these hackers might listen to reason. They aren't asking for money. What is it they want?"

"We'll take this discussion off line," said Creighton. He turned back to Branson. "Do you have the resources you need?"

Branson considered a wise crack. A rabbit's foot? A crystal ball? But those kind of jokes weren't for this room. "Yes sir," he responded, trying to project a sense of confidence that wasn't really there. They weren't looking for a needle in a haystack here. It was more like all the wheat fields in Kansas.

The meeting was over. He left the conference room and walked briskly back to the temporary office he had been assigned, sat down in the creaking swivel chair and took his laptop out of his briefcase. A minute later he was looking at twenty three lists of potential suspects, some of them with thousands of names. Branson found a pad of yellow paper is his borrowed desk and set about prioritizing the lists, at least on a preliminary basis. That done, he called the FBI's Washington field office and was put through immediately to the Assistant Director in Charge who ran the office, one Carl Cox. The ADIC had a young, energetic voice and seemed ready to cooperate. This was a break. Branson needed good people to winnow down this mountain of leads, and he had neither the time nor the familiarity with the WFO personnel to make good choices on his own. He had already decided not to directly tap the NSA unless he had to. Ever since the surveillance scandal they had become sticklers for following the rules, and that was not how Branson operated.

Half an hour later, as he put the phone's receiver back in its cradle, a wave of panic washed over him. There were several hundred thousand people in the world who could have mounted this exploit! For all he knew, the one who was responsible wasn't even on any of the voluminous lists the techs had provided. He stared at his yellow pad. There were lists of known hackers, of libertarian extremists, of employees within the IRS who had access to the compromised applications, of individuals who had IRS judgments against them of over ten thousand dollars, of individuals who had sent email messages with suspicious combinations of keywords. It went and on and on. Sheer human persistence could reduce the number of names substantially, and so-called Big Data correlation algorithms could push some names to the top of a list and others to the bottom. But at the end of the day, all the math in the world might not be enough.

At seven fifteen his civilian cell phone chimed. It was a text message from Natalie.

I'm ready.

He typed in the address of a nearby café and hit reply.

Natalie Pearson was a group head in the Department of Commerce whom he had met two years ago at a conference on cloud computing where he was a featured speaker. Like him, she was involved in a lukewarm marriage and was ready for sex without emotional involvement. But they did become involved. They soon found themselves talking on the phone almost every day, and meeting regularly for lunch or drinks to discuss departmental politics and strategize about their careers. She was, if anything, more ambitious than he. And although he was higher on the totem pole at present, she was climbing fast.

He entered the Palermo Caffè and found her immediately, sitting at a table near the window. With her sensible-if-expensive beige suit, neatly coiffed blonde hair and business-like glasses, she blended into the crowd, just another bland bureaucrat having a quick bite before an evening at the office. The men at the next table didn't seem to notice her. *They would if they knew what she was like in bed,* he thought.

A moment later they were sitting face-to-face in the dim light, sipping Perriers and waiting for their over-priced sandwiches to arrive. At times when he felt overwhelmed and started to think of himself as just another a bureaucrat wading through a swamp of regulations and standard procedures, she had the power to make him feel like a hero. Tonight, he had real hero potential if he could come through.

She put her hand on his in a rare public gesture of affection. "You look tired."

"This one isn't going to be easy." He gave her a quick overview of the situation, ignoring the fact that her security clearance was nowhere near adequate to hear what he was telling her. It was reckless on his part, but she wouldn't blow the whistle on him. They had a relationship based on trust, which was rare in Washington. And if they ever split up, he had enough dirt on her to be sure she would keep her mouth shut about these security violations or anything else. He hoped it would never come to that.

"What's your next move?" she asked

Branson was about to respond that he didn't know when the sandwiches arrived, large kaiser rolls sliced in half, their contents of exotic meats and cheeses held in place with large, flat toothpicks.

The two ate in silence and then ordered espressos to finish the meal. Just as the coffee arrived, Branson's secure iPhone buzzed. He looked at the screen and shook his head.

"What?" asked Natalie.

"There was a new communication. He took down Atlanta and Denver, and then Philadelphia later on in the afternoon.

"What does that mean?"

"He's decided to move faster. I was hoping for the one-a-day brand."

"How do you know it's a he?"

"I don't, of course. But the I.T. world is male-dominated. That's just how things are."

"So now what?"

Branson surveyed the restaurant. Many of the patrons were youngish couples on dates. He had a moment of guilt. Shouldn't he be in his office under the harsh artificial light, making phone calls or looking at computer print-outs? No, he had nothing more to do right now. And he knew this break would help him stay sharp as the night wore on.

"It's a numbers game. I have a list of about a hundred and twenty thousand suspects."

Her face fell, and he knew what she was thinking. It was a huge number.

"We just have to grind through the names and hope something turns up. I have people putting together some big data algorithms so we can prioritize who to investigate first."

"You mean like the ones Target uses to figure out when a woman is pregnant?"

"It's the same technology. In fact, I have an ex-Target guy working on it as we speak."

"How long will it take to investigate a hundred and twenty thousand people?"

"With my current manpower, about three weeks."

"That's too long! Won't they give you more people if you ask?"

He shook his head. "It's not how many people you have."

She finished the thought for him. "I know, it's how good they are. But still, it seems impossible. If he's taking down three districts a day, that's basically three states, right? Then, in three weeks...."

"The whole country will be down, and people will have figured out that there is something very, very wrong with the agency that collects about twenty-five percent of their salary every week or so."

On this grim note they stood up. She bent forward and kissed him, a light peck of friendship for the benefit of any onlookers.

"See you soon, I hope," he said. "Keep your fingers crossed."

"Is there anything you can do to make this not a numbers game?"

"Yes," he said. "I could get lucky."

Keyed up and exhausted at the same time, Stone climbed up the stairs to his darkened bedroom for one last night's sleep in the bed where he had struggled to find sleep so many times in his old life. It was a lot harder to say good bye to the trappings of that life than he had ever imagined, and that wasn't the only pain he was feeling. In spite of what his common sense told him, he felt like he was running away from a fight. Reason, supported by the most trusted precepts of warfare, had led him into this lopsided guerrilla war, where secrecy and stealth were necessities. Still, he longed for a public forum where he could tell the world how the bastards at the IRS had brought this trouble down upon themselves, and show the American citizenry that it was possible to fight back.

He sat down on the bed and put his head in his hands, wishing for a moment he could fast forward to the small country house in southern Italy that was to be his future life. Much as he wanted to speak out, he was uncertain that he had the skill to win a war of words with White House experts in propaganda. Instead of a David citizen pitted against a Goliath government agency that ruined people's lives with impunity, he could be painted as a cyber wacko who wanted to put the entire government at risk, not to mention blocking millions of tax refund checks.

On impulse he pulled out the phone and took out Nevada early, just to keep up the pressure. Then he tapped out a quick text to Briggs

Detroit is next.

"Herb would be proud of you." It was Laura. Her voice came from the direction of the walk-in closet on the other side of the bed. He turned on the bed lamp, but of course there was no one there. These hallucinations. There was no other word for them. They always sounded so real.

"Things have gone far beyond Herb," he said, addressing the slatted closet doors.

"Yes, but he's the one who started the ball rolling."

Stone stared at the closet. Was there a dark silhouette behind those slats? There couldn't be. He stood up and walked around the bed to open one of the closet doors. His eyes fell on a familiar collection of suits and sports jackets. He was having a conversation with thin air, hearing a voice no one else would ever hear.

He sat back down on the bed, shaken. He had to be able to distinguish between what was real and what was not. And he could, damn it. It was just when she caught him by surprise.... *When my mind catches me by surprise*, he thought, correcting himself. *She* was not real.

He took a couple of deep breaths, trying without success to calm down. He needed help. After a long moment of hesitation, he picked up the phone and dialed a number he had known by heart for years.

"Hello?" said Ginny.

"It's Matt. How are you doing?"

"Matt! What a surprise. I'm okay. How are you? You don't sound so hot."

"I should have called sooner. I'm so sorry about what Stetson did. You didn't need that."

"You're right, I didn't. He thought he was doing the right thing, Matt. But it didn't help anybody. In fact, it hurt a lot of people, including me."

"It's good to hear your voice." *The voice of a real person*, he thought.

"Yours too. I... Maybe I shouldn't ask, but... is everything going okay with you and your girlfriend?"

"My girlfriend?"

"Matt, it's obvious. You didn't have to say anything."

Stone thought, *Sure, she's fine. She's left the country under a false identity and I'll be joining her in a couple of days.* But he couldn't say any of that.

"It's all good."

"Well, you're calling me at bedtime That has to mean something. But I won't pry. You can tell whatever you like." She paused. "Matt, did you want to come over? If you say yes, though, you have to stay all night."

It was an invitation he hadn't expected, but somehow it didn't surprise him. And it was welcome. He usually thought of himself as tough and resourceful, but tonight he was truly frightened.

"Stay all night?" he asked.

"Hey, it's safe. And we'll have complete privacy. All the cops and agents and whatever are gone. They won't see your car and think you're part of some conspiracy."

He thought, *Why did she mention a conspiracy?* At the moment, Stone couldn't really bring himself to care. He needed all the help he could get to make it through the next twenty-four hours.

"We don't have to, you know, *do* it," she said. "We'll just keep each other company. I'll wear long johns if you want."

"Flannel pajamas will be enough," he said with lightness he didn't feel. "I'll be over in a few minutes."

A little after eight o'clock the next morning Branson got lucky. He had just finished shaving and putting on a fresh set of clothes when his secure Blackberry buzzed. It was Carl Cox from the FBI. A programmer from an IRS subcontractor had walked into the Washington Field Office out of the blue to report a "strange meeting" with a young woman at a local bar about a month earlier. Cox hadn't talked to the programmer directly and wasn't clear about all the details, but it looked like there was a chance this woman was connected to The Hack. "I thought I should call you immediately," he said.

"I'll be right over." He ended the call and then pumped his fist like Logan Paulson when he caught a touchdown pass for the Redskins. He loved these moments. There was nothing like a breakthrough to give you a sense of power.

The coder was waiting for him in a small interrogation room on the building's fourth floor, seated at a metal government-issue table with a white plastic top. Nathan Clouse was his name. He was thin, with blue eyes and the pale skin that came from too many hours spent in front of a computer monitor and too few outdoors. He had put on a blue blazer and a tie for this visit, clothes Branson guessed this thirty-something almost never wore. Clouse looked scared, and well he should be. This piece of shit in a blazer had probably put the whole United States government at risk.

Branson weighed his options. More intimidation? A good cop approach? What he needed was details, which a mind in a state of fear might not be able to provide. It was time to play good cop. He approached the coder and extended his hand. "Charles Branson," he said. "Sorry for the lack of hospitality. They just automatically treat everybody like a suspect, which you're not, by the way. Can I arrange for some coffee? You hungry?

Clouse shook his head.

Branson sat down facing Clouse and rested his elbows on the cold, white table. He wouldn't pull out a pad and take notes. That reinforced the sense of us vs. them he had decided against. Besides, the conversation would be automatically recorded anyway.

"So, what's the story here? You came to us."

Clouse described his encounter with a young woman named Samantha he had met on a Sunday night at the Mecklenburg Inn in Shepherdstown. He was "almost sure" a month ago Sunday. He *was* sure she was a Java coder.

"How do you know that?" asked Branson.

"She could talk the talk. When I explained the project I was working on, I could tell from her questions that she understood me."

"You explained the project you were working on?" asked Branson, raising his eyebrows.

"Nothing we do is classified, Sir," Clouse replied. "She said she was looking for work in the area and I was trying to give her an idea of what kind of opportunities were available at my company."

"That's DataTech, a subcontractor to the IRS, is it not?"

Branson thought, *This could be big.* But it could also be nothing. He struggled to contain his excitement.

"So let's see," he continued. "It's Sunday night. You're having a beer or two at a bar, you meet a pretty girl, she chats you up, asks about work opportunities, you take her to dinner. It sounds pretty normal. What was it that made you put on a jacket and tie and come down to FBI headquarters this morning?"

"She stole my phone. Or borrowed it, or whatever. She said she accidentally put it in her purse when we left the restaurant. The next morning she was waiting for me in the DataTech parking lot and gave it back. She seemed embarrassed. To tell the truth, at the time I thought the whole thing was a little weird, but then I thought maybe she had just made up some excuse to see me again. She seemed interested in me. Anyway, after that I didn't hear from her, and I really didn't think about it anymore until I heard about the trouble in the Delaware Maryland district."

Shit! thought Branson. *How does this Clouse know about The Hack? Is the cat that far out of the bag already?* "Are you working on that issue?" he asked, affecting a casual tone.

"No, a guy I used to work with told me about it. Apparently it's something security related. That's when I thought of Samantha and the phone thing, because if you had physical possession of that phone it would make hacking our system a lot easier, and from there you could get to a lot of government networks – including the IRS."

"Was your system hacked."

"No."

"You're sure about that."

"I reviewed the log files for anomalies myself. The log files are our record of –"

"I know what log files are," snapped Branson, a little too impatiently.

Clouse seemed taken aback. "We weren't hacked."

"But you think somebody tried?"

"There's no evidence of a penetration. Nothing." Clouse went on to explain how he had called in and locked his account the moment he had discovered the missing phone, leaving at most a forty-five minute of opportunity, not enough time for a brute force attack against a strong password.

Branson knew that modern malware could erase its tracks, but it was also possible that Clouse was right, and that there was no attack on that night. Was the girl's questionable story true? Branson didn't think so. He had a strong hunch she was somehow connected to The Hack.

"Did she give you any contact information? An email address?"

"No. She said she'd be in touch, but like I said, I've never heard from her again."

"We need to find her," said Branson, "and I need you to go through that night in as much detail as you can."

Branson spent the next forty-five minutes meticulously grilling Clouse, while in his mind he built a block diagram. Clouse was in the central box, and from it radiated half a dozen lines to other potential sources of information about this Samantha: Clouse's friend, who had also met her, the Mecklenburg Inn's parking lot surveillance cameras, the bar's credit card receipts from the night in question, hotels and motels within a ten mile radius, car rental agencies.... He had unlimited resources. Why not use them?

Branson's first instinct was to incarcerate the coder on general principles for being so careless. Instead, he took the kid's mobile number and warned him to pick up if he called or face the consequences. Then he took the elevator up to ADIC Cox's office. Working together in an office with multiple secure direct lines, the two men had half a dozen data analytics teams on standby in less than fifteen minutes, as well as agents on the ground headed to Shepherdstown where the coder met this "Samantha," if that was even her real name. Branson also sent two of his top digital forensics people over to DataTech, equipped with intrusion detection tools not commercially available to get a lead on the malware itself.

In less than an hour, an analysis of credit card charges matched against vehicle license plates captured by surveillance cameras positioned in the Mecklenburg Inn parking lot had identified Katherine Glen of White Lake, Ohio as the prime suspect. Employment records, some from an IRS database that was still working, placed her in the IT department of an Ohio manufacturing company called Numerica, also a government contractor. *A coder!* With this data, Branson was ready to act. He had Cox mobilize a dozen FBI agents out of the Detroit office. Then he called Briggs' private line. The secretary picked up. She said her boss was waiting for a call and that she would put him through immediately.

"Please do," he said. "And get a jet for me. I need to get to Detroit ASAP." It didn't get any better than this.

Connie Winston had great tits. That was the first thing Branson noticed about her when she walked into the conference room he had commandeered at Numerica's headquarters. That, and the fact that this attractive woman with not one hair out of place was rattled. Good. Her nervousness would play into his hands.

"Sit down," he commanded.

She took a seat opposite him at the long oval table, which could comfortably seat twelve. The walls, the chairs and the table itself were all varying tones of gray. The air was cold, and the woman was obviously uncomfortable. Branson didn't ask her if she wanted to go get her coat. The more uncomfortable she was, the better.

"Ms. Winston, I understand you're the person who rents the various apartments around town for visiting guests, customers who need to stay for extended periods and the like?"

"Yes," she said through tight lips. "I explained that to the other agents."

"Well, can you explain how it is that an ex-employee is living in one of those apartments? Actually, it's a detached structure several miles from here. I think you know the one I'm talking about."

"Yes. We thought it would be popular because it's isolated and quiet. But that didn't work out. It was too far away. So she took it over."

"She took it over? How did she know it even existed?"

"I wouldn't know."

"Who authorized the acquisition of this particular property in the first place?"

The woman glared at him.

"Don't tell me you don't know."

"I do know. It was our CEO, Mathew Stone."

"Did she and Stone have a relationship?"

"That I don't know."

Branson leaned forward and lowered his voice. "I think you do."

"There were rumors. But there were rumors about him and a lot of women, including me."

"Did you sleep with Stone?"

"I don't think I have to answer that question."

"I can make you answer any question I want to ask. Believe me." He watched her ponder this threat. In fact, he had already gotten what he needed, but evoking fear was part of the fun.

"I don't have any special knowledge about his private life. Or hers."

Branson pulled his cell phone out of his pocket. "You can go now," he said without looking up. When she was out the door, he spoke into the phone.

"We need to track down Mathew Stone, the CEO here at Numerica. I think he might have been involved with the girl. You find anything at the cottage?

"No obvious smoking gun, Sir. And no clues as yet as to where she might have taken off to."

"Send a team to Stone's house, and try to get a fix on his mobile ASAP. I'm headed over to this cottage myself if anybody asks."

Racing along an unfamiliar road in the back seat of high-powered black limousine, Branson pondered his options. Stone was hiding. He sensed it. Stone had been fucking Katherine Glen and now he was protecting her, probably planning to run. She was a sexy little bitch, judging from the photos his teams had dug up. If luck was on their side, they could be out of the country in less than twenty-four hours. They probably wouldn't make it with the alerts Branson was about to launch. But they might. Like it or not, it was time to get the local police involved. He hoped to Hell he wasn't sending them on a wild goose chase.

Stone had slept soundly for the first time in weeks, waking only once, very briefly, to feel Ginny pressed sweetly against him. As he showered, he could sense that Herb's ghost had been expunged from the house along with his possessions. Ginny had meticulously given everything away, perhaps with a touch of anger. She had also bought a new bed which she had shown off to him with great pride, explaining how the mattress was specially designed for "people our age."

He came down the stairs dressed in the previous night's clothes, but otherwise feeling fresh. Ginny was in the midst of cooking a breakfast of bacon and eggs. Spring sunshine slanted in through the glass doors that led to the patio.

"Thank you," he said as Ginny sat down at the dining room table across from him and poured coffee into their mugs. "I really needed this."

"I know. I could hear it in your voice last night. You look so much better. You should make this a habit."

They ate in silence for awhile.

"Do you ever think you'll see Kimmie again?" she asked. He had talked about his trip to California the night before, mentioning his daughter's somewhat mysterious Christian retreat.

"I truly don't know."

"Matt, I know I said I wouldn't ask, but is something wrong? You seem distracted."

Stone considered how to answer this caring, honest woman. When he disappeared, Ginny would surely be questioned. What should he give her to say?

"I'm involved in a potential deal with a foreign government," he said. "It would be hugely beneficial to the company, but there are security issues. I have to be careful, That means doing what's right, but also what's legal. And that isn't exactly clear."

Ginny reached across the table and put her hand on his. "Your job is so hard. I wish I could help."

"You gave me aid and comfort when I needed it," he said, squeezing her hand. "And now, I have a company to run. They're all going to ask me why I got in so late."

She came around the table and gave him a hug. For a moment it felt like they had been married for decades.

"The world is a better place because you're in it, Ginny."

"See you soon, I hope." Stone saw a question in her eyes.

"Yes, soon," he said, hating the lie. She suspected this was their final good bye. He could sense it. When he opened the front door he wasn't heading off for another day at the office. He was heading to the nearby town of Troy where he would abandon his car, *and* his identity. He would drive to the airport in the cheapest vehicle he could purchase, and at three twenty Eastern time or thereabouts, take off for Rome.

Standing on the porch, Ginny called after him. "You're a good man, Matt. Don't forget that."

Stone had parked his car in front of the fatal garage. As he approached it, he stared at the white door with its peeling paint and the gap at the bottom where Herb had stuffed rags to prevent the carbon monoxide from escaping. Stone could feel his anger building once again. If Briggs wouldn't involve the President in fixing what was wrong with the IRS, Stone would do it himself.

He was halfway to Troy when he realized he had left his escape passport in the bedroom of his home the night before. He felt a moment of panic. No, he told himself, it wasn't a problem. He was learning to make allowances for lapses like these, and had allotted several hours in this morning's schedule for things to go wrong. He made a quick U-turn and headed back to the home he thought he had seen for the last time. Two minutes later, his work mobile chimed. He didn't recognized the number. He hesitated. Was the call a trap? A means to trace his position? It was unlikely, but not out of the question. On impulse, he took the risk.

"Hello, this is Mathew Stone."

"Matt, it's Connie."

She was obviously calling from her mobile. Why?

"Listen, Matt, the FBI was here. They're looking for Kat. I told them about the cottage. I had to. She's living there, right?"

Stone hesitated for a moment, trying get a grasp on what this meant.

"Yes, she is. And she's planning to start paying the rent. She's also going to reimburse the company for the past three months or whatever it is. You knew that, didn't you?"

"I don't think they care about the rent. I don't know what's going on, Matt, but if you're there I think you should leave right now, and maybe call your lawyer. And I wouldn't come into work either. They're going to connect you two, and I just don't like the way this feels. I think you need to protect yourself."

Stone blinked back unexpected tears. "Connie, you're a true friend."

"That I am. You take care."

Stone fought an urge to floor the gas pedal. The last thing he needed was to get pulled over for speeding. He did some quick mental calculations. If Connie had phoned right after the agents left Numerica, they were about twenty minutes away from the cottage. If Kat had been careless and they found a clue that identified him, it would take them another fifteen to get to his house, which was the obvious first place they would look for him - *unless they could track his mobile.* Stone rolled down the window and tossed the device into the bushes by the road. He glanced at his watch. He would be back home in ten minutes tops, and on his way to Troy where he would be rid of his car in another twenty.

I can do this, he thought grimly. He would have felt safer in a drab beige mini-van, but in fact no one was looking for him. Not yet.

Two miles from his home, Stone pulled over and killed the motor of his Crossfire. *This isn't safe,* a voice kept telling him, and it was no hallucination. It was the voice of the second sense that had kept him alive in Viet Nam. The cottage was only one out of dozens links between him and Kat, and as soon as the Feds discovered any one of them they would be after him as a *suspect.* He and Kat had been relatively discreet, yes, but anybody with eyes could figure out what was going on. He hadn't really cared who knew what because his days as Numerica's CEO were numbered anyway. Now, one way or another, it was his hours that were numbered.

He had to hide, he had to get a new set of documents, and he had to get new money to pay for his escape without any transactions that the feds could trace. In other words, he had to hack into his own bank accounts. There was only one person who could help him now. He started the car and headed for the freeway that would take him to Detroit.

Gaviot Avenue where The Drummer's store front was located had depressed him on prior visits, but today its empty lots and boarded-up homes felt like a sanctuary where he'd be safe for awhile, or as safe as anybody could be in this part of the city. He glanced at his watch. Eleven-thirty. There was no question in Stone's mind that they were closing in on him. They were casting a net, one they estimated would catch him in two to three hours. It was time to ditch the Crossfire.

He turned off onto a side street and managed to find a healthy tree with branches broad enough to hide his car from helicopters, which they might very well deploy as spotters. The Drummer's office was less than half a mile away. He walked briskly along the cracked sidewalk, passing occasional groups of middle-aged black men gathered in doorways, smoking cigarettes and drinking beer from bottles hidden inside brown paper bags. They probably used to work for Ford or GM or Chrysler back in the day. There were women with battered baby carriages and grandmothers carrying shopping bags, but few young men.

He was about half a block away from The Drummer's storefront when he realized something was wrong. The cream-colored venetian blinds behind the windows were gone and had been replaced - he could not believe his eyes - by displays of dresses and women's shoes. His heart sank. The Drummer had been his last hope. Although he knew it would be useless, he entered the store. There was only one person minding it, an attractive young woman in her early twenties who was obviously confused by the arrival of a middle aged white guy. She managed a smile, but when he asked about the computer business that used to be there she could offer no help. He wasn't surprised. The Drummer was cautious beyond cautious.

He found an old-fashioned cafe down the street, complete with a Formica counter and stools. He slid into one of the booths and picked up the menu. *Was this his last meal as a free man?* When the waitress came over, a woman in her 'sixties who might well have worked there for decades, he ordered a cheeseburger and a coke even though he wasn't really hungry. It was five minutes to noon. He was out of options. They would track him down. It was only a matter of time. He didn't even know how to carry out his threat to go public. For years, when he communicated with the media, everything was arranged by his small but very talented PR group. They wrote the press releases, arranged the interviews, sent announcements over the Internet and in general handled the mechanics of getting a message out into the world.

He pulled out the weaponized phone and called up the map display. So far, he had taken out half a dozen facilities. If he wanted to, he could take down the entire nation in about ten minutes. He didn't want that. It would be chaos. Not only the IRS, but the nation itself would be at risk. No, he wasn't going to destroy the IRS, but he was going to give it a black eye that would last for years. It was the best he could do. That, and put a spotlight on the awful injustice Herb and Ginny had suffered.

Tap by tap, he took down what he estimated to be twenty-five percent of the system. His food arrived, and he took a few bites. Then, he picked up the phone again and in its normal mode looked up the main number of the Detroit Free Press and hit the call button. He navigated to the extension of Galen Cook, hoping the only business reporter he knew who had survived the paper's repeated staff cuts still had a desk and a land line. Over the years, Cook had done him a number of favors. If he was in, he was about to get a payback he could never have imagined in his wildest dreams. Cook picked up on the third ring. Stone told him where he was, and in exchange for a ride downtown to FBI headquarters he offered him the story of a lifetime.

Stone's own life, at least his life as he had known it, was about to end. The curtain was coming down, as Laura used to say when one of their European vacations was coming to a close. He had no idea what lay ahead. He only knew that he had to maintain his sense of purpose no matter what might happen. He did regret that he had not been able to say good bye to Kat. Instead of making a choice, they were being separated by forces they didn't understand and couldn't control, the same forces, he now realized, that had thrown them together in the first place. It wouldn't have worked, he told himself. For awhile, yes, but at some point his age would have caught up with them, and she would have become nothing more than the dutiful nurse to some old man who had run away from his past in America for reasons no one would ever learn.

"I don't have any choice," he said aloud, as though Kat could hear him. The waitress looked over, but he ignored her.

Stone had to admit that he now felt a certain kinship with Stetson. The man had murdered an IRS agent, and that was wrong. But he had owned up to it, had taken responsibility for his actions. That was the right thing to do: stand tall. He picked up the weaponized phone, longing to call Kat, or at least send her a text message. But that was too dangerous. What if Briggs' men had pierced the veil of anonymity he believed was protecting them from being traced? And, if he could talk to her, what would he say? He knew what she would say to him: *Run*.

Branson was standing in the middle of Katherine Glen's single-room cottage, which the forensics team was combing for clues, when his mobile buzzed in his pocket. It was the Detroit SAIC, now functioning as liaison to the Detroit PD as well as supervising his own agents.

"We have the car."

"Where?"

The SAIC responded with an address that Branson of course didn't recognize.

"I'm not from Detroit," he snapped.

"It's just off Gaviot Avenue, which is a main drag not that far from the lake. I've got four teams canvassing the surrounding neighborhoods."

"I want to know in five seconds if you find our man."

There was a pause. "Am I clear?" said Branson.

"Loud and clear," said the SAIC, ending the call with more than a hint of annoyance in his voice. For the second time in two days, Branson thought, *If he only knew what was at stake*.

Galen Cook looked rather frazzled as he entered the café, as though he had just gotten out of bed and thrown on yesterday's clothes in a rush to get to an appointment on time. Stone had long suspected that Cook cultivated this disorganized look over the years to appear less than competent in front of the high-level executives he so frequently interviewed, all the better to catch them off guard with a piercing question. Stone knew better. There was no one in the Midwest he could better trust to tell his story.

He waved Cook over to his booth and stood up to shake hands.

"This had better be good," said Cook as he slid in. "A man takes his life in his hands driving through this neighborhood."

"It's the last place the cops would look for me," he replied, only half joking.

"The cops? said Cook, adjusting his gray plastic glasses. It was a familiar mannerism that Stone remembered from the past, and somehow comforting.

"The Feds, actually. I don't really know."

Cook stared at him. "You're serious, aren't you." He pulled out a spiral note pad and fished a pen out of his pocket.

"I'm serious."

At that moment the waitress came over, pad in hand, to take Cook's order of a diet Coke. When she had left, Stone began to tell the story of his friend's suicide and where it had led him. He omitted Kat's part in the IRS exploit, and made no explicit reference to The Drummer. He wouldn't be able to hold back those details once he was in custody, but for the first story, which would get the most public attention, he wanted the focus to be primarily on Herb rather than the shameful vulnerability of the IRS. That could come later.

Old-fashioned reporter that he was, Cook took diligent notes as Stone spoke, asking few questions. At the appropriate moment, Stone produced the weaponized phone for Cook's inspection. "I'll give you a demonstration," said Stone.

"Wait," said Cook. "I can't have you committing a crime in front of my eyes."

"Don't worry, I won't. I'll just show you how it works and cancel out before the signal gets transmitted." He tapped on the drum icon to display the U.S. map with its color-coded IRS districts. "The blue districts have been shut down."

Just at that moment, the door swung open and two men entered. They were both in their early 'forties, neatly dressed in dark suits, neither wearing the cliché sun glasses he had half-expected, and neither equipped with ear buds. They scanned the cafe and locked in on him, walking quickly to the booth, where they briefly flashed their badges.

"Mathew Stone?" said one.

Stone nodded.

"We're here to take you into custody for questioning related to a matter of national security. I'll need to take that device at this time."

Stone tapped on the glass screen, a rhythm that The Drummer had made him practice what seemed like a hundred times. Then he handed it over with a smile.

The two turned their attention to Cook.

Cook, Detroit Free Press," said Cook. "Would
see my credentials?"

necessary," said the agent who was taking the lead.
coming with us as well."

this exchange took place, the lead agent dropped the
into a plastic zip-lock bag produced by his partner.
he began counting the seconds. Through the plastic he
uld see the icons coming into view, but they were now
arked with flame-shaped red badges. This was intended as
a warning. As he watched, the bottom of the bag holding the
phone began to melt, and the phone itself fell onto the floor.

"What the fuck?" said the lead agent.

The four of them watched as the phone literally melted
into the dark red carpet.

"Gentlemen, you just witnessed the destruction of about
twenty-five percent of the U.S. government's ability to
collect taxes." Without the phone, and without The
Drummer as backup, there would be no way to unlock any
of the encrypted data. For all practical purposes, it was gone
forever.

The two agents looked at one another, not fully
comprehending what had happened, but clearly aware that it
wasn't good.

"You're coming with us," said the lead agent to Stone and
Cook.

"Gladly," said Stone.

Epilogue

The young woman was stylishly thin – "Paris thin" as she thought of it now – and dressed to fit in with the intellectual crowd at Café des Phares: old jeans, a light sweater and a scarf against the chill. All the women wore scarves here in Paris, even on warm days, which were all too rare. "You'll get used to it," her friend had said in that accented English that never failed to charm her. "And besides, this way you appreciate the sun more when it appears."

She squeezed into a seat well back from the noisy morning traffic circulating around the towering bronze Colonne de Juillet, the "July Column" that celebrated the overthrow of King Charles X and with it, the concept of hereditary right. Earlier, the famous Bastille prison had stood here, the one whose fall had initiated the French Revolution. It was a fitting spot for what she was about to do.

She ordered an espresso and opened her iPad. With its clip-on keyboard it looked like a miniature laptop. Inside, of course, it had been modified beyond recognition. She angled the screen away from the swarthy-skinned middle-aged man sitting next to her and paused. France had a calming effect on her. There were routines and rhythms built into the days that didn't exist in the States. And if anybody started looking for her, all the clues would point to Italy. She was safe here.

She wondered if she would ever return. That would be impossible under her own name. And even if she snuck in, visiting her sis or her parents would be too dangerous. Who knew how long they'd be under surveillance? Of course, over time things might change. For now, it wasn't worth thinking about. Better to focus on learning French and staying out of trouble. And keeping her promise to herself, which she was about to do.

The tiny clock on her screen told her it was 10:08 a.m. in Paris, which made it a little after four in the morning in Washington DC. Stanton Briggs would still be in bed in his fancy house in Bethesda. He would wake up to a message that would have him calling the White House before breakfast. A message the President himself couldn't ignore.

She addressed her message to the U.S. Secretary of the Treasury's private mobile phone, a number that she had stolen months ago. For a moment, her thin fingers hovered above the keyboard. Then she typed:

Los Angeles is next.